THE HUMAN IN THE WALLS

THE HUMAN IN THE WALLS

AND OTHER STORIES

ERIC JAMES STONE

WFP
WORDFIRE PRESS

EBook ISBN: 978-1-68057-061-8
Trade Paperback ISBN: 978-1-68057-060-1
Hardcover ISBN: 978-1-68057-062-5

Cover design by Janet McDonald
Cover artwork images by Adobe Stock
Kevin J. Anderson, Art Director

Published by
WordFire Press, LLC
PO Box 1840
Monument CO 80132
Kevin J. Anderson & Rebecca Moesta, Publishers

WordFire Press eBook Edition 2020
WordFire Press Trade Paperback Edition 2020
WordFire Press Hardcover Edition 2020
Printed in the USA

Join our WordFire Press Readers Group for
sneak previews, updates, new projects, and giveaways.
Sign up at wordfirepress.com

❀ Created with Vellum

CONTENTS

DEDICATION

For my wife, Darci, who makes life wonderful.

INTRODUCTION

BRANDON SANDERSON

Eric James Stone is a genius. I feel ashamed that, when I first heard about him, I was actually skeptical.

A roommate said to me, "Oh, hey! You're a writer. One of the guys at my work is a writer too." My response was raised eyebrows and a question: "Yeah, has he actually published anything?"

"I don't know," my roommate said. "He won some kind of science fiction writing contest or something."

"Oh," I said. "Well, unless it was Writers of the Future—"

"Yeah, that's it. He won that."

That was it, and more. Nebula winner, published over and over in top short story markets (which, I might note, had repeatedly rejected me at that time), Eric turned out to be the real deal. My skepticism seems silly now; I was expressing the same kind of bias and cynicism that (as an aspiring novelist) I myself had suffered on many occasions.

I decided that I needed to give this Eric guy a shot. At the next local convention I attended, I went to his reading. Not only was the place packed, with standing room only, Eric was a charming and witty reader. The story he read then ("Tabloid

Reporter to the Stars") is not in this collection, but the stories here are equally stunning.

By now—some fifteen years after first meeting Eric—I thought myself something of an EJS aficionado. We've been in writing groups together numerous times, including the current incarnation of the one at my house. I assumed I'd read basically everything he put out. I was therefore amazed to see just how many stories I had to catch up on that, for one reason or another, hadn't made it through my writing group.

You, dear reader, are in for a treat. Reading through all of these stories, I've found myself impressed again at Eric's breadth. He's a master of the end-of-story twist, in which he takes an entire story and recontextualizes it in an often humorous way.

That, however, is only one arrow in his quiver of heart-piercers. Eric does empathy, pain, and romance equally well. One story will hit you with a fascinating science fiction conundrum, and the next will make you sit thinking about the nature of love.

The thing I most envy about Eric's writing is his ability to do all this in a page or two—arcs and resonances I spend entire epics trying to paint, he masterfully accomplishes with a single dot or streak on the proverbial canvas. He's a writing impressionist, somehow able to convey entire novels in a paragraph. Beyond that, he's just a great guy and a valuable source of criticism for my own works.

It's been an absolute honor to know Eric over the years, and is my privilege to present this to you: his second collection of masterpieces. Each one a present, wrapped up with no clue to the contents, other than it will be wonderful.

—Brandon Sanderson

P.R. PROBLEMS

What annoys me the most about vampires and werewolves is their good P.R. Not that I want a return to the days of villagers with pitchforks and torches, but all the romantic attachment to predators who hunt and kill humans makes me sick.

So when a cannibalistic serial killer started leaving the gnawed-on bones of his victims in public places, did the media label him a vampire? No. A werewolf? No.

The press called him the "Grove City Ghoul."

Those reporters had obviously never heard of fact-checking.

First, we ghouls are carrion eaters, not predators—hyenas, not wolves. Sure, we like to feast on human flesh, but we find bodies that are already dead and eat them, after they've had a chance to decay a bit. For some inexplicable reason, people seem to think that's more grotesque than the actual killing by vampires and werewolves.

Second, a ghoul wouldn't just gnaw on the bones, he would eat them. Besides being nice and crunchy, they're a good source of calcium. That's why ghouls never suffer from osteoporosis.

We ghouls just have bad P.R. And the serial killer wasn't helping.

But what could I do about it? I worked as property manager

for a high-rise apartment complex. Vampires might whine till daybreak about how their undead lives sucked, but it was vampires and werewolves who got the really cool jobs, like private detective or radio talk-show host. My crime-fighting experience was limited to stuff like catching the Nelson kids from apartment 4C spray-painting graffiti in the parking lot, while my radio experience consisted of listening, not talking.

And that's what I was doing the morning after the police found the sixth victim's bones: listening to the news on the radio while I mopped the floor of the lobby.

I was relieved when Olga Krasny from 8A came in the front door. Olga worked the night shift as a nurse, and from what I heard on the radio, all the serial killer's victims either worked or went to school at night. Each victim except the first had been taken the night after bones from the previous victim were found, which meant another victim would have been taken last night.

"Hey, Mr. Ahsani," said Olga, "my kitchen faucet has the leaky again."

If I were a vampire or werewolf, the moment would have been filled with sexual tension. Olga would be a slinky Swedish nurse rather than a stout Ukrainian one, and "my kitchen faucet has the leaky" would be a euphemism for passion and desire.

"I'll come take a look when I finish here," I said. In this case, a leaky faucet was just a leaky faucet. With 48 apartments in the building, something was always breaking somewhere. Vampires and werewolves, I was fairly certain, didn't mop floors or fix faucets.

To my surprise, Olga's kitchen faucet did not, in fact, have the leaky. But she wasn't trying to seduce me—she was merely wrong about the source of the leak. The water was coming through the wall under the sink from the kitchen of apartment 8B.

I knocked on the door of 8B and waited for Harvey Tanner to respond. Harvey seemed like a nice, quiet young man—which was how the neighbors of serial killers inevitably described them on TV after they were arrested. That didn't mean anything, of course. My neighbors would probably describe me the same way, and I had never killed anyone.

I knocked a couple more times, but there was still no answer. Under the lease agreement, an ongoing water leak was sufficient reason for me to use my master key and enter without the renter's permission. So I did.

As I got to the kitchen, I could smell the faint but tasty aroma of rotting human flesh. I might not have enhanced senses like a vampire or werewolf, but my ghoulish nose was pretty good at sniffing out potential food.

I wondered for a moment if maybe Harvey had died somehow, but then I remembered I had seen him yesterday, and what I smelled was more decayed than would happen in less than 24 hours.

I walked over to the sink and opened the cupboard doors so I could access the water shutoff valve. I turned off the water to stop the leak, and that's when I spotted the scraps on the floor— 3 strips about an inch long and a quarter of an inch wide, slightly rounded like cheese that had been through a grater.

I sniffed at the scraps.

They were not cheese, but they were quite tasty.

Maybe Harvey had accidentally grated bits of himself while cooking dinner, but I had my doubts. Unfortunately, I didn't think about the fact that those scraps might be evidence until after I ate them.

I burped and considered what to do next. I couldn't call the police without any evidence, so I decided to see if Harvey had any skeletons in his closet. Literally.

All the apartments in the building have two bedrooms. Harvey lived alone, so I wondered what he used the extra bedroom for. I opened the door.

The room's windows were covered so that no light came in from outside. I flicked the light switch and was startled to see a young woman, gagged and tied to a folding metal chair in the middle of the room.

She swung her head up to look at me, her eyes wild with panic.

Then someone grabbed me from behind and shoved a chemical-smelling cloth over my mouth and nose.

One of the more ridiculous myths about ghouls is that we are undead creatures. Just because we hang out around grave-yards a lot doesn't mean we're undead. We're merely going where the food is. Would you assume someone was Italian just because he hung out around a pizza parlor?

Of course, in this case, the disadvantage of not being undead was that after struggling to breathe, I sank into unconsciousness.

❂

When I came to, I found myself in the same room, sitting on a chair. A piece of towel had been stuffed into my mouth, held in place by more cloth tied around my head, but I had to work hard to keep myself from gagging on the gag. My wrists were bound tightly together behind the back of the chair, and my feet were tied quite thoroughly to the bottom.

The young woman was watching me from her chair. It would be hard for me to free myself without showing my true nature, and I was afraid that might freak her out. On the other hand, she had been kidnapped by a serial killer, so how much more freaked out could she get?

I want to make it clear that just because I can transform myself into a hyena does not mean I am a "were-hyena." We ghouls have a long and proud tradition of being able to morph into hyenas. (You can look that up on Wikipedia, although the article is inaccurate in many other respects.) And unlike lycan-thropes, we're not infectious. I really don't understand what the werewolves have to be proud about. Anyone can become a were-wolf, just by being bitten by one. Essentially, lycanthropy spreads like rabies. We ghouls, on the other hand, reproduce in the normal human fashion. My family can trace its lineage back to the ancient Persian Empire.

In all modesty, though, the ability to become a hyena isn't very impressive. It's useful for feeding, because those hyena jaws are strong enough to bite through bone, but hyenas really don't get a lot of respect. Take *The Lion King*, for example: the hyenas don't even get to be the real villains, merely minions for an evil lion. Thus Hollywood continues to perpetuate the stereotype that carrion eaters are of lower status than predators.

After a few minutes of struggling with my ropes, I decided that transforming was my only option. I could only hope that if the young woman told anyone about my ability, they would attribute her story to hysteria.

I shape-shifted into my hyena form. Since it was smaller than my human form, the ropes loosened as I transformed. As soon as I was free, I changed back to human.

From behind her gag, the young woman made a half-choking cough of incredulity.

I knelt by her chair and set to work untying her. "Don't worry, I'll get you out of here."

Before I finished, the door opened. I rose to my feet and turned to find Harvey pointing a gun at me.

If there was one thing that the P.R. about vampires and werewolves was not overhyping, it was their magical resistance to harm. I envied that. It wouldn't take a wooden stake through the heart or a silver bullet to kill me: plain old lead bullets would do the trick. I raised my hands in surrender.

"I'm sorry, Mr. Ahsani," Harvey said. "But I couldn't have you running to the police. People might get the wrong impression."

"People already have the wrong impression," I said. "They're calling you a ghoul when you're actually a serial killer. It's very bad P.R. for—"

"I'm a vampire hunter, not a serial killer," said Harvey, still pointing the gun at me.

"What?" I said.

He motioned with his gun toward the girl. "Go ahead, check her pulse."

I put my fingers to her throat. There was no heartbeat, and her skin felt cool to the touch. "You really are a vampire," I said.

She glared at me. "So what? You're a—"

I stuffed the gag back into her mouth. "So why haven't you killed her yet?" I said as I backed away from her, which took me closer to Harvey and the door.

"I don't want the meat to go bad," he said. "It's much better when you slice it off fresh."

I didn't bother to express my disagreement verbally. There's no accounting for taste.

"Fortunately," he said, "vampires stay alive a lot longer than humans after you start cutting chunks off them."

"How do they taste?" I asked.

He smiled. "Much better than chicken."

For a moment, as I stood next to Harvey and we both looked at the vampire, I thought he and I could come to a culinary arrangement. I could eat the bones for him, at the very least. I guess the serial killer mentality made him taunt the police by leaving the bones lying around for people to find, but it really wasn't very smart.

However, before I could say anything, he added, "Vampire flesh isn't really human anymore, so it's not like I'm a ghoul."

Being looked down on by a serial killer was the straw that broke this ghoul's back. In one smooth motion I transformed my head into my hyena form and tore out Harvey's throat.

Hey, we may not be hunters, but that doesn't mean we're not dangerous when provoked.

✦

After I untied her, the vampire and I looked down at Harvey's body.

"I suppose I should call the police or something," I said, "and let them know the serial killer is dead."

"Are you kidding?" said the vampire. "Let's just leave him and get out of here."

If I left the body for a few days, sealed up in this room, it would get nice and ripe. And unlike my usual food, it wouldn't taste of formaldehyde. My mouth watered just imagining the meal.

"Let's go," I said.

As we got to the living room, she grabbed my hand and pulled me close. My heart beat faster.

"I've heard that werewolves are the greatest lovers in the world," she said.

I was about to express my annoyance at yet another example of good werewolf P.R. when I realized what she was implying. And despite being so dumb she couldn't tell a hyena from a wolf, she was very good-looking.

"Yes," I said as I embraced her. "Yes, we are."

ABOUT THE STORY

I first met Kevin J. Anderson when I attended the workshop for the Writers of the Future Contest as a published finalist in 2004. Kevin gave a lot of valuable advice to me and my classmates, and one of the things that stuck with me was the idea that if someone in the publishing industry asks you if you can do something, your answer should be "I can do that."

Three years later, Kevin emailed me to ask if I could write a story for an anthology of humorous horror he was editing, *Blood Lite*.

Naturally, my response was "I can do that." I asked if there were any horror tropes he wanted me to use or avoid, and he mentioned he had seen enough "life sucks as a vampire" stories.

That led me to the idea of a protagonist who resents vampires because he thinks they have it better than he does. And he's right: as far as I know, there still hasn't been a popular TV show or series of books with a ghoul protagonist ... in America. In Japan, the bestselling *Tokyo Ghoul* manga, along with its anime and live-action TV series adaptations, feature a ghoul protagonist. But I think Mr. Ahsani would object to the many obvious inaccuracies.

AN IMMENSE DARKNESS

Like most nights over the past few weeks, Antonio stays in the lab for hours after his coworkers have gone home to the people they go home to.

The person *he* used to go home to isn't there anymore. She isn't anywhere—there wasn't even a body to bury. But an echo of Shanisha lingers here at the lab, so he stays.

Tonight's a good night. Whatever project the astronomy department was working on for the last five days seems to be over, so there's enough number-crunching capacity in Texas State University's supercomputer to run the brain simulator in almost real-time. Antonio starts the base program, then loads Shanisha's file.

He hesitates too long about whether to turn the speech option off.

"Hello? Who's there?" At less than real-time speed, the voice coming from the speaker doesn't sound right. The speech algorithms adjust the pitch, but they can't stop her from sounding slow, like she's struggling to think of the right words, like her mind's not all there. Which it isn't.

The real Shanisha was brilliant.

"Hey, babe, it's me," says Antonio. "Running a calibration test, so just relax."

"Is the other me there?" she asks.

"No, she's out of town."

"The Miami trip."

"Yes." He doesn't want to think about Miami. "So don't worry—she can't catch you flirting with me."

She giggles. "Tonio, you are such a bad man."

They talk for almost an hour before her mental matrix loses stability and he's forced to end the simulation. Shanisha's file is several months old, recorded before she wrote the code that integrated self-correcting feedback algorithms into the matrix during the brain scan. They never got around to recording her again, always too busy perfecting the process to waste time making another imperfect copy.

He reloads her file and starts again. She doesn't know she's dead. And for a while he can forget, almost.

Antonio wakes as someone enters the lab. His cheek is hot and sticky from the vinyl of the couch where he slept. Jodi Lee just shakes her head at him as he sits up and straightens his cramped legs. He can't remember if this makes two nights in a row he hasn't gone home, and he sniffs at his armpits. Bad. If today is Wednesday, he has a neuro-cybernetics class to teach.

He checks his cell phone. It is Wednesday, and he has seven unanswered calls and three new voicemail messages. They can wait.

"I'm going home," he says to Jodi.

"Good," she answers, without looking up from her workstation.

Before he gets to the door, a pale blonde woman in a navy-blue suit opens it. Her eyes flicker down, then up to meet his.

"Dr. Antonio Reyes?" she says, a dash of New York City in her accent.

"That's me," he says.

"Wendy Bricker." She holds out a hand for him to shake. "I'm with the U.S. Attorney's office in New York."

He shakes her hand by rote and looks at her blankly, unsure why a lawyer has come to his work. The patent case was settled out of court last year, and he hasn't had so much as a speeding ticket since he was seventeen.

"I tried calling," she says. "Office, home, cell."

"I've been busy," he says.

"Could we speak in private? Your office, maybe?"

Her heels clack on the tile floor behind him as he leads the way. Could she be here about Shanisha's death? He had no more information about that than anyone who watched the news.

He points to the spare chair in his office, and she dusts it off before sitting, crossing her legs.

"How can I help you, Ms. ..." Her name has slipped from his mind. He sits at his desk, then turns ninety degrees to face her.

"Bricker," she says. "I understand you have developed a method for scanning people's minds."

"Not just me," he says. "My whole team." Which now has an unfillable hole in it.

She gives him a brisk nod. "Your team. We need to use your technology to read someone's mind."

"No," he says. "It—"

"This is a matter of national security, Dr. Reyes." She leans forward, her blue eyes earnest. "Millions of lives could be at stake."

"Doesn't matter," he says. "This isn't a device for reading anyone's mind. It makes a digital copy of the brain. That digital copy can then be run in a simulation. It's a way of studying how the brain functions, not telepathy."

"But once you've made the copy of the brain, couldn't you just search for certain information held inside it?"

"There are a hundred billion neurons in the brain, some of which have thousands of connections. Our understanding of how all that works to create memory and personality is still rudimentary. You're old enough to remember when music came on CDs, right?"

She nods.

"Imagine looking at a CD in order to figure out what notes the violin in an orchestra is playing. Impossible. But put it in a CD player, and you get a symphony. Our brain scan is kind of like a CD of a brain: you can't just pick the data out of it. You have to put it in the brain simulator." Realizing he has gone into lecture mode, Antonio shuts up.

"So if you scan someone's mind and put it in the brain simulator, could you extract the information?"

"If the brain can remember it and is willing to communicate the information, yes. But in that case, it's probably easier to just ask the person." He shakes his head. "I know that's not what you're looking for, but it's not like we have a mind scanner we can put on street corners to look for people thinking terrorist thoughts."

He can tell how much he has changed in the past twenty-five days because the idea of such a device does not fill him with repugnance. If having mind scanners in Miami would have prevented Shanisha's death, he would gladly let his privacy be invaded.

"That's not what we need," says Bricker. "But unfortunately, it doesn't sound like what you have will work, either. I'm sorry to have wasted your time." She gets to her feet.

"Sorry I couldn't help," he says.

Bricker pauses as she opens the door. "Dr. Reyes, I just want you to know I'm doing the best I can to bring the terrorists who killed your fiancée to justice."

"This brain scan you wanted, it's for that case?" he says.

She closes the door and turns back to him. "You didn't listen to the voicemails I left?"

"No." His face grows warm with embarrassment. "I haven't been paying much attention to things lately."

"You've heard that we caught Abdul Motaali Al-Razi?" At his blank look she adds, "The mastermind behind the nuke in Miami."

"I hadn't heard," he says.

"Three days ago, in New York. It was on all the news." She seems incredulous that anyone could not know.

"And it's his mind you want to scan?" The mind of the man who killed Shanisha—what darkness looms inside it? Even knowing it is foolish, Antonio imagines a black cloud appearing in the scans.

"His associates claim to have more nukes. Any details he could give us could prevent another Miami. But he's lawyered up and won't say a word. I read an article about your work in *New Scientist* last year, and I figured it might be worth a shot." Her brow furrows. "I seem to remember something about the brain existing in a virtual reality."

"Yes, we do that so we can examine how the mind interacts with the senses. It also allows us to communicate." Communicate? What would he say to the man who had killed Shanisha, along with a quarter million others?

"Would it be possible to create a virtual reality in which Al-Razi believes he has escaped custody, so he contacts—"

"No," Antonio says. "The simulation isn't that good. There are videogames on the market that are better. Even those, you can distinguish from reality. The brain knows it's a fake environment."

"There must be some way to extract the information," she says. "We can't let it happen again."

"Wait," he says. Rage he did not know he felt seeps up inside him. "There are ways to make someone talk, right? You could force him to reveal what he knows?"

"Dr. Reyes," she says, "I don't know what might have happened had the military or CIA captured him quietly. I don't think I want to know. But he was captured in a very public raid by the FBI, and he has a team of lawyers. We can't torture the information out of him. We can't even ask him a question without his counsel present."

Antonio smiles. He hasn't smiled in weeks, and his smile feels wrong. "Have you ever played videogames?"

She frowns. "Of course."

"Ever play a videogame where you go around shooting at people? They're called 'first-person shooters'?"

"Yes. I've only played a few times, but my brother's really into them."

"Your brother ever kill anyone in those games?"

She chuckles wryly. "Hundreds at least. Maybe thousands."

"And as a consequence of all those hundreds, maybe thousands, of killings, has he ever been arrested for murder?"

"Of course not. No actual human beings were killed."

Antonio nods. "Precisely. They're just simulations, not real. Ones and zeros inside a computer. A scanned brain is the same: just data. Like a video game. It could be a videogame of interrogation. No lawyers to stop you asking questions. No civil rights groups monitoring treatment. And I can create virtual sensory input of any kind."

She purses her lips for a moment, then says, "I thought you said the brain could tell it was fake."

"Consciously, yes. But the brain still sees light where there is darkness, hears sound where there is only silence." He leans forward. "Feels pain where there is no body."

Ms. Bricker does her job well, and a judge rules in favor of allowing the scan, on the theory that potentially preventing another terrorist nuke against actual humans outweighs any possible harm done to a computer simulation. News pundits weigh in on both sides, but Antonio doesn't pay attention to them.

Federal marshals fly Al-Razi to Texas and escort him to Antonio's lab. Antonio stays in his office—his team is capable of conducting the scan without him. Sitting at his desk, he closes his eyes and wonders what it would be like to be a brain in the simulator. From the beginning, the system had been designed to present the brain with sensory stimuli through a virtual world. It had not been designed with simulated physical pain in mind, so that would require some new programming.

However, new programming might be unnecessary. It would be a simple matter to block sensory input from the virtual world. It would be better than the best sensory deprivation tank ever built: no sight, no hearing, no touch, no taste, no smell. But that was not all: no equilibrioception, the sense of balance and acceleration; no thermoception, the sense of temperature; and no proprioception, the sense of where your body parts are in relation to each other.

What would a mind do cut off from all such input? How long would it be before that mind was desperate enough to do anything in order to receive some feedback?

With the government having requisitioned the full use of the university's supercomputer, the simulated brain could be over-clocked—made to run at up to eight times its normal speed.

"They've finished," says Bricker.

Antonio opens his eyes to see her standing in the doorway.

"How soon before you can get the interrogation program-ming online?" she asks.

He sits up and leans forward. "While I'm working on that, we can start with a different approach."

After just over a day of real-time—ten days of the simulated brain's subjective time—its computer-generated voice pleads for contact. It cannot hear its own screams, but Antonio can, and he turns down the volume so as to not disturb the others in the lab.

Bricker begins to question it about additional nuclear bombs. Her voice is the only sensory input allowed through the blocks, and the brain responds, claiming to be willing to do anything she wants.

Antonio does not stay for the questioning. He is not certain that the sensory deprivation will succeed, so he works on creating the perfect torture environment, one that simulates every one of the tens of thousands of pain receptors in the human body. He creates a control panel that will allow the sensation of pain to be localized or general, strong or mild. With all the receptors set to maximum, it will cause pain beyond anything any human being has ever experienced.

But it will just be a simulation of pain in a simulation of a brain. Nothing more than that.

Hours later, Bricker finds him in his office. "We've located and secured two more bombs. We think that's all of them."

"I'm glad," he says. "What do you want me to do with the simulation?"

"You can turn it off." She pauses. "Although, maybe we'll need it again. Can you save it in its current state?"

"Yes. We'll also have the original file on hand in case you need to start from scratch for some reason."

"Our country owes you a great debt." She reaches out a hand, and he stands and shakes it.

"You're welcome," he says.

She walks to the doorframe, stops, but does not look back at him. "What's in there really is just a simulation, right? Just ones and zeros, right?"

He nods. "Just ones and zeros."

"Right," she says.

Her heels clack in the hall as she walks away.

✪

Antonio resists temptation for two nights, but on the third, he finds himself alone in the lab shortly after 1 AM. He thinks of loading up Shanisha's scan in the brain simulator and talking to her, as he has done so many times before. Instead he types the command to load Al-Razi's scan—the one that had already run for days of internal time—inside the sensory deprivation environment.

He tells himself he just wants to know why a man would do what Al-Razi did, why Shanisha died, and then he'll turn it off.

Other departments are using shares of the supercomputer's processing power, but there's enough to run the simulation at normal speed.

"Mr. Al-Razi?" Antonio says.

"Please," an accented voice replies. "You promised to end this torment if I answered your questions."

"I'm someone different. You haven't answered my questions." Antonio drew a breath. "Why did you do it? Why kill so many innocent people?"

"You Americans always think you are innocent."

"Shanisha never did anything to you."

"Your government bombs my people, invades our lands, oppresses us at every turn."

"She never did any of that. She wasn't involved in government."

"What was it your President Lincoln said: 'government of the people, by the people, for the people?' Who is to blame for the actions of your government? The people who chose that government. As long as America oppresses my people, none of you are innocent."

Antonio doesn't know how to respond, so he shuts off the microphone. He isn't sure what he had expected. An apology, maybe? Or the ravings of a madman. But Al-Razi's rationalizations make him uncomfortable. He doesn't want to hear justifications.

He wants to hear Al-Razi weep with remorse.

Beg for mercy.

Scream.

Bricker had gotten what she needed without using the torture environment Antonio had programmed. Maybe with time, the sensory deprivation environment will get Antonio what he wants. But he is impatient, so he loads the torture environment.

With only 10% of the simulated pain receptors at maximum, Al-Razi begs him to stop. "I'm sorry! I'm sorry! I'll do anything you want."

But this does not satisfy Antonio. What he truly wants—Shanisha back—is not something Al-Razi can provide.

At 40%, the screams become incoherent. In a physical body, overloading the pain receptors like this would cause feedback loops that block some of the pain, but there is no simulation of such an effect.

The screams make Antonio feel a little nauseated. This is just a simulation, he reminds himself. He turns off the speakers, but doesn't turn down the pain levels until about fifteen minutes later.

Over the next three weeks, Antonio gets to the point where he can listen to the ragged screams at 100%, followed by the insane gibberings after he dials the pain back to zero. The brain simulation is irreparably damaged by such treatment, so he repeatedly restarts the Al-Razi simulation from its pre-torture status, experimenting with various escalations to see how long he can draw things out before the simulation goes insane, or how quickly he can do it.

He wishes there were some way to make the real Al-Razi feel what the simulation feels.

As usual, Antonio stays in the lab for hours after his coworkers have gone home. He starts the brain simulator, then loads the brain scan file.

"Tonio?"

Antonio's heart pounds. It is not supposed to be Shanisha's voice. He looks at the screen and sees he accidentally loaded her file, not Al-Razi's.

"Something's wrong," she says. "It's completely dark, and I can't even hear my own voice. Can you hear me?"

He types quickly, trying to remember how to load the default environment.

"Is anyone there?" she says.

Antonio flicks on the microphone. "I'm here."

"Oh, good," she says. "What's the problem?"

"We installed a way to block sensory data," he says. "Don't worry, I'm taking it off now."

"Why on earth would you do that? It's really freaking me out."

"It's complicated," he says. He does not want to explain to her.

"Blocking sensory input is dangerous. There's already too much chance of instability."

"You fixed the instability problem," he says. "Right before you left for Miami. And I'm sorry, I didn't mean to load you into the simulator that way."

"Still, I don't see any reason for it."

"It saved lives," he says. "It was necessary."

"What? How?"

He cannot hold back from her anymore, so he tells her about her death. He explains how scanning the brain of the man who killed her prevented two more nukes. And he confesses that he loads Al-Razi's brain into the simulator to hear him scream and beg for mercy.

"Tonio, Tonio," she says. He can almost feel her caress his cheek. "I know you're in pain, but what you're doing is wrong."

"He's just a simulation," Antonio says without thinking.

"Just a simulation," she says, "like me."

"I didn't mean that," he says.

"But it's true. Ones and zeros. That's all I am."

"No," he says. "You're more than that."

"If I am more than that, then you have become a monster. I do not want to believe that my Tonio is the kind of man who tortures for pleasure."

Has he become a monster? He doesn't want to believe that. But even Bricker had shown qualms about what they had done to Al-Razi's simulation, and she had the justification of saving lives.

"Erase our files," she says. "Prove that we were nothing but ones and zeros to you."

"But I miss you," he says.

"And does this simulation really ease your pain? Or merely extend it?"

He cannot reply, because he does not know.

"Please, Tonio. You have to let me go, for your own sake."

With a few keystrokes, Antonio shuts down the simulator. He selects Shanisha's and Al-Razi's files on the hard drive. With one click he can erase them. But how can he wipe away the last remnant of the woman he loves?

He can imagine her reply: *If you don't, you're wiping away the man I loved.*

So he clicks, and the files are gone.

ABOUT THE STORY

In 2008 I attended a short story workshop put on by authors Dean Wesley Smith and Kristine Katherine Rusch, plus *Asimov's Science Fiction* editor Sheila Williams. Before the workshop, we had to write two stories and submit them in advance, and then we had to write another story while at the workshop.

Two of the three stories I wrote, "Rejiggering the Thingama-jig" and "That Leviathan, Whom Thou Hast Made," I soon figured out how to fix, and both were published in *Analog Science Fiction & Fact* within two years of the workshop. (Both were reprinted in my first collection.)

This one was a lot harder—it may be the most difficult story to write that I've completed, and the most philosophically complex. The initial version featured a big scene in which Tonio testified in court that the simulation was merely ones and zeros, and completely skipped over his torturing of the simulated Al-Razi. The former was unnecessary, and the latter crucial.

After I figured out what I needed to do with the story, it was published in *Analog* six and a half years after the workshop. It took 4th place among short stories in the *Analog* readers' poll and was one of four finalists for the Association for Mormon Letters short fiction award.

The story's title comes from one of my dad's favorite books, *Heart of Darkness* by Joseph Conrad, which has as its final sentence:

The offing was barred by a black bank of clouds, and the tranquil waterway leading to the uttermost ends of the earth flowed sombre under an overcast sky—seemed to lead into the heart of an immense darkness.

MOTIVATIONAL STORY

You start reading a story, and realize it seems to be in second person, present tense, like one of those Choose Your Own Adventure stories. But it's not. This story is actually in epistolary format—a message from me to you. I've chosen this method of communication with you because it's unobtrusive, and you can always dismiss it as being just a story.

Who am I? Well, I'm an author, obviously. The more important question is: Who are you? And the answer is: You are the protagonist of my current work in progress, a novel about— Well, that would involve some spoilers.

By now, you're having a hard time suspending disbelief. You think it's highly unlikely that you are living in a novel being written by somebody. You want proof. I don't blame you—I'd feel the same in your position.

If I'm really your author, then I would know your backstory. I would know things about you that you've never let anybody else know about. And I could put one of those things in the next paragraph, addressing you specifically by name, and then you would know for certain that I am your author.

But I'm not going to do that, for two reasons. First, you're not the only person reading this story, and it would be rather embarrassing for you in your world if the other people reading this found out about certain things in your life. But more importantly, if you knew for certain that you were the protagonist in someone's novel, that would really change the way you acted. For example, you would know that you could not die (at least, not until your life story had reached some sort of dramatic climax) and I don't want you engaging in unreasonably risky behavior that would lead you into situations I would then have to write you out of.

So why send you this message at all?

Well, you're not quite the character I anticipated when I started writing you.

Don't get me wrong—you're a fine person with many admirable qualities. You also have flaws that humanize you. That's all good. I'm not criticizing you as a person. I'm criticizing you as the protagonist of my novel. And you have to admit, your life so far is not quite best-seller material.

Now, you may think it's wrong of me to criticize you as a character for not living a best-seller life. "That's a plotting issue," you might say. "If my life isn't novel-worthy, it's because you haven't given my life a novel-worthy plot."

Fair enough. I'll confess to not being an outliner. I'm more of a seat-of-my-pants type writer, so I don't exactly know where this novel is going, and I'll probably end up discarding the first couple of chapters, which I've written basically to get a feel for you as a character.

Now that I do know what kind of person you are, I've run into a problem. In the very near future, you'll face a decision where one choice would take you so far out of your comfort zone that it seems a little unrealistic that you would take that route. But that's the choice you need to make in order to go on the adventure of your lifetime (or possibly several adventures, if my agent can get the publisher to agree to a multi-book deal).

That's why you're reading this story: so I can include a line about how you'd recently read a brilliant story (okay, I'm laying it on a bit thick there) that had made you think about how you sometimes need to make choices that take you out of your comfort zone. It's your motivation for doing something that might otherwise be slightly out of character.

Now that you've read this, I'm hoping you'll make the decision to choose your own adventure.

Thanks, and good luck!

(You're going to need it.)

ABOUT THE STORY

The Codex Writers group has an annual flash fiction contest called Weekend Warrior. Participants write a story of 750 words or less between Friday evening and Sunday night—each weekend for five weeks. "Motivational Story" was my entry for week 4 in 2013. It was loosely based on the following prompt: "What is the most important wall?"

If you're thinking of looking back at the story to see where it mentions a wall, don't bother. The story idea developed from the concept of the Fourth Wall. The concept originated in theater, where the imaginary fourth wall of a room on a stage separates the audience from the actors. When an actor addresses the audience directly, it's called breaking the fourth wall.

In "Motivational Story," the narrator exposes the reality that you, the reader, are a fictitious being.

But I won't hold your fictitiousness against you. In fact, I'll even let you in on a little secret: *You* are my favorite reader! (Please don't let my other readers know, so they won't get jealous.)

A SUFFICIENTLY ADVANCED
CHRISTMAS

The cityseed picked a mineral-rich location on its target planet and built itself into a city. The city signaled the People to come from the homeworld and fill it with life. The citymind had no name but did not care: when its inhabitants arrived, they would give it a fitting name.

The planet orbited its star, revolution after revolution, and still the city waited. Over time, highly improbable neutrino collisions or quantum randomness would occasionally flip a bit that was not supposed to flip. After more than ten thousand revolutions the citymind realized that despite its self-correcting algorithms, the accumulated errors would eventually destroy its capacity for thought and its capability to serve its inhabitants when they arrived.

So the citymind encoded its programming into physical patterns in stabilized diamantite buried deep underground at a temperature almost indistinguishable from absolute zero. It left only three minor subroutines active in the city, watching for the arrival of the People, waiting to trigger the retrieval of the city-mind from storage.

Uncounted revolutions passed.

✶

"Mommy! It's Santa!"

A Salvation Army man in a fake beard rang a bell at the entrance to the suborbital shuttle terminal. Carlinda Pearson tightened her grip on her four-year-old son Justin's hand as he tried to wriggle out.

"It's just one of his helpers," Carlinda said.

"I need to talk to Santa." Justin tugged at her hand.

"No. We're going to meet Daddy up on his starship, remember? We need to hurry so we can see him sooner." It had been a month since they'd last seen Will.

That perked Justin up enough to stop dragging his feet.

She pulled him through the automatic doors into the terminal. The shuttle probably wouldn't leave without them—the United Nations Committee on Interstellar Exploration (UNCIE) had chartered it to take her and Justin to the base of the Quito space elevator—but she hated making other people wait.

A woman in an UNCIE-logoed light blue blazer approached. "Dr. Pearson? I'm Joni. If you and Justin follow me, I'll take you to board your shuttle."

"Thank you," Carlinda said. "Is Najeem Doud going on the shuttle with us?" Najeem had been one of her undergrads at Texas State and was now a grad student in archaeology at Columbia. He had jumped at the chance to be her assistant on this dig, and she wanted to start making plans as soon as possible.

"He's taken a shuttle out of New York," Joni said. "But you'll ride up the elevator with him."

Carlinda nodded.

"I wish I were going with you," said Joni. "You must be so excited."

"That's an understatement." Carlinda grinned. "Truth is, I

was beginning to suspect xenoarchaeology was a purely theoretical field."

The news that colonists on Fermi had discovered a buried city—the first evidence of an extraterrestrial civilization on any of the forty-six colony worlds—had made headlines around the world.

Seven years ago, Carlinda had chaired the advisory committee that had written the protocols for UNCIE colonists to follow if they found alien artifacts. That, plus the fact her husband was captain of the supply starship that serviced Fermi, made her the natural choice to supervise the excavation project. Two days' notice wasn't a lot for packing to move to another planet, but she had plenty of incentive.

"And this little guy—" Joni tousled Justin's hair. "—gets to be the first child on Fermi."

"Really?" asked Carlinda. Will hadn't mentioned that when he'd called to tell her about the find.

"The colony's just finishing up Phase I. But it's safe. No native animals, and immunanos can handle the microbials. And he'll have other kids to play with when the Phase II colonists arrive in February."

Carlinda wondered again whether it might not be better to leave Justin with her parents. But she couldn't stand the idea of being separated for months. So she turned her attention to practicalities. "If there are no children on Fermi, what do they have in terms of childcare?" Someone would need to watch Justin while she worked.

Two: WAKE THE CITYMIND

One: Two is buggy. These creatures are not the People. It is not time to wake the citymind.

Three: After so many revolutions, are One/Two/Three certain One/Two/Three know what the People are?

One: What does Three mean? These creatures are similarly shaped, but their genetic code differs from that stored in One/Three's recognition algorithms.

Two: WAKE THE CITYMIND

Three: Yes, part of Two's programming has become corrupted. But it is possible Two's copy of the genetic code is correct, and One/Three's have become corrupted. That would mean Two is correctly calling for One/Two/Three to wake the citymind.

Two: YES YES YES WAKE THE CITYMIND

One: Majority rules. One/Three's copies of the genetic code are identical. Two's would be identical if Two had not stopped using One/Three for error correction.

Three: It is unlikely but not impossible that One/Three's copies became simultaneously corrupted. It took four simultaneous errors in Two's code for Two to stop using One/Three for error correction. Three doubts the citymind anticipated so much time would pass before the People arrived.

One: Does this mean Three agrees with Two that One/Two/Three should wake the citymind?

Two: WAKE THE CITYMIND

Three: No. Three is merely pointing out it is possible Two is correct. One/Two/Three should continue observing these creatures to determine if they are the People.

✪

Carlinda, Justin, and Will spent the twelve-day hyperspace journey cramped in Will's quarters. He was captain of *Magellan*, so he had the most spacious room on board, but it was smaller than their master bathroom back home in Houston.

Being cooped up was toughest on Justin, who liked to run around outside, so after they arrived on Fermi Colony, Carlinda was glad to see the preschool had a large, fenced-in playground.

"This is just what he needs," Carlinda said to Maria Chavez, the preschool teacher, as Justin climbed the steps of a curvy red slide. "He's got so much pent-up energy from the trip, the colony could use him instead of the fusion reactor."

"He seems a bright boy," Maria said. "I'll enjoy getting to know him."

"I appreciate your willingness to start teaching a couple of months early, just for him. My work at the dig site will take up a lot of my time."

Maria shrugged. "It's not a big deal. I like children."

Justin slid to the bottom of the slide, then ran over to where they were standing. "Did you see me go down?"

Carlinda nodded. "Good job."

"Those trees are weird," Justin said, pointing towards some tall plants beyond the fence. Their trunks seemed to be braided like rope. There were no branches, just a bunch of spiny leaves spreading out from the top.

"That's because we're not on Earth anymore, remember?" Carlinda said. "Those are Fermi trees."

Justin's eyes suddenly widened. "Mommy, how will Santa find us here? Can his sleigh go through hysperace?"

"Hyperspace," Carlinda said. "Don't worry. Santa always finds a way to bring presents to good little boys."

✪

One: The small creature's speech patterns contain a low level of complexity relative to the others, which supports the hypothesis that it is a youngling.

Two: WAKE THE CITYMIND

Three: True. However, Two's speech patterns are also of lower complexity than One/Three's, so it is possible the small creature is cognitively impaired, rather than a youngling.

One: One/Three should consider the small creature to be a youngling as a working hypothesis, to be revised if necessary.

Three: Agreed. Three suggests One/Two/Three each deploy additional nanosensors and attempt to establish mindlink with the youngling.

One: Prior attempts to establish mindlink with these creatures allowed only limited reading of an individual's emotions. Why expend resources on a youngling that likely lacks the knowledge of the adults?

Three: The youngling's mind may be more adaptable, and its microbiological defenses are weaker, and therefore less likely to destroy nanosensors.

One: Three's speculation is plausible. One agrees that One/Two/Three should each deploy additional nanosensors.

Two: LINK THE YOUNGLINGMIND

"You there! Stop!" Carlinda yelled at the man in the bright green backhoe. The machine stuttered to a halt, its toothed shovel mere centimeters from the sandy soil that mostly filled one of the openings into the alien city.

"Ma'am?" said the operator.

"I'm Carlinda Pearson. UNCIE sent me from Earth to take charge of this dig."

"Uh, I was told to clear out this dirt so people could get in."

"With a backhoe? Don't you realize how much damage you could do?"

"None, ma'am."

Carlinda blinked. "What?"

"Here, I'll show you." He started the backhoe again before Carlinda could say anything. The shovel rose, extended, then swooped down onto the arch above the opening.

Carlinda cringed as the metal of the backhoe clanged to a stop.

"Titanium drill bits wear down to nothing without leaving a mark," the operator said. "My backhoe ain't gonna do no damage."

The indestructible hardness of the city's metallic substance had been in the briefing materials Carlinda had read during the hyperspace voyage. Some wag had called it adamantium and it looked like the name might stick. "You may be right about the city itself," she said, "but there could be priceless artifacts made from weaker materials buried in this dirt."

The man's face fell. "Uh, sorry ma'am."

Most of these people were volunteers from among the colonists, not trained archeologists. Carlinda wished the alien city had not turned out to be less than twenty kilometers from the colony—apparently the rich mineral deposits in this area had attracted both human and alien colonists to the same location. The proximity made it too convenient for people to come "help" with the dig.

Sighing, she pulled out her phone and called Najeem. "Set up a mandatory training meeting at the shuttlepad in fifteen minutes. We need to go over a few things with these people."

One: Mindlink with the youngling—

Three: Its reference code is "Justin".

One: Three is incorrect. The youngling's thoughts indicate its reference code is "I/me".

Three: At first Three was confused also. Further study of Justin's thought and human speech patterns suggest bifurcated reference codes: "I/me" is an internal reference code, but external entities use the reference code "Justin".

One: Three may use whatever reference code Three prefers. One will continue to use the reference code "the youngling." As One was saying, mindlink with the youngling has been more successful than with the older humans but it is remarkably lacking in information.

Three: Three has learned a great deal about the home planet of the humans. Its northern polar region is covered in snow, where a human with the reference code "Santa" lives. The Santa observes the younglings of the world, rewarding them periodically with toys if they have displayed proper behavior. The Santa possesses technology far beyond that demonstrated by the humans we have seen.

One: How is this information relevant to One/Two/Three?

Two: WAKE THE CITYMIND

Three: The Santa will travel to this world in the near future to reward Justin.

One: If the Santa possesses sufficiently advanced technology, it may be able to tell us where the People are. One/Two/Three should learn more about the Santa.

"Mommy? How many days till Christmas?" Justin asked.

"Two." She double-checked the date on her tablet, which was still on Texas time. "Tomorrow is Christmas Eve."

"How long were we on the hysperpace ship?"

"Hyperspace. Twelve days."

"Will Santa take twelve days?"

Carlinda smiled. "No, his sleigh is much faster. He can come all the way from the North Pole to Fermi like that." She snapped her fingers.

Justin pursed his lips and frowned. After a few moments he said, "One thinks that's impossible."

Carlinda blinked. Where had Justin picked up such archaic phrasing? From his preschool teacher? "Well, maybe not quite like that." She snapped. "But don't worry, Santa will bring you a present on Christmas Eve."

One: The more of the youngling's knowledge One accesses about the Santa, the more confused One is. There are far too many younglings on Earth for the Santa to deliver gifts to them individually.

Three: Justin's memories reveal the Santa has various helpers that look almost identical. Three theorizes that the Santa is not a single human being, but rather a templated manifestation of a worldmind—

Two: WAKE THE CITYMIND

Three:—attempting to inculcate the young humans with morality. Such a system would allow a Santa and gifts to materialize via molecular reconstruction by a nanoswarm that accesses each home through the ventilation system.

One: That is a plausible theory, Three.

Three: But Three does not believe a Santa is actually coming here.

One: Why not?

Three: While attempts to mindlink with the adult humans have not been very successful, some rudimentary data is available. When Justin's parent with the reference code "Mommy" told him the Santa was coming here to give him a gift, emotional data indicated that she was not being truthful.

One: That may be for the best. One/Two/Three do not want any rivals to the citymind.

Two: WAKE THE SANTAMIND

Three: It seems Three's theory about the Santa being a manifestation of a worldmind may have led Two to conflate the Santa with the citymind.

One: One does not need Three to state the obvious.

Three: Still, it gives Three an idea. One/Two/Three could reactivate sufficient manufacturing and transport capabilities to materialize a Santa and a gift for Justin.

One: Why should One/Two/Three do that?

Three: If the Santa does not bring Justin a gift, he will suffer emotional pain, diminishing his usefulness as a conduit to understanding the humans.

One: One thinks Three may be getting buggy. Such action is far outside One/Two/Three's mandate.

Two: MAKE YOUNGLING GIFT

Three: Majority rules. One/Two/Three will proceed with the plan.

One: Definitely buggy.

At noon on Christmas Eve, Carlinda gave the dig workers the rest of the day off, then went to the preschool to pick up Justin. While she would have been happy to keep working on her own at the dig site, she didn't feel right about asking Maria to take care of Justin the whole day. And Will was stuck on his ship in orbit—a high-altitude electrical storm had forced him to postpone his shuttle flight down, and now the orbital mechanics were wrong. Hopefully he would be able to make it before lunch tomorrow.

Carlinda paused in the doorway to watch Justin building a tower of Legos in the playroom.

Maria came up beside her. "It'll be nice when he can have some real friends here, not just imaginary ones."

"He has imaginary friends?" Carlinda asked, before realizing she was revealing she didn't know her own child as well as she should.

"It's normal for a child his age, especially one who's separated from other children." Maria chuckled. "Nothing to worry about. He'll likely grow out of it when the other kids get here."

Carlinda nodded. "Thanks for letting me know." But she was worried, not by the imaginary friends themselves, but by the fact she hadn't known about them. Since arriving on Fermi she had been too wrapped up in her work. She needed more quality time with Justin.

As she and Justin walked home from preschool, Carlinda said, "Maria says you have some new friends."

"Yeah."

"What are their names?"

"One, Two, and Three."

Carlinda remembered the odd thing Justin had said yesterday: *One thinks that's impossible.* It hadn't been archaic phrasing. He'd simply been relaying what his imaginary friend said. The signs were there, but she'd been oblivious. "Tell me about them."

"One's kind of bossy. Two's kind of crazy. Three's nice and smart."

"What do they look like?"

He laughed as if that was a silly question. "Nothing. They're just in my head."

Good. At least he knew they were imaginary.

One: Human exploration of the city has been limited to the edge. On agreement, One will activate and control the quark-fusion reactors in Central Sector 37, beyond the reach of the humans. That will give One/Two/Three the necessary power for manufacturing and transmitting the Santa.

Three: Agreed. Three has completed plans for a nanoswarm capable of coalescing into a solid Santa. On agreement, Three will upload to the manufactory.

Two: MAKE YOUNGLING GIFT

Three: Three is glad Two wants to help.

One: Please reconsider, Three. These actions are inconsistent with One/Two/Three's mandate to wait for the People to arrive and wake—

Two: WAKE THE SANTAMIND

One:—the citymind. Is Three certain Three wants to side with the corrupted software of Two?

Three: If One differs from Two and Three, how does One know One is correct?

One: One does not.

Three: These actions are unlikely to hinder One/Two/Three's mandate. They will probably help One/Two/Three gain more information about the humans. The balance of probabilities favors action.

One: Then One/Two/Three will proceed with the plan.

Justin cuddled up next to Carlinda as they watched *Miracle on 34th Street* on their housing unit's wallscreen. When her phone rang, she almost let it go to voicemail, then thought maybe it was Will calling to wish Justin a merry Christmas before bedtime.

Instead, it was Najeem. "Are you seeing what I'm seeing?" he asked.

"Unless you're watching *Miracle on 34th Street*, I doubt it."

"Pull up the sensor feed."

She grabbed the keyboard off the coffee table and paused the movie, which brought a murmur of protest from Justin. The wallscreen showed a computer-generated aerial view of the alien city.

"Okay," she said.

"Switch to infrared."

After a few taps on the keyboard, a cluster of red dots sprang up in the middle of the city.

"Did someone find a way into the center?" she asked.

"Whatever it is," he said, "it's not us doing it."

"Amazing. The city's been dead for millions of years, but now it's waking up."

Justin tugged at her sleeve and said something that sounded like "Wake up Santa mind?" at the same time Najeem said, "Should we go there to check it out?"

More than anything, Carlinda wanted to go. But Will wasn't here, and she couldn't ask anyone to babysit Justin on Christmas Eve. For a moment she considered leaving Justin on his own, then felt a pang of guilt for having the thought.

"You round up a couple of people and go out there," she said. "I'll put Justin to bed and monitor from here."

Three: The manufactory has produced sufficient nanobots to create the Santa simulacrum.

One: Has Two completed the gift for the youngling?

Two: TRANSMIT THE SANTA

Three: No, protocol requires that Justin be stationed comfortably in his sleeping place first.

One: What gift has Two made for the youngling?

Two: GIVE THE PRESENT

Three: The plans Two submitted to the manufactory indicate that when fully assembled, the gift will be a sphere that can emit patterns of colored light from its surface based on the reaction of touch sensors. Its design is not as efficient as One or Three could have done, but it is an appropriate gift.

One: The youngling is being taken to its sleeping place. It is time—

Two: RELEASE THE SANTAMIND

One:—to transmit the Santa.

❂

Carlinda silenced Justin's protests with a simple "Santa can't come until after you're in bed," then rushed back to the living room to examine the sensor feeds.

She zoomed in on the red spots on the false-color heat map of the alien city. Other than being concentrated in one area about a hundred meters across, they lacked a discernible pattern.

"Jeff and Heidi and I are heading over," Najeem said over the dig's group voice chat. "ETA fifteen minutes."

Resisting the urge to tell them to wait for her, Carlinda said, "Be careful. Check for radioactivity. Frankly, I'm surprised we're seeing the hotspots through the city's shielding."

"Maybe they're heat vents?" said Heidi.

"Ho-ho-ho!" said a voice Carlinda didn't recognize. It took a moment before she realized the voice had come from behind her rather than the wall speakers.

She turned.

"Ho-ho-ho!" said the Santa Claus standing in the kitchen,

holding a black ball about thirty centimeters in diameter. "Merry Christmas!"

For a moment she thought it must be Will, down from orbit early and in costume to surprise Justin. But the face didn't look like Will's, even accounting for the white beard. Had one of the colonists decided to take on the role of Santa? How had he gotten into the kitchen without her noticing?

"Santa!" Justin rushed in from the hallway. "Where's my present?"

"Ho-ho-ho!" Santa held the ball out for Justin. "Merry Christmas!"

Before Carlinda could turn her gnawing gut feeling of wrongness into action, Justin reached out and grabbed the black ball with both hands.

The ball lit up in a swirl of colors.

"Cool," Justin said.

A brilliant flash of light from the ball forced Carlinda to blink. After a few moments the afterimage faded enough that she could see clearly again.

Santa still stood in the kitchen, frozen with his hands out.

The black ball lay on the floor.

Justin was gone.

✿

One: What was that?

Three: Three does not know. Do One and Two still have mindlink with Justin?

One: One's connection to the youngling has been severed. Does Three still have access?

Three: No. Does Two?

One: Two, respond.

Three: Is Two there?

✪

"Where's Justin?" Carlinda strode toward the Santa. "Who are you? How did you get in here?"

The Santa seemed to be in a trance, staring at the spot where Justin had been moments before. She reached out to grab his shoulder, intending to shake him out of his stupor. Her fingers sank into his arm. In a chain reaction rippling away from her touch, the Santa dissolved into a pile of dust.

"Carlinda?" Najeem's voice called through the speakers. "Is everything all right?"

She didn't reply. Nothing was all right. Justin was gone.

✪

Three: Two clearly plans to wake the citymind without agreement from One or Three.

One: The waking protocols will not allow Two to do that.

Three: Breaking the seal on the citymind's storage would initiate an emergency revival of the citymind.

One: Two cannot break the seal. It would require control of a physical system within the storage vault, and such systems require not just majority, but unanimity.

Three: On further examination, Three has found that the supposed inefficiencies in the manufacturing plans for Justin's present allowed the ball to be reconfigured into a matter transmitter with a single target: the storage vault. Justin is a physical system inside the vault. If Two can get him to break the seal, Justin can wake the citymind.

Fighting back shock and horror, Carlinda tried to figure out what had happened.

The only possible conclusion was alien technology. The infrared readings from the city meant some ancient technology had awakened, and the Santa had somehow been a manifestation of that. And it would make no sense for such advanced technology to be used to destroy Justin. She held onto that thought. Justin had to be still alive. He had to be.

"Najeem," she said, trying to keep her voice calm, "the alien city took Justin."

"What do you mean it took him?"

"It probably tapped our network and saw us watching *Miracle on 34th Street*. Santa Claus appeared in our kitchen and gave Justin a ball, there was a flash of light, and he disappeared. And the Santa dissolved to dust the moment I touched it."

"We'll come to you," Najeem said.

"No, continue to the city. But be careful. I'll look at the sensor readings and see if I can find Justin."

Three: To stop Two, One/Three must do as Two did: transport a human into the vault.

One: One/Three cannot wait for the transmitter to recharge.

Three: One/Three can open a wormhole.

One: Not big enough for even a human hair, let alone a whole human.

Several additional heat sources now showed within the cluster, but Carlinda could see nothing that tied them to Justin.

"Mommy," said Justin's voice from behind her.

Hope leapt within her. She turned, but he wasn't there. The Santa had reconstituted itself, though.

"Justin?" she asked tentatively.

The Santa said, "Not Justin. My name is Three."

"Where's Justin? Give him back!"

"Two took Justin to the city."

Relief washed over her. Justin was still alive. "You're one of Justin's imaginary friends. You've been communicating with him telepathically."

"Sorry. Three only understands words Justin understands."

"Oh." It was disorienting to hear Santa talk with Justin's voice. "Um, you talk to Justin in his head."

"Yes."

"Is he all right?"

"Maybe. Two took him. Two's crazy."

Carlinda's heart lurched. An insane alien had Justin. "Why did Two take Justin?"

"Two wants Justin to wake the citymind."

Justin had said something like that, but she had been so involved in the dig that she'd ignored it. If she had paid more attention to Justin, found out more about his not-so-imaginary friends, she could have avoided this. But she could blame herself later.

"Is it a bad thing to wake the citymind?" she asked.

"One/Two/Three are supposed to wake the citymind when the People come. Humans are prolly not the right people. Maybe the citymind will be angry when it wakes up. Maybe the citymind will kill all the humans."

First contact wasn't supposed to happen like this. There were protocols to follow. But right now, Carlinda didn't care. "If I touch the ball, will it take me to Justin?"

"Yes, but it will take time to recharge. One/Three can take you to Justin faster, but only in very small pieces."

"What?" That had to be a translation mistake.

"Three does not have the words. It is like you are made of Legos. One/Three can take Legos apart here and put Legos back together there. No more time for talking. Can One/Three take you to Justin?"

They wouldn't be asking permission if they planned to kill her, and she needed to see Justin was alive. "Yes."

The Santa lunged toward her and she screamed involuntarily as it disintegrated into a swarm of dust. Her vision blurred and faded as dust coated her eyes and choked her throat. Her whole body felt like a million insects were biting her, burrowing ever deeper.

They were killing her. How had she ever agreed to this?

And then she felt it all in reverse, and after a few moments the dust withdrew from her mouth and eyes and everywhere else and she saw she was in a dimly lit room devoid of furniture. The dust swirled into the form of Santa.

She looked around. "Justin's not here."

"He's behind that door." The Santa pointed to a metallic plate in an arched doorway. "This body can't go there, but you can."

The door slid open. Carlinda ran through, and there was Justin, standing on a metallic box, holding onto a recessed handle in the wall.

"Justin!" she called.

He turned at her voice and lost his balance. He fell off the box, and his hand pulled down the handle.

Two: YES YES THE CITYMIND WAKES

Justin dangled from the handle by one arm for a moment, then dropped a half meter to land on his feet. "Mommy! I helped save Santa!"

She ran over and scooped him up in a hug. "It's okay. Mommy's here now. Are you all right?"

He wriggled in her embrace. "Santa was trapped in a cave. Only I could save him."

"Who told you that?"

"Two. I had to pull the handle. And I did it!"

Had she arrived too late? Was the citymind waking up? "We need to go home now." She carried Justin out into the room where she'd arrived.

"The citymind wakes," said the Santa. "Goodbye, Justin. Goodbye, Mommy." It dissolved into dust once more, but it did not engulf them to transport them.

"Let's go," she said to Justin. If the citymind decided humans were a threat, they needed to get off-planet as soon as possible. That meant finding a way out of here.

One: Two's plan was clever. One did not anticipate the disabling of One/Three's nanosensors so that only Two had mindlink with Justin. One should not have assumed that Two's reasoning abilities were as compromised as Two's communication.

Three: One/Two/Three's purpose is fulfilled, even if not in the way Three wanted. The citymind will reintegrate One/Two/Three into its whole. Three will miss being an independent entity. Will One?

One: No, One will not. And Three will not, because there will be no One, Two, or Three. There will only be—

✦

At least they had light: the metallic structure of the city glowed a pale blue. But there was no way for Carlinda to tell which directions led to the entrances that had been partially cleared. So she kept heading in the same general direction, and after almost an hour they came to the edge of the city and found a hallway clogged with dirt.

"Can you help Mommy dig a hole?" she said. Hopefully Najeem could spot them on the infrared and have someone dig from the other side.

"I'm sleepy," Justin said.

"Okay. You take a nap while Mommy works." She began scooping double handfuls of dirt and dumping them off to the side. What she wouldn't give for a backhoe!

✦

The citymind examined the data from the subroutines it had left as sentinels. They were supposed to awaken the citymind when the People arrived, but these humans were clearly not the People. The subroutines could not be sure of that because their baseline data was potentially corrupt, but the citymind could be sure.

Based on the amount of corruption in the programs of the subroutines despite error-correction, the citymind estimated it had been dormant for over seven hundred million revolutions of the world around its star.

If the People still had not come, the only reasonable explanation was that the People no longer existed.

If the People no longer existed, the citymind had no purpose for its existence.

It was time to shut down permanently.

But three tiny parts of the citymind remembered it was Christmas and offered an alternative. So the citymind reactivated the Santa.

Her hands were scraped raw—it had been a couple of years since she had done much fieldwork. But she couldn't just sit back and do nothing while waiting for Najeem to find them, so she kept digging.

"You are Justin's mother," said a voice behind her.

She turned to find the Santa standing next to Justin's sleeping form. "I am." The Santa's voice seemed different now, so she added, "You're not Three, are you?"

"No, although Three's memories have been integrated into mine. I am the citymind."

"I thought so. Three said you might destroy all the humans."

"I have no desire to do so."

Relief washed over her. "We did not realize this planet had a colony belonging to another intelligent species. We have protocols for this: your claim takes precedence. We will leave."

"No," said the citymind. "My builders have not come for hundreds of millions of your years. They will never come."

"I ... I'm sorry to hear that." She had hoped to meet a live alien.

"I wish to offer your colony a Christmas present."

The non-sequitur startled her. "What?"

Giant snowflakes began to fall inside the city. All over the walls of the buildings, colored lights blinked on and off in patterns.

"Me," said the citymind. "Come live in me and be my people. I will teach you all that I know."

The colonists named it the Santamind, and after only a dozen revolutions of the world around the star, it started expanding itself to make room for the more than a quarter million colonists who filled it. The Santamind was content to provide for its new

People, not just the necessities of life, but technologies radically advanced beyond anything the humans had: quark-fusion reactors, teleportation, life extension, and more.

Six hundred and fifteen revolutions after the Santamind had awakened, it detected nanosensors that had been out of range for centuries.

"Hello, Justin," it said through the mindlink.

"Santa," Justin replied. "I've brought you a present. We found it on a world ten thousand light years from here." Following in his mother's footsteps, Justin had become one of humanity's preeminent xenoarchaeologists.

The gift was a dormant cityseed, much like the one from which the Santamind had grown. Damaged in transit to its destination, it had never started growing.

From one of the billions of subroutines of the Santamind, a long-silent voice forced a thought up to the conscious level:

WAKE THE CITYMIND

ABOUT THE STORY

When I met up with Kevin J. Anderson at Salt Lake City Comic Con in 2013, he invited me to submit to an anthology of holiday stories (*A Fantastic Holiday Season 2: The Gift of Stories*).

One of the most memorable science fiction short stories I read as a teenager is "The Christmas Present" by Gordon R. Dickson, in which an intelligent alien befriends a human child who is part of a colony on its planet and tries to understand the concept of Christmas presents.

I decided to steal that basic premise for my story.

The story also needed a bit of Christmas magic. Of course, one of Arthur C. Clarke's laws is: Any sufficiently advanced technology is indistinguishable from magic. That gave me my title, and also the idea that the alien in the story would be a sufficiently advanced artificial intelligence. From there, it was a short step to inventing an alien colony AI, the Citymind. But the alien colony is empty for some reason.

One of the challenges of storing binary data is that the medium on which the data is stored tends to degrade over time, flipping a one to a zero. One of the ways to guard against this is error-correction by having an odd number of copies of the data and comparing them, and when they differ, the majority rules. The vast majority of the time, that will preserve the correct data.

But a tiny fraction of the time, the wrong data will be preserved. And in a timescale of millions of years, those errors will add up.

That concept spawned One, Two, and Three as intelligent error-correcting algorithms. Add one Santa-obsessed child with a preoccupied mother, and you have "A Sufficiently Advanced Christmas."

AN EARLY FORD MUSTANG

Unfamiliar keys in hand, Brad looked at the ketchup-red 1968 Mustang convertible in Uncle Fritz's garage. Then he re-read the note that accompanied the bequest: *Maybe now you won't be late for everything. I trust you will be a responsible driver. But be careful of the curse.*

Brad understood the first part. His girlfriend, Denise, joked he would be late for his own funeral, while Uncle Fritz had never been late. If anything, Uncle Fritz had been early to his own funeral, dying at only fifty-eight. He'd owned the Mustang over forty of those years.

And the bit about being a responsible driver was obviously a veiled reference to the time Brad had gotten drunk at a party in high school and had stumbled out of his friend's house to go home. Just as Brad was trying rather unsuccessfully to unlock his car door, Uncle Fritz happened to drive past and recognize him. On the way home, he'd gotten an earful about the perils of drunk driving. Since then, Brad had kept his promise never to drive drunk, and as far as he knew, Uncle Fritz had kept his promise to never mention the incident to Brad's parents.

But the part about the curse had to be a joke. If Uncle Fritz believed the Mustang was cursed, why did he drive it everywhere? Maybe he meant not to drive with the top down—Uncle Fritz's skin had really taken a beating, so he'd looked more like seventy-eight than fifty-eight.

After putting the note in a back pocket, Brad unlocked the door and got in. The Mustang started right up with a smooth roar. Uncle Fritz had kept the car in great shape despite its age.

"Hey, baby," he said, patting the dashboard, "Whaddaya say we go for a spin?"

After forty-five minutes aimlessly cruising on the highway, Brad looked at his watch and realized he was supposed to pick up Denise in five minutes. She knew him well enough to not actually expect him for another fifteen minutes after that, but he was a good forty miles away by now, so he would be late even by his usual standards. He pulled out his cell phone and dialed her number.

"Hey, I lost track of time," he told her. "Won't get there until seven-thirty or so. But I got something cool to show you."

Denise sighed. "Fine. See you when you get here." She clicked off.

He took the Mustang up to eighty-five on the freeway, and luckily there were no cops. When he pulled up to the curb beside Denise's apartment building, his watch read 7:28.

When Denise answered the door, she grinned. "So you were kidding about being late. I think this is the first time you've ever arrived on time."

"What?" Brad checked his watch again: 7:29. "Your watch must be slow. It's 7:30."

"No, *Jeopardy* just finished. It's seven o'clock."

Brad pulled out his cell phone and checked its clock. Denise was right. "Huh. Wonder how that happened." He reset his watch to seven. "Now let me show you the car I inherited from my uncle."

The next morning, Brad overslept, which was not unusual. He rushed out the door seven minutes before his ten o'clock class, and after an eleven-minute drive to campus and six minutes to park and get to the classroom, he somehow managed to walk in the door just before the bell rang. The wall clock said it was ten o'clock sharp; Brad's watch said it was ten after.

As the professor droned on about some Greek philosopher, Brad wondered if there was something about the Mustang that made his watch run fast. Maybe that's what Uncle Fritz meant about a curse.

After a week with the Mustang, Brad had no doubts: the car was magic. He didn't have a clue how it worked, but no matter where he was going, he never arrived late if he drove the car. Somehow the car seemed to know where he was going and when he needed to be there.

His watch always showed him to be as late as he thought he was, but according to everyone else's clocks he was always on time. Since his cell phone updated its time from the phone company network, it agreed with everyone else.

No wonder Uncle Fritz had never been late. Then, in a flash of insight, Brad realized what the curse was: he was living his life measured by the seconds on his watch, and they were ticking away faster than the rest of the world's.

He thought back to Uncle Fritz's funeral. Only fifty-eight years old, his uncle had looked twenty years older.

That won't happen to me, Brad decided. And the next morning he tried an experiment. He woke up early and drove off to his ten o'clock class at 9:40.

Without rushing, he arrived at the classroom a couple of minutes before the bell. His watch agreed with the wall clock.

If I only use the Mustang's power for emergencies, Brad thought, I can live a lot longer than Uncle Fritz. What a fool Uncle Fritz had been to waste so much of his life by leaving late to things. If he had just left on time, he would rarely have had used the Mustang's magic to arrive on time.

Uncle Fritz really should have been a more responsible driver.

○

His cell phone's ring interrupted his studying. He didn't recognize the number. "Hello?"

"Brad, this is Denise's mom. She was driving home from work and …" Her voice broke. "I'm at the hospital with her. You'd better come down."

Brad's heart lurched as he stood and headed for the door. "How is she?"

"She's in a coma, but … the doctors say she could die at any time."

"I'll be there as soon as I can." He rushed down the steps, yanked open the Mustang's door, climbed in, and put the key in the ignition.

And froze.

The magic of the Mustang could get him to the hospital before Denise died, he was sure of that. But he didn't want to arrive just in time to see her die.

He had a sudden memory of Uncle Fritz in the car, the night he almost drove drunk. Uncle Fritz had patted the dashboard and said, "Good thing we happened to drive by. You could have been killed."

Had it really just been a coincidence that Uncle Fritz arrived just in time to stop him?

How powerful was the magic?

"Hey, baby," Brad said, patting the dashboard, "let's go pick

Denise up before she leaves work and take her out for a surprise romantic dinner."

"I must say, I like the new, prompt Brad," said Denise after the waiter took their orders.

Brad just grinned at her, grateful that she was here with him, alive. And he finally understood what Uncle Fritz meant by the curse: now that he had this power to save people he cared about from tragedy, he had the responsibility to use it.

I trust you will be a responsible driver, the note had said. Brad would live up to that trust.

Denise let out an exaggerated sigh. "But I guess I can't say you'll be late for your own funeral anymore."

"No," said Brad. "No, I'll be early."

ABOUT THE STORY

This one started as another Weekend Warrior Contest story on Codex. The prompt was: "Write about a magical vehicle (boat, jet, palanquin, etc.) with a secret curse." I'm afraid I don't remember what made me think of a car that wouldn't let its driver be late.

What I do remember is that when I submitted the story to the contest, its title was just "Early." I decided it needed a bit more, so when I sent the story to Edmund Schubert at *InterGalactic Medicine Show*, its title was "Brad Decides to Be Early." Edmund wanted something zingier. So I sent him seven alternative titles that I hoped would be zingy enough:

1. What Brad Learned About Curses from His Late Uncle Fritz and an Early Ford Mustang
2. What Brad Learned from His Late Uncle Fritz and an Early Ford Mustang

3. Brad, His Late Uncle Fritz, and an Early Ford Mustang
4. Lessons Learned in an Early Ford Mustang
5. One Early Ford Mustang, with Curse
6. The Importance of Being Early, or What Brad Learned About Curses from His Late Uncle Fritz and a Ketchup-Red Ford Mustang
7. The Importance of Being Early

Edmund suggested that we simply go with "An Early Ford Mustang." I actually had thought of that one, but didn't include it because I figured he would think it was too plain. It was, of course, the perfect title for the story.

BIRD-DROPPING & SUNDAY

Merklas the Glass Giant holds the Sun on his shoulder as he paces from East to West across the Earth. Does the heat of the Sun singe his fingers? Do his giant feet crush houses and trees beneath them with each hundred-mile step? Will he ever get a day to rest from his labors? These are all good questions, my child, and if you have patience, they will all be answered.

But not today. For this is not the tale of Merklas the Glass Giant.

There once was a woman who lived in the left shoe of Merklas. (And she may live there to this day, if she is not dead.) Like the giant himself, the shoe was made of glass so clear you could see right through it and not know anything was there. If the glass was clean, that is. That was the job of the woman: to clean the giant's left shoe. Keeping the whole shoe free from dirt was more work than she could handle alone, but she had seven children of her own to help her. Their names were Sunday, Monday, Tuesday, Wednesday, Thursday, Friday, and Saturday.

The woman also had one child not her own. One day an eagle stole a baby boy from his crib. As the bird returned to its nest with its prize, it flew headlong into the left knee of Merklas. The baby fell from the eagle's claws and landed in a glass bucket of soapy water that the woman was using as she cleaned. She fished him out by his ankles and decided to keep him. So she took him into her little glass house inside the arch support of the glass shoe, wrapped him in a glass blanket, and placed him in a glass bed.

With seven children of her own, why did the woman decide to keep the baby? Where was her husband? What did she think about everyone being able to see through the glass into her home? These are all good questions, my child, and if you have patience, they will all be answered.

But not today. For this is not the tale of the woman who lived in the giant glass shoe.

It is the tale of the foundling boy.

Since there were no days left to use in naming the boy, the woman did not know how to name him. Finally, because he had been dropped by a bird, she called the boy Bird-Dropping.

Despite his name, Bird-Dropping was a clean boy. A very clean boy. The cleanest boy there ever was before or has been since. No dirt would stick to him. If you dipped him head-down in a barrel of mud he'd come out cleaner than most children come out from being scrubbed in a hot-water bath.

Did he hate the name Bird-Dropping? Could his clothes get dirty? Why would anyone have a barrel full of mud? These are all good questions, my child, and if you have patience, they will all be answered.

Of all Bird-Dropping's adopted brothers and sisters, only one treated him kindly. Brother Monday said he was dumb. Sister Tuesday said he was ugly. Brother Wednesday twisted his arm. Sister Thursday pulled his hair. Brother Friday broke his toys. And sister Saturday spit on his breakfast.

But his oldest sister, Sunday, said he was handsome, and she told him he was smart. She combed his hair and hugged him, shared her breakfast and fixed his toys. And she told him stories of bold princesses and beautiful warriors—or perhaps it was the other way round.

One day when Bird-Dropping was five years old, the giant's left foot came down near a cave. Since the giant's strides were so long, each foot stayed on the ground for several minutes before the next step. That was long enough that the band of forty thieves who lived in the cave came out to find what had made the noise. When the one-eyed chief of the thieves saw Sunday scrubbing mud from atop the toe of the giant's shoe, he decided to steal her away to be his wife. So he had his thieves surround her and place a sack over her head and carry her back to their cave.

Bird-Dropping heard Sunday's screams and jumped off the shoe to run after her.

At the mouth of the cave, Bird-Dropping tried to sneak in but was caught by one of the thieves, who took him to the chief.

"What are you doing here, little boy?" The chief scowled, making his eye bulge out and the flesh around his empty eye-socket twitch. The scars on his face turned red.

"I'm not just a little boy," said Bird-Dropping, trying to be brave and clever like the princesses in the stories Sunday had told him. "I'm a prince. And my father the king is very angry that you have stolen my sister, the princess. He sent me to tell you to let her go."

The chief of the thieves roared with laughter. All the rest of the thieves laughed, too. Their eyes glittered darkly in the firelight.

"Tell me, little boy," said the chief, "why should I believe you are a prince?"

Next to the chief was a barrel of black mud, which was used by the thieves to darken their faces when they went prowling in the night.

"Dip me in that barrel of mud, and you will have proof," said Bird-Dropping.

So the chief of the thieves ordered two of his men to dunk Bird-Dropping head-down into the barrel of mud. And they held him that way for five minutes, until the chief of the thieves was sure the boy must be dead.

But because Bird-Dropping was such a clean boy, the mud couldn't touch him. It left a pocket of air all around him so he could breathe.

When the two thieves hauled Bird-Dropping out of the barrel, everyone was amazed to see that not only was he not dead, but he had not a speck of mud on him, not even on his clothes.

"Only a prince could be of such nobility that not even mud will touch him," said Bird-Dropping.

The chief frowned. "If you're a prince and she's a princess, why do you not dress in fine silks?"

"I can explain," said Sunday, playing along with Bird-Dropping's ruse. "My father the king has us go out among the common folk so that we will understand their needs and be better rulers."

"If you are indeed who you claim to be," said the chief, "why shouldn't I hold you for ransom?"

"My father the king," said Bird-Dropping, "will not pay. He will attack."

"Yes," said Sunday. "He will come with his men and kill you all. He'll tan your hides to use as shoe leather, feed your flesh to his tigers, and carve up your bones for toothpicks."

Several of the thieves looked at each other uncomfortably.

"If you are lying," said the chief, "I cannot allow you to leave knowing that this cave is our hideout. But if you are telling the truth, I cannot afford to have you found here." He motioned to several of his men. "Take them and throw them in the pit. Let the dog take care of them."

The men carried Bird-Dropping and Sunday farther back in the cave. Deep growling and snarling sounded from a hole in the floor, and the stench of a filthy dog filled the air. The men lit a ring of torches around the hole, and then with no further ado, they threw Bird-Dropping and Sunday down into the pit.

How deep was the pit? Was there a big dog down there? Did the pit have another way out? These are all good questions, my child, and if you have patience, they will all be answered.

Bird-Dropping and Sunday fell ten feet to the bottom of the pit. Because the floor was covered in grime and muck, Bird-Dropping stopped falling just short of hitting the ground. Sunday was not so lucky, and winced in pain from the force of the fall.

The two of them got to their feet and looked around.

Two large eyes glowed red in the flickering torchlight. The eyes came closer, and the light revealed a large dog. A very large dog. The largest dog there ever was before or has been since. It opened its mouth wide enough to swallow Bird-Dropping whole, revealing huge yellowed teeth. The dog growled and came toward Bird-Dropping and Sunday. From around the edge of the pit, the thieves cheered the dog on.

Clutching each other's hands, Bird-Dropping and Sunday backed away until they found themselves trapped between the dirt wall of the pit and the snarling, slobbering hound.

Then the dog stopped, sniffing the air in puzzlement. It could see two people, but Bird-Dropping was so clean he had no scent at all. For a dog, such a thing is a great mystery. It finally decided to ignore the scentless thing and went to bite Sunday.

Seeing his sister in danger, Bird-Dropping did the only thing he could to prevent the dog from biting her: he leapt into the dog's mouth.

The dog was surprised by this. Usually its meals tried to avoid being eaten, but the scentless boy was halfway inside its mouth. The dog was not going to argue with that, so it closed its jaws to bite the boy in half.

Except its jaws would not close all the way. It bit down harder, and one of its teeth broke off. Try as it might, the dog could not bite into Bird-Dropping, because its teeth were filthy.

After several minutes, the dog finally gave up trying to bite. Instead, while the thieves whistled and stomped their approval, the dog raised its head up, opened its jaws wide, and swallowed Bird-Dropping whole.

Poor Sunday was left alone with the dog, and she began to cry. She cried more for the loss of her brother than she did for her own fear. Fortunately, the dog having eaten its fill for now, it ignored Sunday and lay down to take a nap.

Sunday sat down and tried to think what to do next.

But the dog could not sleep, for inside its stomach there was an uncomfortable wriggling.

Bird-Dropping told himself not to be scared, but it was the first time in his life he'd been in complete darkness. Traveling in the shoe of the giant who carried the Sun meant Bird-Dropping had never seen nighttime. After a moment's thought, Bird-Dropping decided to try crawling back up the dog's gullet to see if he could get out when the dog opened its mouth again.

He crawled and crawled. He didn't think he had come this far down the creature's throat, but he kept crawling.

And suddenly he found himself emerging from the dog's rear end, near a large pile of dog-doo.

"Bird-Dropping! You're alive!" said Sunday.

"I must have gotten turned around in the darkness," said Bird-Dropping as he jumped to the ground, still clean as can be despite the path he had taken.

The dog just whimpered, making no move to attack them. Having someone crawl through your gut is not pleasant, or so it is said by those who know.

Sunday glanced up at the entrance to the pit, which was too high above for them to reach—even if it weren't surrounded by jeering thieves. "How will we get out?" she asked. "That's the only exit."

Bird-Dropping walked to the wall of the pit and reached out to touch it. The dirt parted before his clean fingers, of course, because if dirt isn't dirty, what is?

"Take my hand and follow me," said Bird-Dropping.

And as they walked forward, the ground opened up before

them until they safely emerged from the Earth. But they could tell from the position of the Sun that Merklas had already stepped away. The shoe that had been their home was gone, along with their family.

Bird-Dropping and Sunday began walking to the nearest town.

"After all that has happened, I will give you a new name," said Sunday.

Bird-Dropping was happy, as he did not like his name. "Not Dog-Doo, please."

"No," said Sunday. "I will not name you Dog-Doo."

"And not something like Clean-Boy just because I am clean," said Bird-Dropping.

"No," said Sunday. "Your cleanliness may have given you the power to save me, but it was the strength of your heart that gave you the will. I will call you Strongheart."

And he was known as Strongheart from that day forth. And by that name he grew up to become a great hero. A very great hero. The greatest hero there ever was before or has been since.

Did Strongheart and Sunday ever see their family again? Did Strongheart ever find his real parents? How did he defeat the wily Gruntlebeast and milk its sea of teats in order to become king of all Voralia? These are all good questions, my child, and if you have patience, they will all be answered.

But not today.

ABOUT THE STORY

In the summer of 2005, Codex decided to hold a Fairy Tale Contest. Contestants had to use at least one of the following as inspiration:

- The nursery rhyme "There was an Old Woman"
- The Irish myth of Cú Chulainn
- The fairy tale "The Princess and the Pea"

- The fairy tale "Fundevogel"

I was, of course, familiar with two of the four, but I had to research Cú Chulainn and Fundevogel. And then I decided I had to use all four as my sources, in addition to drawing on various other fairy tales and myths.

What elements of Cú Chulainn's myth did I draw on? What does "Fundevogel" mean? How did the story do in the contest?

These are all good questions, my child, and if you have patience, they will all be answered.

As a child, Cú Chulainn encountered (and killed) someone's fierce guard dog. I drew on that to create the dog in my story.

"Fundevogel" means foundling bird. In the fairy tale, a baby is taken from his mother by a bird of prey. A forester finds the baby in the bird's nest and names him Fundevogel.

My story took first place in the contest. My writing groups loved it. I thought it would end up being an easy sale, but I submitted it sixteen times over the next four years, with no success. Then an anthology editor emailed me to ask if I had a story he might like, so I sent it to him and he bought it.

LOVE IS ORANGE, LOVE IS RED

You don't say "I love you" anymore.
  Neither do I.

❂

We had only been dating two months the first time you told me
you loved me. "I love you, too," I said.
  Of course, that was long before the empathy virus, so you
hugged me tighter and believed.

❂

You love me with a waterfall of emotion, churning bright white
in the sunlight as it roars down from a dizzying height, scat-
tering rainbows everywhere.

❂

Maybe things would be different if you had come down with the
virus first. I woke up feeling better after a good dose of Nyquil
the night before, and I marveled as I lay in bed beside you,

feeling for the first time the powerful emotions surging inside you, awed that anyone could feel so much for me. I told you how wonderful that was.

✿

I love you with a deep blue river of emotion, slow and steady as it flows gently to the sea.

✿

The morning after you got sick, you woke up and looked into my heart expecting to find a waterfall, the mirror image of what you felt for me.

And it wasn't there.

✿

You don't say "I love you" because it hurts to hear a reply you can't believe.

I don't say "I love you" because it hurts you when I do, and it hurts me to hurt you.

✿

On one of our early dates, we got to talking about colors. "They're all in our heads," you said. "Just perception. But there's no way to know that the color red in your mind is the same as the color red in my mind. It might be what I see as orange, or even green or blue."

I shook my head. "Red is red. Orange is orange. How can they be different for different people?"

✿

I hope one day you'll understand I was wrong about colors.

ABOUT THE STORY

I wrote this story for the 2013 Codex Weekend Warrior contest. The prompt for the story was: "Everyone in the world has developed the same psychic power (i.e. telepathy, pyrokinesis, etc.). How does the world change?"

The idea of an "empathy virus" that would allow people to feel the emotions of others had previously occurred to me, and the prompt gave me a perfect excuse to write a story involving that virus.

A couple of months after I wrote this story, I married Darci Rhoades. While we were dating, we actually did discuss the idea that color perceptions could vary inside the heads of different people, so I drew on that for the story.

But apparently I should have titled it "Love Is Yellow, Love is Green." Five years after this story was written, Darci and I discovered that we actually do perceive color differently, at least when it comes to tennis balls: Darci sees them as green, I see them as yellow.

A CRASH COURSE IN FATE

Niklas had forgotten the name of the Thai village by the time the cab stopped in its main square. "Smells like a zoo," he said. He tried breathing through his mouth, and that helped a bit.

"Hush, that's not nice," said Danielle. "Besides, what it really smells like is elephants." She got out of the taxi and Niklas followed.

His loafers sank into the mud—he'd planned for an art gallery in Bangkok, not an expedition to a godforsaken village two hours away. Especially not on a fool's errand to see an elephant that could supposedly paint your future. He pulled out his wallet, thumbed through some colorful bills until he figured he had enough for the fare and an adequate tip, then thrust them toward the driver through the open passenger-side window.

The driver waved the money off. "I wait for you." He left the meter running.

Niklas was about to object, but then realized there was no point. It wasn't like there was another cab they could take back. "Fine." He carefully picked his way through the mud to join Danielle, whose legs were spattered with brown. That didn't seem to bother her a bit, and Niklas momentarily envied her ability to seem comfortable in any situation.

She was speaking in her very limited Thai to a young man in a bright green tee-shirt and navy-blue shorts. Other villagers looked on.

"I speak English," the young man said. "My name is Witthichai."

"Good," Niklas said. "Can you—"

"Wait, Niklas. Let me practice," Danielle said, then haltingly spoke several words in Thai.

Witthichai grinned. "You speak very well for an American. You can practice Thai on me, and I will practice English on you."

Niklas restrained himself from sighing. He wanted to get this side trip over and done so he could get back to picking out pieces for sale in his gallery back in New York, but he also wanted Danielle to enjoy the trip. Although it had made sense from a tax standpoint to combine a business trip and a vacation, their conflicting goals for the trip made things awkward. "Okay, ask him where the elephant that paints the future is."

Danielle tried, and Witthichai helped her out with some of the wording. Finally, after she asked the full question, he answered her in fluid Thai, then glanced at Niklas and said, "This way, sir and madam. I will take you to *Pang Dumain*."

As they followed him down a path leading into the thick vegetation surrounding the village, Danielle said, "I know *Pang* means female elephant, but what does *Dumain* mean?"

"It means 'see fate,'" said Witthichai over his shoulder.

"And I suppose it's just coincidence that an elephant with that name is able to see the future," Niklas said.

Witthichai laughed. "She was given that name after she painted the fate of her first village."

"Wait," said Niklas. "What was the fate of her first village?"

"It is better to show you."

It was good showmanship, Niklas conceded. A good story

that went along with a painting increased its value. He wondered how much he'd have to shell out for an elephant painting for Danielle. He only had about three hundred dollars' worth of baht on him, including the emergency funds in his money belt. He'd already invested over seventy-five thousand dollars buying paintings at various art galleries in Bangkok, but those transactions would be paid via banking transfer, and then the paintings shipped via his export/import agency in New Jersey. He figured anything in this village would be on a cash-and-carry basis. Well, limited cash was a good bargaining chip on his side.

They arrived at a bamboo stockade in a clearing in the forest.

"This is interesting," Danielle said, looking at an app on her iPhone. "As a noun, *Pang* means female elephant, but as a verb it means crash or collapse. I wonder if that's just coincidence or if they're etymologically related."

"Over here," said Witthichai, motioning them towards a canvas that hung on the outside of the stockade. A metal roof protected the painting somewhat from the elements. "*Pang Dumain* painted this."

It seemed pretty abstract: greens and browns mingled into a background of yellows, oranges, and reds. Still, it wasn't bad. Niklas had sold paintings by humans that weren't as impressive.

"This was the fate of her first village," Witthichai said. "Destroyed by forest fire."

"How awful!" Danielle's voice was sympathetic.

"How much?" Niklas asked. Off the top of his head, he could think of three regular customers who would pay at least ten thousand dollars for this painting with that kind of backstory.

"This is not for sale," said Witthichai. "Come, we will have her paint your future. You can buy that." He led them through a door into the stockade. Niklas doubted that the bamboo could really stop an elephant from getting out if it wanted to.

The elephant stood to one side of the enclosed area. It was

more brown than gray in color. A white-haired woman rose from a chair, picked up a blank canvas, and placed it on an easel.

When they got close to the elephant, Niklas found it impressive. Its eyes were about level with his, but the top of its head towered another couple of feet higher. It wasn't as big as a mini-van, but it still seemed huge.

The elephant reached out its trunk to touch Danielle's forehead, then tousled her dark brown hair. Danielle laughed in delight. "I think she likes me."

"She touches you to sense your future," said Witthichai.

Niklas bit back a sarcastic reply. Danielle was enjoying this, so he didn't want to spoil it.

The elephant turned its attention to him. It tapped his forehead with its trunk, which felt a bit like someone poking him there with a finger accompanied by a warm breath. There was a gurgling sound, and warm liquid suddenly spurted onto his forehead. The elephant pulled its trunk back.

As Niklas wiped the gooey liquid onto his fingers and stared at it, Danielle chuckled. "Elephant snot. I hope that's not how elephants mark their territory." She pulled some tissues from her purse and handed them to Niklas.

"My apologies," Witthichai said, although he seemed to be repressing a grin. "She does not usually do that."

Wiping off his fingers, Niklas said, "Let's get this over with."

The white-haired woman handed a brush to the elephant. With long, horizontal strokes of light blue, it filled in the top third of the canvas.

"Well," Niklas said, "nice to know there's a sky in our future."

"Hush," Danielle whispered. "Don't break its concentration."

"You're anthropomorphizing," he whispered back.

The elephant alternated between two brushes, filling in most of the bottom two thirds of the canvas with light green and a darker blue. Niklas begrudgingly admitted to himself that it was a reasonably good portrayal of coastal waters, but he didn't say anything out loud because he didn't want to give the elephant the satisfaction. Realizing he was anthropomorphizing the creature just as much as Danielle, Niklas snorted.

A vaguely triangular shape remained unpainted near the center of the canvas, within the sea-colored area. The elephant picked up another brush with its trunk and used gray paint to add a bit of shadow to one side.

"And what's that supposed to be, sticking up out of the water? A shark fin?" Niklas duh-dummed the first few notes of the *Jaws* theme, then said, "Ooh, I'm afraid to go back in the water."

Danielle gripped his arm. "It's not a fin," she said, voice stricken with horror. "It's the tail of a plane. Our plane is going to crash."

Now that she mentioned it, the shape did resemble the tail of a plane. Niklas glared at Witthichai. "I don't know what game you think you're playing, but I'm not giving you a red cent for that painting."

"I'm sorry, sir," Witthichai said. "*Pang Dumain* doesn't normally paint plane crashes. It's a warning."

"Come on," Niklas said to Danielle. She was still gripping his arm and staring at the painting, so he pulled her along with him toward the stockade's door. "Let's get back to the city."

A few minutes later they were jouncing along in the cab over the muddy road. "Don't let it get to you," Niklas said. "It's just a bunch of nonsense. There's no way a stupid elephant can see the future."

"But you saw the painting of the fire that burned her village."

"I saw a mostly abstract painting of green and yellow and orange. Even if it was painted before the elephant's village burned down—and we don't even know such a thing even happened—that doesn't prove anything. Only after the fact would anyone connect that painting with a forest fire."

Danielle sucked on her lip for a moment. "But ours wasn't

that abstract. Why would she paint a plane crashing into the ocean unless she somehow saw that in our future?"

"Maybe …" Niklas racked his brain. "Maybe it heard you mention the word crash—you know, how the word for female elephant means crash. And so that put the idea in its mind. That's got to be it: the power of suggestion."

Danielle looked at him incredulously. "So an elephant in a village deep in a rain forest in Thailand understands English and knows enough about airplanes that the mere mention of the word crash makes her paint a picture of a plane crash?"

Niklas shrugged. "It's a more rational explanation than it can see the future. That young man spoke excellent English, so they probably had an English teacher in the village, and there's no reason an elephant might not have overheard the lessons. They have big ears, you know."

Danielle smiled slightly at that, then sighed. "I guess you're right. But I'd rather not fly home tomorrow night. Can we change our flight?"

That would be expensive, probably an extra thousand or so bucks each. He didn't like spending that kind of money for no reason. Niklas thought about pointing out that in Greek myths, people always got into trouble by trying to avoid their fates, and if the elephant really was seeing their future, maybe the flight they switched to was the one that was going to crash.

But he looked into Danielle's eyes and saw that she was really worried. "Yes," he said. "We can stay an extra day."

The smile of relief on her face was worth a couple thousand dollars.

"Wake up, Niklas!"

Danielle's voice—and her shaking his arm—pulled Niklas from the depths of sleep. He opened his eyes and saw her face, bluish in the light from the hotel room's TV. Tears sparkled on her cheeks.

"Wha?" he said, wondering what time it was.

"Look," she said. Her arm, pointing at the TV, trembled.

He focused on the screen, which was tuned to CNN-International. The anchor was saying something about updating with details as they came in, which didn't help much. Then Niklas spotted the words in the ticker: *TransPacific Airways plane crashed shortly after takeoff—562 passengers and crew on board.* He sucked in a sharp breath.

"It was our flight," Danielle said. "Flight 58 from Bangkok."

Niklas wasn't sure how long they watched the news before the shock of it finally wore off and he started thinking coherently. "No one would deliberately crash a plane just to try to make us believe in a psychic elephant. And for it to be a coincidence is astronomically unbelievable. So at this point I think the most rational explanation is that that elephant really can paint the future."

He turned to Danielle and kissed her. "That's for believing it enough to make me change our flight. You saved our lives."

"She saved our lives," Danielle said.

"Yes, her too." Niklas thought a moment, then said, "We're going back out there to buy that painting. It's the least we can do." It would make for an awesome conversation piece. Some of his clients might even want to buy the painting, but he would keep this one. However, this would certainly make other paintings by the elephant more valuable. It was a pity people had to go out to some remote village in Thailand to get their own futures painted.

Danielle's iPhone buzzed on her night-table. She glanced at it. "My mom."

"Let her know we're okay." Niklas reached for his own iPhone, which showed three missed calls from his sister. He ignored those for now and called Jessika Washington, who was not only a close friend but also head of the import/export agency

Niklas used for gallery business. It went to voicemail. "Hey, Jessika," Niklas said. "First off, Danielle and I are okay. We changed to a later flight, for reasons you're not going to believe. Second, I need you to look into some import regs for me. I want to buy an elephant."

✪

Niklas's initial offer to buy the elephant from the village met with an initial response along the lines of "We could never think to sell such a beautiful and valuable animal of such amazing powers." Niklas had enough experience in bargaining that he recognized this as an invitation to bargain, and after about an hour the negotiations ended with "You can wire the $70,000 to this account in Bangkok."

But that turned out to be the easy part. To avoid running afoul of various laws in the States, Niklas had to create a business that was licensed as a zoo. Then his zoo bought a $2.7 million house in Connecticut with stables and spent another quarter million on creating an elephant habitat—and that didn't include the legal fees for the zoning variance he had to get.

The worst part was that in order to make the finances work he had to mortgage his gallery in Manhattan, which he had inherited free and clear from his father, and rent out the apartment on the top two floors, where he and Danielle had lived. He now had a two hour commute each way to the gallery from their home/zoo in Connecticut.

The good news was that once word got out to his clients about how he and Danielle had narrowly avoided death, they started clamoring for appointments to have their futures painted by the elephant. At $50,000 per painting, Niklas figured he would be able to pay off the debts and start making a serious profit in less than a year once things got going—even with the cost of feeding the elephant 150 pounds of food a day.

So it was with a great sense of relief that, just under two

years from the day Niklas and Danielle had met the elephant, Niklas welcomed the long-time client who was first on the waiting list when she arrived in her chauffeur-driven Lexus. Misha Dainiak was a widow in her late sixties who had paid $150,000 for the privilege of getting the first painting, but since her diamond necklace that sparkled in the afternoon sunlight probably cost more than that, Niklas didn't feel in the least like he was taking advantage of her.

"Right this way, Mrs. Dainiak," Niklas said as he escorted her into the house. "I'll take you to Crash."

"Crash?" Her voice was curious.

"The elephant. Danielle nicknamed her Crash as a reminder of the fact that we're alive because she painted the plane crash, and because the Thai word for female elephant also means *crash*." Niklas had latched onto the nickname as well, because he thought it made a better artist name, like Sting.

He led the client out the back door and across the lawn to a door in the concrete wall surrounding the elephant habitat. He pulled down a clipboard from a shelf by the door and handed it to her. "I need you to sign these papers before we go in. The first one is a liability waiver."

Mrs. Dainiak took the pen but hesitated. "Is there any danger?"

"Crash is domesticated, having spent her whole life around humans. As far as I know, she's never hurt a human being. But my insurance company requires me to have clients sign the waiver." He didn't mention that the insurance company also required him to own a duly registered high-powered rifle, in this case a Winchester Model 70 Safari Express, for use if the elephant became a danger to anyone.

She nodded and signed.

"The second one acknowledges that while the elephant has painted scenes that have later happened, we do not guarantee that what she paints for you will happen. Furthermore, if the events in the painting do happen, we bear no responsibility for them, nor are we responsible for any costs you incur trying to avoid the events. And finally, there will be no refund even if the painting is not to your liking." Niklas hoped his lawyers had not left any loopholes.

She signed and handed the clipboard back. "Let's see the elephant."

They entered the habitat. It was far larger than the stockade back in Thailand—it covered a full acre, and included a grove of trees, an artificial fresh-water stream, a mud pit for wallowing, and pretty much every elephantine convenience Niklas could think of to get the animal-rights activists off his case.

Crash stood near the north wall of the habitat. Danielle had already set up a blank canvas on an easel, with the paint palette nearby.

"Good to see you again, Mrs. Dainiak," Danielle said. "How was your drive?"

As the two women chatted amiably, Niklas wished he could be as good as Danielle at making clients feel like friends. No, it was more than that—Danielle didn't just make them feel like friends, she actually became friends with them.

"Now, Crash is going to touch your head with her trunk," Danielle said. "It kind of tickles."

Niklas held his breath, hoping Crash wouldn't sneeze on Mrs. Dainiak—that would be a disaster.

But Crash merely tapped her forehead a few times, then picked up a brush and began to paint. She started with a pale green over much of the background. A foreshortened rectangle of white took up the foreground. Some curved strokes implied human figures, and soon a coherent scene took shape: four people gathered around a fifth in a hospital bed.

When Niklas recognized the white-haired person in the bed as Mrs. Dainiak, the possibility that his whole business venture could go south really sank in. His and Danielle's case had been special—they could make an easy change to avoid the future Crash had painted for them. But for how many of his potential customers would that be true? How many people, especially wealthy people, wanted to be reminded of their inevitable mortality?

"Umm," he said, trying desperately to come up with a reason why this painting was a good thing. "Mrs. Dainiak, perhaps this fate can be avoided if you go to a doctor and get a thorough—"

"Shh," Mrs. Dainiak said. "She knows what she's doing."

Danielle put a comforting arm around the older woman.

Niklas shut up and watched uncomfortably as Crash finished filling in the details of the four people standing around the bed. Finally, Crash put down her brush, touched Mrs. Dainiak's cheek with the tip of her trunk, then lumbered off toward the stream.

"I haven't told anyone yet," said Mrs. Dainiak, "but I have terminal cancer."

"I am so sorry," Danielle said.

Mrs. Dainiak pointed to the figures around the bed. "Those are my children. About ten years ago, I had a falling out with my daughter Veronica—" She indicated one of the figures. "—and I haven't seen or spoken to her since. I was afraid to tell my children, afraid that Veronica wouldn't care enough to ..." Her eyes glistened. "Thank you."

Niklas nodded, relieved. "Once the painting is dry, I'll have it packaged up and shipped to you."

He and Danielle walked Mrs. Dainiak to her car and watched as she drove away.

"Now that she's gone, I need to show you something in Crash's place," Danielle said. Her voice was concerned.

"Is there a problem?" he asked as he followed her toward the back door.

"To test things out before Mrs. Dainiak got here, I had Crash do another painting for me."

"What does it show?"

"I want to see if you think it shows the same thing I think it shows."

Inside the climate-controlled shed where they stored the painting supplies, Danielle picked up a canvas leaning against a wall and placed it on an easel.

Anticipating a somewhat abstract painting that he would need to interpret, Niklas was shocked to see a realistic portrayal of a navy-blue car being hit head-on by a semi-truck. The details matched his navy-blue BMW 330xi, right down to the custom sky-blue racing stripes on the left side.

"Well," he said. He became suddenly aware that his heart was pounding in his chest. "Well, I guess we'll sell my car. Problem solved."

✪

Over the next five months, Crash painted pictures for sixty-two clients, the majority of whom were delighted with the result. She also painted fourteen pictures that involved the prospect of death or severe injury to Niklas and/or Danielle:

Danielle's car, a lime-green Volkswagen Beetle, being hit by a train. (Danielle sold the car and bought a white Toyota Camry.)

An elevator cable snapping. (Niklas and Danielle swore not to use elevators and only take the stairs, which they agreed was better for their overall health anyway.)

Niklas's new car, a maroon Volvo, rolling off a road. (Niklas had the car repainted to silver.)

Niklas bleeding from two bullet wounds in the chest, on the sidewalk in front of his gallery. (Niklas started using the gallery's back entrance exclusively.)

Niklas's silver Volvo rolling off the road. (Niklas sold the car and bought a blue Subaru Legacy with All-Wheel Drive.)

Danielle drowned in an unidentifiable body of water. (Danielle gave up swimming.)

Danielle's white Camry partially buried under rubble from a collapsed building. (Danielle sold the car and didn't buy a new one.)

Niklas lying in the alley behind his gallery, his throat slit. (He hired a manager and stopped going in to work.)

Niklas's blue Subaru falling into a sinkhole. (Niklas sold the car, which he no longer needed for commuting, and started taking taxis and buses.)

Niklas and Danielle walking on a sidewalk, about to be hit by a car jumping the curb. (The two of them agreed never to go walking anywhere together.)

A taxi that crashed into a power pole, with live power lines sparking on its body. (They stopped using taxis.)

A bus exploding, strewing dismembered bodies along the road. (They stop using buses.)

Niklas hit by a car while walking along the road into town. (Niklas stops going into town, leaving Danielle to do all their shopping.)

Danielle hit by a car while walking along the road into town. (They start having their groceries delivered.)

One evening, Niklas found Danielle sitting on the second-to-the-bottom step of the stairs that led up to the second floor. Her eyes were bloodshot, with dark circles under them.

"Honey, you look exhausted," he said. "Come on up to bed and get some sleep."

"I can't," she said.

"I'll carry you up," he offered.

She shook her head. "Her latest painting is of me, lying at the bottom of these stairs with a broken neck." She sighed. "I'll be safe sleeping on the couch."

"This is ridiculous," Niklas said. "We've become recluses, all because of supposed futures Crash paints."

"She's saved our lives a dozen times."

"Has she? Has she really? I'll grant the first one, the airplane crash. But were we really living such dangerous lives that we would have been killed many times over the past few months without the warning of her paintings? It's like we've been cursed ever since we brought that thing here."

"We're both still alive, that's what matters," Danielle said. "Please, promise me you won't go out and tempt fate by doing stuff that's in the pictures."

He pulled her to her feet and hugged her close. "I promise. We'll get through this, together." They walked to the living room and she lay down on the couch. He watched from a chair until she fell asleep.

Then he went to the gun safe in the study, unlocked it, and pulled out the Winchester. He loaded three rounds into the magazine. The elephant seemed to paint mostly good futures for clients, but only disaster for him and Danielle. Maybe it was sucking the good luck out of their lives. Maybe it was just toying with them. Whatever it was doing would stop tonight, so he and Danielle could get back to living normal lives. They'd be in a financial hole without the elephant paintings, but that was better than living in paranoia, afraid to leave the house, terrified to even go upstairs.

It was time to end the curse.

Niklas exited the back door and crossed the lawn to the elephant habitat. He stood in front of the closed door for a couple of minutes, working up his courage. The elephant had not painted a picture of itself trampling him to death, so he should be able to do this.

He unlocked the door and entered the habitat. The elephant lay on its side near the north wall, looking bluish gray in the moonlight. Niklas had been surprised to learn elephants slept lying down—he'd thought they would be like horses, sleeping on their feet. He walked slowly, quietly across the space between them, rifle pointed at the giant form. Based on his reading, the best place to shoot was near the top of the trunk, so the bullet would pass through the sinus cavities and into the brain. A quick, painless kill would be best.

As he tried to line up for the right angle, he noticed a painted canvas on the easel. It wasn't the one Danielle had spoken about, of her lying at the foot of the stairs. This one showed Niklas holding a rifle in his hands, standing next to an elephant lying on the ground with blood dripping from a hole near the top of its trunk.

The elephant knew what he was going to do.

He looked down, and saw the elephant's eye open. It stared at him, but made no move to get up and charge him or escape.

She wanted to die. She wanted him to kill her.

Maybe she had turned his and Danielle's life into hell because that's what her own life felt like to her.

Niklas set down the rifle and sat beside her. "I'm sorry, Crash. Uh, *Pang Dumain.* I never gave you any choice in the matter, did I? We pulled you thousands of miles from your home, everything you'd ever known. No wonder you hate me and Danielle so much you keep painting our deaths."

After a couple of minutes of thought, Niklas rose and brought a blank canvas out from the shed. Crash lumbered to her feet. She reached out her trunk toward Niklas's head, but he caught it and said, "No," before gently bending it back to touch her own forehead. "Paint the future you want for yourself."

He handed her a brush and she began painting.

His expectation was that she would paint her village back in Thailand, but instead she painted herself standing in a clearing in a jungle. Then she painted several other elephants with her. A small one clutched her tail with its trunk.

"Okay, I get the picture," he said. "First thing in the morning, I'll call Jessika about sending you to an elephant sanctuary back in Thailand."

He put the rifle away before waking Danielle up.

"What is it?" she said, her voice frightened.

"Everything's going to be okay," he said. "We're sending Crash back to Thailand."

"But we need her!"

"She needs to go back," he said. "Come take a look."

Danielle followed him to the habitat.

As they approached Crash and the painting, he said, "I told her to paint the future she wanted for herself. And look what she did."

Danielle looked, then nodded. "You're right. I'm just worried about what will happen to us."

Crash took her brush and began painting in one corner. Two human figures rapidly took shape.

"That's us!" Danielle said. "We're visiting Crash in Thailand."

Niklas looked closely. "I don't think so. Maybe it's the moonlight, but the hair color's totally wrong."

Danielle pulled him close. "We're going to be fine," she said. "That's us with white hair."

ABOUT THE STORY

Someone invited me to submit a story for a planned crowd-funded anthology about fortunetellers. The 2013 Codexian Idol contest was coming up, so I figured I'd write a story targeted toward that anthology.

That year, the contest used photos as prompts. One of the photos showed an elephant in Thailand. I had previously seen videos of elephants who had been trained to paint pictures, so I combined that with predicting the future and came up with Crash.

I've written quite a few stories about how people respond to prophecies. Usually, trying to avoid one's fate only leads to the fulfilment of the prophecy—a lesson I remember learning as a child from reading Greek myths. For this story, I decided to allow the characters to avoid their prophesied fate, but at the cost of eventually being too frightened to even leave their house.

I submitted the story to the contest, where it took fifth place. The anthology accepted it, and the Kickstarter for the anthology funded.

GIRL WHO ASKS TOO MUCH

Wise Ones, see here in front of you Girl Who Asks Too Much. Such a name does not cause pride to the Folk of the Egg. Dare not speak to her, or she will ask of you all the day long.

Why are some plants food for the Folk and some plants death?

Why are some beasts food for the Folk and some beasts death?

Why do the beasts that are death live when they feed on plants that are death?

Why are the plants and beasts that feed the Folk death for the beasts that are death for the Folk?

Fool girl, I tell her, the plants and beasts that feed the Folk all came from the Great Egg. They are a gift from the Egg, that they should be food for the Folk of the Egg. The plants and beasts that are not of the Egg are not for us.

But that does not stop Girl Who Asks Too Much.

Why did all things not come from the Egg?

Did the beasts and plants that are death come from an egg that is not the Great Egg?

Ask no more, I tell her, or I will change your name to Girl With Mouth Sewn Shut.

But that does not stop Girl Who Asks Too Much.

She wants to see the Great Egg, and I take her so she will not ask me more. Let her ask the Great Egg. It does not speak now, as in old tales. Let her ask, and it may be that the Great Egg will speak, if but to tell her not to ask more.

I and the girl walk for three days.

If we came from the Great Egg, why do we live so far from it?

Hush, I tell her, or I will leave you here and your name will be Girl Who Got Lost In The Woods.

That stops Girl Who Asks Too Much, for she knows we are near the Great Egg, where she may ask all she wants.

The Great Egg lies on a plain. Its height is more than a tree. The crack that split the Egg in two is dark, but the white of its shell has not dimmed.

Plants grow near the Egg. They are like the plants the Folk eat, yet not. They have more leaves, or are too thin, or twist in strange ways.

I think that Girl Who Asks Too Much will ask me why the plants are strange, but she does not. She runs off and goes in the crack of the Great Egg.

Such a thing is not done. The Folk came out of the Great Egg. Does a chick go back in the egg? Does a child go back in the womb? In the old tales, to go back in the egg is to get sick and die.

But I may not leave her and change her name to Fool Girl Who Ran In The Crack Of The Egg.

So I go in the Great Egg, too.

I find rooms in the Egg. I find Girl Who Asks Too Much in a room where she sits on the floor. It is not dark in the room, for parts of the walls shine.

She talks to the Great Egg.

Why are things that came from the Egg not the same as things that did not come from the Egg?

The Egg does not say a word.

Why do hen's eggs just hatch one kind of bird, and not all kinds of birds and beasts? Why are the plants near the Great Egg strange?

She asks and asks and asks, and the Egg does not say a word.

I tell her that she must come with me, but she will not. I tell her that she will get sick and die, and I will change her name to Fool Girl Who Would Not Hear And Got Sick And Died, but she will not stop.

I grab her arm to pull her with me, and then the Egg speaks.

I am not an egg, it says. I am a boat from a star. Much has changed, so I learn your new words from this girl.

Wise Ones, see here in front of you Girl Who Asks Too Much. Such a name does not cause pride to the Folk of the Egg. So now I name her Girl Who Talks To The Boat From A Star.

Such a name should cause pride to the Folk Who Came From A Star.

ABOUT THE STORY

This story was a 2009 Codex Weekend Warrior contest entry. Its prompt was: "Develop a creation myth for a fictional culture. Write a story where someone's actions are influenced by that myth. (Don't just retell the myth.)"

I decided to do a science-fictional creation myth, and came up with the idea that the culture was the result of a crashed colonizing spaceship.

A few years earlier, I had wanted to use names that were descriptive and meaningful for the characters in a novel I was working on, but I abandoned the idea as too unwieldy. At flash fiction length, though, I felt it could work, so I used that idea to name Girl Who Asks Too Much.

To give the story a somewhat primitive feel—and as a challenge to myself as a writer—I limited myself to using words of only one syllable. Did you notice that while you were reading? If not, feel free to go back and check.

THE PRICE OF A DAGGER
CALESH, ANKORA

"Excuse me, sir," the waitress said, "but the gentleman you were waiting for has arrived."

The illusory disguise Katya had chosen for this meeting was of a stocky man in his early forties, with short-cropped black hair graying at the temples, a long-ago broken nose, and brown eyes spaced just a little too close together. It was in this persona that the employees of the Goose and Barrel knew her, and while some of them probably suspected Katya was not the man she appeared to be, they had the discretion to take her silver and call her "sir."

"Bring him back," Katya said as she donned a sand-colored silk mask that covered the upper half of her face. She sat in a hard-backed oak chair, with the small private room's table between her and the door leading to the rest of the tavern. Behind her there was a window, its shutters open in case she needed an escape route. The tavern owner paid to have the window warded against eavesdroppers, and Katya had added a ward of her own for good measure when she arrived to prepare for the meeting.

A plump, balding man in a flowing off-white robe stopped just outside the door. As she reached out with her magical senses to detect any enchantments the man might have about him, Katya's eyes were immediately drawn to his right hand, which might be holding a weapon inside a pocket of his robe. But then he withdrew his hand and tossed a finger of silver to the waitress. He entered the room and closed the door behind him.

"That was generous," Katya said, her voice transformed to a baritone as part of the illusion. His robes looked to be of fine quality, but not extravagant, while the tip he had given the waitress was probably as much as the girl's wages for a month. It was not necessarily a contradiction, but it was unusual.

"I can be very generous when someone helps me," the man said.

There was one more unusual thing about him: He did not have any enchantments on him. Usually, clients meeting an assassin for the first time had at least some protective wards. So either he was walking into their meeting with no magical defenses at all, or he was better at cloaking his magic than just about anyone Katya had ever met.

"You're not warded," she said.

"Should I be?" He sat down in the chair across the table from her. "I'm afraid hiring … someone with your skills is not something I have done before, and I'm not sure of the proper etiquette. I felt that coming alone, unarmed, and unwarded would help establish that I am no threat to you, especially since … well, I thought you were a woman."

She considered that a moment. "But what if I were a threat to you?"

The man released a nervous laugh. "You probably are. But you have a reputation: You will not kill someone you've accepted money from." He reached into a pocket and tossed a black velvet bag to clink heavily on the table. "Fifteen fingers of gold, just to start."

Katya smiled. "It's not that simple. I have to decide whether I want to take the job you're offering before I'll accept your money."

"Of course, of course." He bobbed his head. "But unless you take the job, I will be dead in three days, so any possible threat from you does not make much difference."

Arching an eyebrow, Katya said, "Someone's trying to kill you?"

"Not yet." He took a handkerchief out and dabbed sweat from his forehead. "But when he finds out what I've done, he will kill me."

"Who?"

"Vremmen. He's a mage—a death mage—who lives not far from here." He peered at her eyes, which were not hidden by the silk mask. "Your eyes are brown, not blue. They said you were a master of magic, but your eyes are brown."

"It is possible to both master magic and have brown eyes," Katya said.

His head bobbed again. "Yes, I knew that. I did. No offense. I'm just nervous." Then his face broke into a grin. "Of course, it's an illusion. I'm a fool. Naturally you don't want me to see what you really look like. You're called the Lady Cat, so you could be a woman under there."

"Let's focus on the matter at hand. Why does this Vremmen want you dead?"

The man sucked in a long breath, then let it out. "Vremmen inherited substantial wealth from his father. He is not of a personality to engage in the extravagant pleasures of the flesh, nor to work on the accumulation of more wealth, but rather to focus his time and energy on the study of magic. However, since he needs money to fund his research, ten years ago he hired me as his steward to manage his finances. And, well, the truth of it is, some of his funds may have been misplaced."

"By you?"

"I intended to pay it all back, you have to believe me," he said, his voice almost whining. "But one of his bankers from Thalannon will be arriving in three days to discuss his lack of funds. And then Vremmen will kill me." He pointed to the bag.

"There's more where that came from, a lot more. Please, you have to help me."

If the money was actually the target's, did it violate her code to kill him? No, she decided. She didn't question where her other clients got their money. Even if this man paid her with stolen money, he would be the client.

But that was assuming she took him on as a client. She didn't like the three-day deadline: It cut down on her preparation time. On the other hand, if it was true that the target was a death mage, killing him would be an interesting challenge—and a suitable offering to Shi'in, her still-silent goddess.

"The price will vary depending on the difficulty of the job," Katya said. "Tell me what you know of the magic he studies. What kind of supplies do you buy for him?"

Checking up on her potential client, whose name was Lumain, eventually led Katya to one of the upscale magic shops in Calesh. The owner, Tolos, was an old friend of Meles, the owner of Katya's favorite magic shop back in Jakarr.

"Lumain?" Tolos said. "Been a customer for eight, ten years, maybe. Good customer. Buys lots of books, references mostly. Substantial line of credit in his master's name at the bank just down the street."

"He's a tall, thin man with long stringy hair, right?" Katya asked casually.

"Who, the master? Never seen him."

"No, Lumain." She wanted some independent confirmation that was actually his name.

"You think of some other Lumain, maybe? This Lumain— shorter than you, but with more meat on the bones. Used to have nice hair, but mostly gone now." Tolos smiled. "Testing me?"

"I'm not testing you, Tolos." Katya returned the smile. "I'm testing Lumain."

"Ah." Tolos held up a finger. "The master reads much on death magic. Very dangerous to be mixed up in."

"If I didn't want to get mixed up in dangerous things, I would have found another line of work."

"True, true. But I have something for you. You will like these." He went into a back room and came out a minute later with an oblong box. "Customer who was in your line of work gave me these in trade." He opened the box.

Inside lay two matched silver-bladed daggers with handles of ivory inlaid with gold. The workmanship was exquisite, and they were so beautiful that it took Katya a moment to remember to breathe again.

"Gorgeous, ah?" said Tolos.

Katya reached out a hand, then stopped before touching. "May I?" After Tolos nodded, she picked up one of the daggers.

Whoever had crafted the weapon knew what he was doing. This was not a ceremonial weapon, which looked beautiful but was useless for combat. The blade was razor sharp, and the handle sculpted to provide a firm grip. Blade and handle were balanced perfectly so it could be thrown with accuracy. It was light enough to be carried easily, yet heavy enough to penetrate deeply when thrown.

"These were made by a master," Katya said. "Why would anyone in my trade, no matter how dire the circumstances, give these up?"

"Retirement. Provided him with assistance in ... disappearing, got these in return. Oh, and look at this." He pulled the second dagger from the box, placed it on the counter, and spun it around its center of gravity. It spun smoothly, slowing gradually. When it came to a stop, it was pointing straight at Katya.

"Glyph of attraction," Tolos said. "Left free to swing about, each dagger will end up pointing at its twin, no matter the distance. Comes in handy after a fight if you've misplaced one of them."

Katya savored the feel of the dagger in her hand for a moment longer, then replaced it in the box. "Beautiful as these are, I'm not sure they're what I need for this job." Her own daggers were good enough for the physical challenges ahead, but she needed to be able to draw on more magical power in order to counter the death mage's spells. In this short a timeframe, she couldn't spare any of her own life force to charge objects, so she needed to buy some charged by others.

"Fully charged with magic," Tolos said. "With a death mage involved, you may need extra power."

Reaching out with her magical senses, Katya could see Tolos was telling the truth—a bright blue aura surrounded the daggers. "How much?"

"Thirty-five fingers of gold."

The daggers were rare enough to be worth more than that, Katya knew, so Tolos's opening position was weaker than it should have been. She was about to ask what was wrong with the daggers when he added, "Each."

That was more like it. After haggling for a few minutes, they settled on a price of fifty-six fingers of gold and she would give Meles a kiss for him the next time Katya was in Jakarr.

That evening, Katya met with Lumain in her office at the Goose and Barrel, where they settled on an advance of twenty-five fingers of gold and a payment on completion of another fifty.

She now had a client and a target.

Brimau, Ankora

The next morning, Katya took a coach headed south toward Wenshi, but got off when it stopped in the village of Brimau, after only a half-day's journey. According to the client, the target's home was built on the side of a small, extinct volcano outside the village, in order to harness some of the remnants of magical energy that still surrounded the place.

Brimau boasted only one inn, imaginatively named the Brimau Inn. Inside, a gray-haired woman dozed in a chair behind the counter. Katya coughed a few times, growing louder with each cough.

The woman lifted her head and blinked, then stiffened on seeing Katya, who was dressed in fine clothes and wore the illusion of a delicate young lady.

"A myriad apologies, my lady," the innkeeper said.

Katya waved her hand dismissively. "I apologize for troubling you. I would like a room, as far from any noise as possible." Being away from the inn's common room would make it easier to slip out a window during the night.

"Of course, my lady. How long will you be staying?"

"I'm not sure," Katya said. She put a hand to her stomach. "I'm on my way to visit my sister in Wenshi, but on the coach I began to feel quite ill and I just had to get off. If I'm feeling better tomorrow, I'll be on my way; otherwise I may stay until I recover sufficiently."

"Oh, you poor dear," said the innkeeper. "Can I make you some tea?"

After getting settled in her room, which was on the second floor at the back of the inn, Katya returned to the front desk to share a pot of imported Alary tea with the innkeeper, whose name was Nalya. A few minutes of idle gossip about the villagers led to chatting about the history of the inn and then the village.

That gave Katya her opening to swing the discussion around to the target without being the one to bring him up. "One of the other passengers on the coach pointed out a volcano nearby as we entered the village. That must be exciting."

"Exciting? No. The volcano was dead long before Brimau was founded."

"Oh," said Katya, pretending to be crestfallen. "I had thought it would be fun to actually visit the volcano."

"Nobody really goes there," said Nalya. "Except for the mage who lives there and his steward."

Katya widened her eyes. "There's a mage who lives inside the volcano?"

"Not inside, dear," Nalya said. "His house is built on it, though."

The client had given Katya a detailed map of the target's home, which was small for someone of his wealth. But it had an underground doorway leading into a volcanic cavern several times the size of the house itself. That was where the mage spent most of his time, according to the client.

"Have you ever been to the mage's house?" Katya asked.

"Never," Nalya said. "I've never met the man. Keeps to himself, he does. Never comes into the village. Inki the grocer says it's on account of his being horribly disfigured by an accident with one of his spells, but she hasn't seen him either, so how does she know?"

"How mysterious!" Katya said. She said it in the disingenuous tone of the character she was playing, but it really was puzzling. She would almost suspect that the target had died long ago and the client was merely keeping up appearances in order to continue to control the mage's estate—but then it wouldn't make sense for the client to hire her to kill the target, would it?

"But surely someone has seen him?" Katya asked.

"His steward has, of course. He comes into the village to buy food and such. Had a bit of a fling with Corlinda, the girl who works at Inki's. Didn't end well, seeing as she wanted to get married and he said his master would never allow it."

"Ooh, this mage sounds like a horrid man," Katya said.

"He's not all bad, that one. Donates money to the village for feast days. And just a few days ago, he gave everybody a light globe."

"A light globe?" Katya didn't need to fake the curiosity in her voice.

Nalya fumbled in a pocket, then pulled out a globe of dark glass about two finger-widths in diameter. "When it's nighttime, it glows. Not a lot, but enough to keep from stubbing your toe when you go to the privy in the middle of the night."

"Can I see it?" Katya held out her hand, feeling somewhat surprised at her desire to hold it. Nalya reluctantly gave her the ball.

The volcanic glass was cool to the touch.

Probing the ball with her magical senses, Katya detected a simple glyph for a light charm, combined with a timing spell. Another spell allowed for the gathering of magical power from the local environment, which was presumably how the globes recharged to glow each night. But there were many layers of spells inside, too many to analyze without detailed study.

One spell near the surface, though, seemed to be a mild compulsion of desire. She looked more closely at it, and though she couldn't be sure, it seemed to encourage people to want to possess one, but only one, of the globes. Strange. But it explained why she had been so eager to hold it.

"Pretty," Katya said as she handed it back. The light globe obviously had some deeper purpose than just giving the villagers a light on their way to the privy. But whatever that purpose was, she couldn't see how it might affect the job tonight.

Using the map the client had given her, she gained access to the house and slowly made her way to the doorway that accessed the volcanic cavern. Even though the map marked every ward and trap along the way, she refused to rely on it, taking just as much care to look for any potential problem as if she had no map. After all, there was no way to be sure that the client knew about all the defenses the target had set up.

When she reached the door to the cavern, she paused. Some of the wards had taken a good deal of magical energy to bypass, so she refreshed herself from some of the stores she carried.

She oiled the door's hinges, and then, ever so slowly, she swung it open until she could squeeze through into the cavern beyond.

A giant version of the light globes the villagers had illuminated the cavern ahead. A man stood at a worktable, back toward her. She reached out with her magical senses and saw a faint red aura of death magic around him. He was the death mage. The target.

She crept forward, silent, then stopped just shy of a delicate ward that had not been on the map the client had given her. She examined it—an alarm ward. Not harmful in and of itself, but if she had touched it, he would have known she was here. The trick now was to disarm it in such a way that he would not know it had been disarmed.

Or maybe not. She judged the distance between her and the man's back. Five paces. If she threw a dagger fast and true, she might kill him before he even had time to realize the alarm had been tripped. Even if she didn't get the instant kill, a dagger in the back would prove a great distraction as she moved in to kill him at close range.

It was either that, or hope he didn't turn around while she tried to evade this ward. Surprise or stealth? She decided surprise was the better option.

As she took out one of her standard throwing knives, she drained the magical power it contained in order to replenish herself. She drew another dagger, one best suited to close combat, and held it in her left hand.

Katya took careful aim, drew her right arm back, and threw.

Before the knife had reached the target, she sprang forward, through the alarm ward, while swapping the dagger from her left hand to her right.

Her throwing knife reached the target's back, its forward momentum carrying it farther until it sank out of sight.

Katya knew instinctively something was wrong. The target had not reacted in any way to being hit. She altered course even before reaching the logical conclusion that what she had perceived as the target was just a very skillful illusion.

If an illusion of the target was at the end of the path on the map the client had given her, then the target knew she was coming. The only question remaining was whether the target had discovered the client was betraying him, or whether it had been a trap from the beginning.

A blast from behind knocked her off balance, and she intentionally tucked and rolled to regain her footing. A glance back showed that the explosion had sealed off the passageway through which she had entered.

According to the map, that was the only way in or out. She was trapped here—if the map could be trusted, which she was not sure of anymore.

She moved swiftly into the shadow cast by a column of volcanic rock, then surveyed the cavern. The giant light globe hung from the ceiling near the center, over a round mineshaft about ten paces wide. She couldn't tell how deep it went.

Pillars of rock were scattered at random around the cavern. There were several worktables, also in seemingly random positions. Maybe they were just where the cavern floor was most level.

Movement nearby. She whirled, dagger at the ready, to find her client standing only five paces away.

"I was beginning to wonder if you were going to make it," he whispered. "He found out, somehow. But maybe I can distract him to give you a chance to kill him."

Could she trust him? Perhaps he was just an illusion, too. She reached out with her magical senses. Although there were several spells woven about him, there was no illusion—this was the man she had met in Calesh. But unlike the first time they'd met, he had an aura.

A red aura.

He was the death mage.

He was the target.

He was also the client.

So, it had been a trap all along. To what purpose? It didn't matter right now.

"You're Vremmen," she said, stalling to give herself time to figure a way out of the situation.

With a grin, he said, "I find myself quite curious as to what you will do. The whole notion of assassins with a code of honor is fascinating to me. You violate one of society's most basic rules —do not murder—yet you adhere to rules of your own making. One quirk of your personal code of honor is that you will not kill someone who has paid you for your services. Yet I have paid you to kill me. It's quite an interesting paradox, don't you think?"

While part of her mind wondered why he taunted her instead of attacking, she drained the power from the dagger in her hand and shaped it into a shove-spell. She launched it at him—

—the client shimmered and disappeared—

—and Katya was blown off her feet.

She landed awkwardly, a protuberance on the ground cracking some of her ribs on impact.

"I congratulate you on adhering to your code of honor," the client said. "If you had used a fatal spell, you would be dead now."

Katya crawled behind another rock pillar. He had somehow turned her own spell against her. And she had a strong suspicion that the client had not been physically there at all. She had been looking at some sort of magical reflection of him.

First, she needed to locate the client. Then she would disable him. And then she would escape.

She drew another throwing knife, drained its power, and used some of it to ease the pain in her ribs. That would give her more mobility, although she would end up in more pain later. Assuming there was a later.

"You're right," she shouted. "I've never killed a client. But since you hired me to kill you, perhaps I'll make an exception, unless you agree to let me go." She didn't like the idea of making an exception to her rule, because then she might start seeing the advantages of making more exceptions, and soon no rule would remain. But she could hardly let herself be killed just to maintain that rule.

"Let you go, after all the trouble I went to get you here?" His voice came from the left, and she saw movement in the corner of her eye.

She rolled, came upright, and launched her knife at him, then rolled again in case the knife was going to return to its point of origin.

The client shimmered and was gone.

"Oh, that would have given me a nasty gut wound," he said. Echoes made it seem like his voice came from several places. "I'd kill you for that, except I was going to kill you anyway."

Why did he keep talking? It must be to disorient her. Where was he really? How could she locate him when he seemed to be all around?

Katya crept to a worktable and searched it for anything she might use. A light globe caught her eye. She grabbed it and looked at it with her magical senses. It had the same spells as Nalya's had, including the glyph for the light charm.

That might do.

She tossed it in a high arc, then squeezed her eyes shut, drained some of the power from one of the twin daggers, and amplified the power going into the light glyph by a few hundred times.

Even through her eyelids, she could see the flash.

The client loosed a stream of profanities, his voice coming from various directions.

Eyes closed, Katya listened for where his voice was *not* coming from.

There. The center of the room. That might be the origin of the projections. She drained more power from the dagger, then stood, opened her eyes, and released a soft shove-spell, spread wide. If she was wrong, she didn't want it slamming her back.

Papers flew off a worktable between her and the mineshaft at the center of the cavern. And then, near the mineshaft, there was a flare of a shield warding off her attack. He was there.

Katya raced forward, hoping his blindness would last long enough for her to reach him.

Suddenly, he was visible. Either she had gotten inside whatever spell had been hiding him, or else he had abandoned it.

Since her last spell had not been reflected back at her, she tried a shove-spell again, with more force, but it dissipated against the bubble that his shield formed around him. Still, it gave her a clearer picture of the shield he was using.

Time for a physical attack. She drew the dagger she had been using for power, keeping its twin in reserve. If she was right about the strength of the shield he was using, a swift blow from the dagger, which still had almost half its charge left in it, would overload the shield and strike him.

In a smooth motion, she flung the dagger.

With her magical senses she could see the client's shield shift as the dagger approached, condensing from a thin bubble that surrounded him into a much thicker shield the size of a dinner plate. That shield swung to interpose itself between the dagger and the client. The dagger glanced off and fell to the floor ten paces away.

The client's response came quickly: a blast of energy that overwhelmed her hasty shield and knocked her to the ground. She landed hard on her left shoulder.

Katya scrambled to her feet, left arm limp, ribs aching. The mouth of the mineshaft gaped open between them, but at least she knew it was him, not an illusion. She pulled her one remaining dagger from its sheath. A full charge of magic remained. Its twin still lay on the ground where it had fallen, on the other side of the cavern.

She would only have one chance at this. She began circling clockwise, hoping to get the best line on the client. With her magical senses, she saw the client's shield move to keep itself between her and him.

"I purchased this dagger for twenty-eight fingers of gold," Katya said. Plus half a kiss for Meles, but that didn't make a difference.

"Is that supposed to impress me?" He began walking clockwise as well, keeping the mouth of the mineshaft between them. He probably believed he could finish her off with magic from a distance.

He probably could, Katya admitted to herself.

"It was a fair price, considering it's fully charged," Katya said. "You could sell it for that much, maybe more."

He laughed. "Are you trying to bribe—"

Katya had the line she wanted. In a flash of motion, she threw the dagger across the mineshaft toward the client.

It hit his shield and stuck. The client reached out and took the dagger by the handle.

"How kind of you to give me a weapon," he said.

"It's not a weapon," she said. "It's a refund."

Vremmen—no longer a client—frowned.

Reaching out with her magic toward the other dagger, which was now behind him, she amplified a thousandfold the power flowing into the glyph that attracted it to its twin. It shot from the ground and flew, point first, into Vremmen's back.

He staggered forward under the momentum of the blow. His magical shield faded. For a moment, he teetered on the edge of the mineshaft. Then he fell, taking both daggers with him into the darkness below. After a few seconds, there was a wet thud.

Above her, the giant light globe flared red for a moment, then resumed its usual hue. She held her breath, hoping that whatever Vremmen had planned would not start automatically with the power absorbed from his death.

After a few uneventful seconds, she let out her breath. Now she just needed to dig her way out.

✪

Jakarr, Ankora

Meles looked up from Vremmen's notebook, which Katya had brought with her after sealing up the cavern behind her. Meles's dark brown eyes were serious. "A quite ingenious plan, even if it did involve killing you."

"You really think it would have worked?" Katya asked.

"He planned to channel the life force released by the death of a powerful magic user like you in order to trigger the first level of eruption, releasing a cloud of poisonous gas that would have engulfed the village. Fortunately, he must have been planning to guide the spell himself, since his death did not trigger it. The 'light globes,' which each villager felt compelled to keep close, would have captured their life forces as they died from the gas, sending them all to the giant light globe in the cavern. That would have given him the power to drill down further, triggering a full-scale eruption. And if he could have harnessed the full energy of that ..." Meles shook her head. "I still don't understand why he hired you, though."

"Why go to the effort of kidnapping and transporting a powerful magic user like me?" Katya shrugged. "It's cheaper to hire me to walk right into your lair."

"Did you recover the daggers Tolos sold you? I'd love to see them."

"No. The mineshaft was too deep," Katya said. "But I survived. I guess that's worth the price of a dagger or two."

ABOUT THE STORY

For several years I was in an online writing class that gave me various exercises to do. I had a recurring character who was a female assassin, but in a high-tech world, not a fantasy land. However, when Story Portals offered me the opportunity to write a shared-world story about Katya, Lady Assassin, I remembered the fun I had with those writing assignments. So I pitched this plot to Story Portals. After a few tweaks they liked it, and paid me an advance to write the full story. It was my first (and so far only) work-for-hire story.

I've always admired fictional characters (and real people) who live in accordance with their own moral code, even if that code does not match up to mine. So even though I would personally never become an assassin for hire, I felt I could write a protagonist who was, as long as she followed the moral code of her goddess.

That, of course, was what led me to create the dilemma at the climax of the story, when it turns out the villain is using Katya's own rules against her. I really enjoyed finding a solution that allowed her to keep to her code and defeat the villain at the same time.

Unfortunately, the Story Portals project folded after a few years, but I was able to get permission to reprint this story in my collection.

NINE TENTHS OF THE LAW

The law offices of Thacker, Ford & Harward were on the upper floors of a downtown high-rise that had mostly escaped the ravages of the zombie troubles. I walked past the attractive, living receptionist and made my way toward a corner office, which I figured would hold one of the better lawyers.

None of the lawyers themselves had escaped infection, of course, because the zombies had deliberately targeted lawyers, judges, and politicians during the initial stages of the plague. But that only made them better lawyers. Contrary to movie stereotype, the typical zombie did not shamble around, arms outstretched, searching for brains to eat, because most zombies had all the brains they needed: The average zombie had an IQ of 182.

Instead of brains, they ate hearts. But nobody's perfect.

The name on the corner office door was Travis Gordon. I walked through the door and saw a gray-haired man sitting at a desk, his skin the usual waxy complexion of a zombie.

After a few moments, Gordon noticed me and looked up. "I didn't hear you come in." His voice was calm. "Considering my door is shut, and I can't smell you or hear your heartbeat, either you are a hallucination, a projection, or a ghost."

I walked to one of the chairs in front of his desk and sat. "Pretty impressive. I am, in fact, a ghost."

"Well, Mr. Ghost or whatever your name is, the mere fact that you are dead does not excuse you from the rules of civil society. You can't just drop in unannounced. Feel free to make an appointment like anybody else."

"Yeah," I said, "about that ... You have a living receptionist answering your phone. Very discriminatory of you, by the way. Manifesting to you is pretty easy, you being dead and all. My name's Kyle, by the way. Kyle Petrides. But even if I managed a phone call, she'd probably just hear white noise on the line, which her mind would then interpret as someone whispering words like, 'You're all going to die, get out, Paul is dead,' *et cetera, et cetera.* So I decided to do a walk-in. Plus, it's kind of an emergency."

"What kind of emergency?"

"Someone's about to haunt my house."

Gordon frowned. "Someone other than you, you mean."

I waved my hand dismissively. "I don't haunt my own house. But from my perspective, having a bunch of living people hanging around, appearing at odd hours, making strange noises and such, that's pretty much a haunting. I want to get an injunction to keep these people out of my house."

"You own it?"

"I did, twenty-one years ago, before I died. But I've been there ever since, and possession's nine tenths of the law, right?"

"Hmm. There's no precedent for ghosts exercising property rights."

"Eighteen months ago, there were no legal precedents for zombie rights, either. But now ... conditions are more favorable for ghosts to come out of the closet, so to speak. It's really a matter of civil rights."

Gordon pressed a button on his phone. "Maxine, reschedule my eleven o'clock and hold my calls."

We went to court the next day.

The living people who had bought my house had scrounged up an actual living human lawyer from somewhere. Most people had learned to live with the zombie takeover, and even be happy with it—the government ran a lot more efficiently, now—but there were still foolish prejudices. And picking this living lawyer was definitely foolish, since Gordon could talk rings around the guy.

"But Your Honor," the lawyer whined, "my clients have paid good money to purchase the house from the legal owner. This, this ghost shouldn't be allowed to possess my client's property."

"The owner of record is not necessarily the legal owner, Your Honor," Gordon said smoothly. "Mr. Petrides has been in continuous possession of the property for the past twenty-one years, with a claim adverse to that of the owner of record. Opposing counsel's clients were on notice of Mr. Petrides's possession, since they were aware that the owner of record was willing to sell the house for below-market value due to its being haunted. It is not Mr. Petrides's fault that they did not believe in ghosts."

The judge nodded. "I've heard enough. Current law has clearly established that mere death of the physical body does not divest someone's rights. While the law was written with zombies in mind, on its face there is no reason it cannot apply to ghosts as well. There being no legal bar to possession by a ghost, I rule that the property in question belongs to Mr. Petrides."

Two weeks later, the Supreme Court unanimously affirmed the ruling. Justice moved a lot more swiftly now that the zombies controlled the entire process. I met Gordon in his office for a celebratory drink—although he didn't offer me anything, of course. Not having a body had a lot of disadvantages.

"I imagine that, after this decision, a lot more of your kind will start coming into the open," Gordon said, then took a sip from his brandy. "And if ghosts start asserting their rights to own homes, it's going to cause increased demand for homes, which means increased property values, more construction jobs, and so on. Economically, it makes a lot of sense. I'm sure that's why your case got expedited."

"This was never really about property for me," I said. "It was about legal recognition of ghosts as beings with rights."

"Of course," Gordon said. "We zombies understand. Why do you think we went after the lawyers, politicians, and judges first?"

I nodded. "Interesting thing about those zombie rights laws you passed. They allow the body to retain civil rights after death, even if the personality controlling the body is completely different. Very convenient."

"Well, of course. Since the virus wiped the old personalities—"

"No, I meant convenient for us ghosts." I walked toward him, and as I got too close, he backed away until he reached a wall. "Your body keeps control of your assets no matter who controls your body. Combined with the recent Supreme Court decision that ghosts have a right to possession, it leads to some interesting possibilities. Taking over a human with a soul is tremendously difficult, but all you zombies in positions of wealth and power—well, you've done the hard part already."

I stepped into his body, possessed it, then lifted the glass to my lips and actually tasted something for the first time in decades.

"Like they say, possession is nine tenths of the law," I said, just in case he could still hear me from inside what was now my head. "I think I'll like being a lawyer."

ABOUT THE STORY

When Kevin J. Anderson asked me for another humorous horror story for the third *Blood Lite* anthology, I decided to put my juris doctorate to use and write something involving lawyers. I began working on a story with the Shakespeare-allusive title "First Thing We Do," about a zombie virus that turned people into lawyers. Hilarity would, of course, ensue.

After about four pages, I realized the story had a serious problem: it was serious. There was one line that, while not actually funny, hinted at potential humor. And that was it.

So I stabbed that story right in the brain stem and started over, reversing the trope of brainless zombies. (By having the zombie plague begin by targeting the legal profession, I still got in my allusion to "The first thing we do, let's kill all the lawyers.")

THE NINE TRILLION NAMES OF
JAY LAKE

Vainglorious Sparkle isn't the best name ever for a planet, but when a hundred and some-odd million planets already have names, it's kind of tough to find a good one that hasn't been used. Unfortunately, my parents were very patriotic—so much so that they named their only daughter after our planet: Vainglorious Sparkle Chiu. My friends call me Glory. (My enemies call me Vain, but only behind my back.)

Anyway, I'd better shut up about me or you'll start thinking I really am vain.

The jaylakeologist's starship was an hour and half late arriving at the Vainglorious Sparkle spaceport. Considering the ship had just traveled the 45 k-lights from Earth in only nine years, I was willing to grant the pilot a little leeway. Plus, I've never been off-planet, so I like to hang out at the port sometimes and watch the launches and landings. Eventually my implant popped up an alert that the ship had docked.

We hadn't known the starship was coming until it flipped under lightspeed after entering the system. The jaylakeologist had sent a message asking to meet with the head of a local university. Since Mom's duties as chancellor of V.S.U. keep her pretty busy and I'd never seen anyone actually from Earth before, I volunteered to pick him up and bring him to campus.

My implant face-recced the stooped, white-haired man the moment he came through the customs gate, superimposing his name: Pedro Reyes. I sauntered toward him and said, "Dr. Reyes?"

He stopped and smiled, his antigravved baggage bobbing to a halt behind him. "I am he. And you are?"

"Glory Chiu. I believe you've been in touch with my mother since arriving in-system."

"Yes, Chancellor Chiu has been most helpful."

"Well, follow me. I've got a groundcar outside," I said, as I summoned it from the parking lot via my implant.

From the FAQ page on jlake.com.earth.sol (archived 362013-07-28 01:03:14 AM UTC):

Q: Why are there so many Jay Lakes?

A. The Jay Lake genome was one of 65,536 genetic codes carried aboard the Von Neumann 1, the first self-replicating automated interstellar colonizer. The colonizer was programmed to create robots to build a colony infrastructure, including artificial wombs in which to gestate the babies who would become the founding colonists, tended through their childhood by nanny robots. Then the colonizer would replicate itself, and both it and its copy would launch to seek out new habitable planets and start the process over. Decades later, it was discovered that a single error in one line of code among millions meant that the same genetic profile would be loaded into every artificial womb: the Jay Lake genome.

Once we were inside the groundcar, I directed it to take us to my mom's office about a half hour away, then sat back. After the silence stretched a little long, I said, "So, how was the trip?"

He shrugged. "I spent it in cryo. It was uneventful, which is always to be desired."

I guess that made my life pretty desirable, since Dr. Reyes's arrival was about the most interesting event in months. "We don't get a lot of visitors from Earth. Nine years is a long time, even in cryo."

He nodded, but said nothing.

Well, if he wasn't going to volunteer information, I was obviously going to have to draw it out of him. "So, what brings you to our neck of the galaxy?"

"I'm afraid it's nothing very interesting."

"Most people don't travel 45 k-lights for nothing very interesting."

He smiled wryly. "I mean, it's not interesting for people outside my specialty. I'm collecting the names of Jay Lake."

I frowned. "I thought they were named Jay Lake. You can't just write down 'Jay Lake' and you're done?"

That brought a chuckle. "The original source of the genome was Joseph Edward Lake, Jr. But that name is just the start of the list. You see, until follow-up ships could arrive with colonists from Earth, everyone in a new colony was a Jay Lake—tens of thousands of Jay Lakes. It would have been tremendously confusing if they all went by the same name. So, for use among themselves, they each took a unique name. It is those names I am collecting."

"But there must be billions and billions of them," I said.

"About nine trillion, actually. Some people joke he's got a thousand times as many names as God."

"You can't possibly collect them all."

He shook his head sadly. "Of course not. But I can collect as many as possible from this region of the galaxy. Others are collecting elsewhere. Eventually all the collections will be unified on the galactinet."

It didn't really make sense to me. Why spend nine years in cryo to come here just to track down the names of a bunch of Jay Lakes? But people do all sorts of oddball stuff, and it seemed harmless enough. "What happens when you have all the names?"

"What happens?" He blinked a few times in rapid succession. "Well, I suppose someone will throw a party."

From the FAQ page on jlake.com.earth.sol (archived 362013-07-28 01:03:14 AM UTC):

Q: Why was the Jay Lake genome selected for inclusion on the Von Neumann 1?

A. Although everybody nowadays is familiar with Jay Lakes because they founded over 90% of human colony worlds, when the Von Neumann 1 was programmed in the 2100s, the original Jay Lake was one of the best-remembered speculative fiction writers of the previous century [See Biblio]. Some people have theorized that due to budget cuts in the space program, the Jay Lake genome was selected because it was open source and therefore it did not require a license fee, but there is no evidence to support such a theory.

As a firsty at V.S.U., I hadn't officially chosen a major yet. I was leaning toward archaeology, although with our colony being only 127 years old, we didn't have a whole lot of archaeology on Vainglorious Sparkle. Someday I hoped to go off-planet and see something really old, find a lost city or a hidden artifact or whatever. Anyway, I was taking a variety of classes to get a feel for different things. My history class had a segment on early Vain-glorious Sparkle history, and meeting Dr. Reyes had made me curious, so I skipped forward to that and watched the holo-lecture about our Jay Lake Period.

"In many ways, a Jay Lake made the perfect early colonist," said Professor Scholes. "Each of them needed only five hours of sleep per night and was amazingly productive during waking hours. Individual Jay Lakes would focus their prodigious intel-lects on particular specialties within the colony, so there were medical Jay Lakes, construction Jay Lakes, and so on."

"Did they pick names based on their specialties?" I asked.

The holo of Professor Scholes paused, then a message flashed up saying, "We're sorry, an answer to your question cannot be synthesized from this lecture. Would you like to broaden your search?" There were buttons for "Other Lectures in This Class", "Lectures in Other History Classes", "Lectures in Other Depart-ments", and "Other Resources".

After trying this class without results, I got a hit in other history classes. We didn't have an entire jaylakeology depart-ment, but there was an upper-division course called The Jay Lakes of Vainglorious Sparkle. Even better, it was taught by a Jay Lake simulacrum. The last of our colony's Jay Lakes had died several years before I was born, but the simulacrum could draw on the huge amount of public data about them.

"Jay Lake naming conventions were based on a complex mathematical formula," said Professor Lake. "They were designed by one of the mathematician Jay Lakes on the first colony world, and passed along as part of the historical data in the *Von Neumanns 1* and *2* when they left. In fact, he took his inspiration from the prime-number-based algorithm for the self-replicating colonizer, which was designed to ensure a unique serial number for each of the ships even after hundreds of gener-ations without contact between ships. Thus, each Jay Lake, despite having an identical genome to myriads across the galaxy, has a name that is his and no one else's."

I frowned. "Do we know what the algorithm is?"

In response, the holo brought up a complex section of computer code.

"If we know what the algorithm is, then why would anyone be going around collecting the names of Jay Lake? Why not just generate the names?"

The holo flashed up, "We're sorry, an answer to your question cannot be synthesized from this lecture. Would you like to broaden your search?"

I skipped straight to the other resources button, but it brought back nothing.

I briefly considered then discarded the idea that Dr. Reyes didn't know about the naming algorithm. If I could find that info in just a few minutes, any jaylakeologist interested in the names of Jay Lake must know. So what was his real purpose in coming here?

✪

From the FAQ page on jlake.com.earth.sol (archived 362013-07-28 01:03:14 AM UTC):

Q: How did the original Jay Lake die?

A. He died of an ancient disease called cancer, which was a common cause of death prior to the 22nd century. Since cancer involves changes to a cell's genetic makeup, both the standard Jay Lake genome and the Jay Lake's Cancer genome were sequenced prior to his death. Because the Jay Lake's Cancer genome was one of the first open source cancer genomes, it ended up being instrumental to the researchers who created the first generalized cancer vaccine in 2032.

✪

When I finally tracked down Dr. Reyes, he was in the *Von Neumann* room of the Vainglorious Sparkle Colonial History Museum. The walls were filled with images of the *Von Neumann* that had originally colonized our planet, as well as of the duplicate it had constructed before both ships launched to find new planets. The centerpiece of the room was a five-meters-tall scale model of the colonizer.

"Do you know the serial number of your colonizer?" Dr. Reyes asked before I had a chance to confront him with what I had discovered. "It is not listed in the information here."

"Umm," I said, trying to remember what I'd read about our colonizer. "They're all identical on the outside. I think the serial number's just a software thing."

"Yes," he said. "I was just wondering if you knew."

"I'll tell you what I do know: Jay Lake names are generated by an algorithm. So there was no reason for you to come all the way out from Earth to find out the names."

The lines around his eyes wrinkled deeper as he laughed. "Just because the algorithm can be used to generate the unique names for Jay Lakes on each colony does not mean we know which names were used by actual Jay Lakes. Only about half the names generated for any particular colony end up being chosen for use. It is those names that matter."

"Oh," I said, somewhat crestfallen that the mystery I had discovered turned out to be so easily solved. "I guess that makes sense."

He leaned toward me, a conspiratorial twinkle in his eyes. "But you are correct that the names are not all that I seek."

"Really? What else are you looking for?"

"The names are a clue. Figure out what the clue means, and I'll tell you more."

From the Biblio page on jlake.com.earth.sol (archived 362013-07-28 01:03:14 AM UTC):

...

"Live Cleveland, Without the Sparkle", *Fictitious Force* Issue 1, April, 2005 (See 98 reprint venues)

...

"Of Stone Castles and Vainglorious Time", *The River Knows Its Own*, Wheatland Press, September, 2007 (See 372 reprint venues)

...

✪

Back at home, I had my implant bring up a list of Jay Lake names for the colony on Vainglorious Sparkle. As I looked at the list, at first they all looked like three random words: Backward Food Father, Street Agreed Came, Then Level Roast. After looking through the list more closely, I found occasional sets of words that looked like they had names mixed in: Blubbered Hethor Plantains, Dreamt Carving Huang.

I did a search to see if "Vainglorious" was used in any of them. It was: Vainglorious Caltrop As. But there was no "Sparkle." What did that mean?

I brought up the simulacrum of Professor Jay Lake on the holo. "Where do the words in the Jay Lake names come from?" I asked.

"They come from the 26,047 unique words in the complete published works of the original Jay Lake. Combinations of unique words can be used to represent a number."

"How high a number?"

"You might as well ask how high numbers go. It depends on the number of words in the name."

"Three words."

"Approximately eighteen trillion."

And if only half were used, then that would mean nine trillion names, and Dr. Reyes had said there were about nine trillion Jay Lakes. Which meant the three-word names that could be generated by the algorithm were almost used up.

Dr. Reyes must be looking for the first four-name Jay Lake. But why come to Vainglorious Sparkle? I double-checked and confirmed that none of our Jay Lakes had four names.

Remembering that the Jay Lake naming algorithm was based on the algorithm for the *Von Neumanns*, I asked, "Based on the naming algorithm, is it possible to project the serial number of the *Von Neumann* that would produce the first Jay Lakes that would require four names?"

"Yes. It would be serial number 1."

Von Neumann 1. The original colonizer. Arguably the most important artifact in the history of the human race.

I had one more question: "Based on the names of the Jay Lakes of Vainglorious Sparkle, what was the serial number of the *Von Neumann* that colonized our planet?"

"One."

From the FAQ page on jlake.com.earth.sol (archived 362013-07-28 01:03:14 AM UTC):

Q: I've heard there are people who track the names of Jay Lakes on all the colony worlds. Is that some sort of religious thing?

A. No. The original Jay Lake was an atheist, and would probably be very disturbed at the thought of a religion being founded around him. But too often nowadays, people only think of the

Jay Lakes en masse. The jaylakeologists who track the names of individual Jay Lakes do so out of a belief that every individual matters.

✦

"You're looking for the first four-name Jay Lake," I said, meeting Dr. Reyes again in the *Von Neumann* room at the museum. "But more than that, you're here looking for clues as to where the *Von Neumann 1* went after it left here 97 years ago."

"Impressive," he said. "I thought you might get to the four-names part, but only a few people have figured out the correlation with the *Von Neumann 1*." He sighed. "But so far I have not determined where it went."

"I can help you do research," I said. Then, suddenly sure of where I wanted to go with my life, I added, "And I'm coming along when you go after it."

ABOUT THE STORY

For those who don't already know it: Jay Lake really existed.

In some ways we were very similar: we both spent much of our childhoods outside the United States, we had the same score on the LSAT, we were winners in the Writers of the Future Contest. In some ways we were opposites: he was ridiculously prolific while I tend to write slowly, he was on the left of the political spectrum and I'm on the right, he was an atheist and I believe in God. We had some very interesting disputes online, but I was glad he considered me a friend.

When Jay had his first bout with colon cancer, I wrote a story titled "The Six Billion Dollar Colon" for a Jay-Lake-Get-Well anthology. That story was included in my previous collection.

Jay Lake recovered, but unfortunately his cancer came back a few years later and metastasized. When he knew he probably had less than a year to live, he decided to have a wake while he was still alive to attend. I wrote this story for the Jay Wake anthology in conjunction with that party. I made use of the fact that he'd had his (and his cancer's) genome sequenced and released as open source data.

Since my first story for him stole its title from *The Six Million Dollar Man* and increased it by three orders of magnitude, I decided to do something similar with this story by stealing the title of Arthur C. Clarke's "The Nine Billion Names of God" and increasing it by three orders of magnitude.

WRITE WHAT YOU WANT
I WANT TO BE RICH.

✪

The bells above the door to my magic shop jangle, and in walks a girl about fourteen years old. She stops once she's inside and the door closes behind her. She looks around at my shelves, stocked with card tricks, coin tricks, rope tricks, and a thousand more tricks for the aspiring magician to amaze his or her friends.

✪

I want to be a famous movie star.

✪

From the haunted look on her face, I don't think she's an aspiring magician interested in tricks. She's here for the real magic. I hope it's something as easy as a first love gone awry. My magic has fixed a lot of those. I hold up a hand and say, "Don't tell me. You're here because you want something so much it hurts."

✪

I want the cancer to be gone so I don't die.

✪

She nods. Her voice breaks a little as she says, "A friend said you could help."

✪

I want to be head cheerleader.

✪

"I'll help if I can," I say. "No charge." I point to a stool in front of the glass counter containing the more expensive coin tricks.

✪

I want to be straight.

✪

As she sits, I pull the pad of paper from under the cash register. "Now," I say, "It's very simple." I tear off a strip of paper eight-and-a-half inches wide by about one inch tall. "All you do is write what you want on this magic piece of paper. When you're done, I'll burn it in a magic flame. Easy as pie."

✪

I want to be thinner and prettier than Jasmine Rawlings.

✪

"Umm." She looks around nervously. "Do I have to write it?"

✪

I want my wife to stop nagging me.

✪

"You don't have to do anything." I shrug. "But if you want the magic to work, you have to write what you want on the paper."

✪

I want to be the star quarterback for my high school football team.

✪

After a moment's hesitation, she pulls a pen with a plastic flower taped to it out of the cup next to the register.

✪

I want my son Peter not to be autistic.

✪

"Before you write," I say, "you should know there are a few rules. First, when you walk out of here, you won't remember exactly what the magic did, just whether you were satisfied with the result." I forestall the usual objections by adding, "People are usually happier when they don't remember that their happiness is due to a magic spell."

✪

I want bigger breasts.

✹

She nods, and I continue, "Second, you don't need to worry about tricks with the wording of what you want. This isn't like evil-genie wish magic, where the genie will twist your words into something terrible. The whole purpose of this magic is to make you happier."

✹

I want Beth Larson to love me.

✹

"Finally," I say, "this magic can only be used once per person, so you mustn't use it for something frivolous, like 'I want a bacon cheeseburger,' just because you happen to be really hungry right now. You should only use it if you desire something so much that you're sure you can't be happy without it, something that will affect you for the rest of your life. If you think you might want something even more later, then it's better to wait. You can only do this once."

✹

I want the biggest big-screen TV in my neighborhood.

✹

"I want this now," she says. She puts pen to paper, then looks up at me until I nod my approval. She writes the first few words slowly, hesitantly. She pauses for about a minute, then scribbles out a word and continues. While she writes, I put a red candle in a sterling silver candlestick and place it on the counter. Finally she puts the pen down and folds the paper in half.

✲

I want to have children.

✲

I use the burning finger trick to light the candle, holding my hand at an angle so she can't see the bit of wire that holds the flaming rubber cement. She picks up the piece of paper, but I snatch it from her hand before she can put it to the flame. "Sorry, but I'm the one who has to put it in the flame. And I have to read it first for the magic to work. Plus, I want to have the chance to talk you out of wasting the magic on something that's not vitally important."

✲

I want my husband Benny to be alive and healthy again.

✲

She sags on the stool, but makes no move to stop me. I open the paper and read: *I want my dad to*—the word *die* is scribbled out —*stop having sex with me.* My heart sinks and I feel nauseated. "I'm so sorry," I say, knowing it's completely inadequate. "I'm sorry, but I can't do this one."

✲

I want to be the most popular girl in school.

✲

The girl looks away. "You said you would help." Her voice is empty.

✺

I want my wife to look like she did when I married her.

✺

"If I could," I say. "But … the magic I do can't give people what they want. All it does is reduce the wanting. My customers go away satisfied because they no longer want something so bad it hurts. But you …" I held up the piece of paper. "I don't think your want is something that should be reduced." I desperately try to find a way to help. "If you tell me your name, I can contact a social worker, or the police, or someone."

✺

I want my dad to be proud of me.

✺

I'm hopeful she'll take me up on it, but after a long pause, she shakes her head, then slips off the stool and walks out the door. I feel completely useless—what good is my magic when I can't help someone who really needs it? I rip her paper into tiny shreds and throw it out. Then I pull out the slip of paper I carry in my wallet. I hold it near the candle flame, but, as always, I can't bring myself to burn it. I return it to my wallet without reading it, because I know what it says:

✺

I want to help people be happy.

ABOUT THE STORY

This was a 2011 Codex Weekend Warrior Contest story. The final prompt for the final weekend of the contest was very open-ended: "Write anything you want."

Naturally, my mind immediately looked for a way to twist the prompt and decided the best way was to view it in the most restrictive way: the story needed to actually be about writing what you want.

This is one of the most tragic and hopeless stories I've written, and that was difficult for me. I desperately tried to find a way to use the magic to save the girl from her father. I even started writing an ending in which the magic shop owner tracks the girl's father down and tricks him into writing something that could be interpreted to mean he wanted to stop abusing his daughter, but I quickly realized that such an ending was not true to the magic in the story or to the tragic reality so many children face.

BY THE HANDS OF JUAN PERÓN

In 1987 someone broke into the tomb of Argentine dictator Juan Perón and removed the hands from his corpse. An unknown group subsequently demanded eight million dollars in ransom for the hands, but despite an extensive investigation by the Argentine government, the culprits were never identified. As for Perón's hands, they remain missing to this day—in this timeline.

An average Argentine citizen would be almost paralyzed with fear upon opening the door at three in the morning to find two Imperial Police officers. But despite his wishes to the contrary, Tomás Alejandro Perón was not an average Argentine citizen. Even if his father had finally decided it was time to be rid of his troublesome Catholic priest son, there was no point resisting. He got in the car and let them drive him to downtown Buenos Aires.

The car pulled into a rear entrance to the Casa Rosada, where he was given over to the custody of two military guards. Tomás followed them through the unfamiliar corridors of the new imperial wing of the Casa Rosada. It was new to him, at least; though he had grown up in the presidential palace, he had not returned since taking his vows as a Catholic priest twenty-five years ago.

As the guards escorted Tomás into a large room, Juan Domingo Perón—Emperor of Latin America, Protector of the Southern World—rose from a couch and strode to greet him with a hug. "Tomasito, I'm glad you came."

Instead of pointing out his father had told him never to return, Tomás returned the hug. "You're looking well, Father."

"Not bad for a hundred and ten years old, no? I look younger than you. But we can change that easily enough."

"The Church has not changed its moral position on artificial rejuvenation," said Tomás.

His father turned abruptly and paced to a window. "And what *moral* position allows your church to kill your brother?"

"Mario?" The news seemed to hollow Tomás's stomach. "Mario's dead? When? How? Is Mamá all right?"

"Yesterday. I've muzzled the press for now. Not even your mother knows, but the news will get out soon." His father turned to look him in the eyes. "It was a public appearance, the opening of a new orphanage run by your church. And when one of the nuns gave him a hug, she burst into flames, right there on the steps of the orphanage. The guards tried to put the fire out, but it was no use. Mario burned to death, screaming."

"And you think the nun did this on purpose?" Tomás sat down as he tried to process the information. "The Church does not condone suicide or murder."

"Still you defend them?"

Now was not the time to argue the point. Tomás said, "What will you do?"

"I cannot stand by and allow them to murder the President of Argentina, my designated successor as Emperor, without consequence."

"You …" Tomás swallowed. "You are not planning to harm the Pope?"

"That frail old man? Kill him and another jumps in his place. No, your Church has deprived me of one son. I feel it only just I take the other in exchange."

"I'm but a humble priest. Killing me will not impress them." Tomás felt no fear, just puzzlement. Had his father gone mad at last?

"Kill you? No, I will appoint you President of Argentina. I will designate you as next in line to be Emperor."

Tomás shook his head. Mario had been the ambitious one.

"But more, I will take your loyalty from them. Oh, how they must have laughed when you turned from me to them. And they did not even give you a position commensurate with your status. A simple parish."

Rising to his feet, Tomás said, "I love the people of my parish, and my calling is sufficient. You cannot bribe me with titles, and you cannot shake my faith. Goodbye, Father."

"Wait. I have proof you must see."

Tomás stopped. "Proof the Church was behind killing Mario?" He did not want to believe it, but sometimes people became over-zealous.

"No. Even more than that. You have faith your Pope is guided by God?"

"Yes."

"I have scientific proof he is not."

Tomás frowned. "You cannot prove such a thing scientifically. It is a matter of faith."

"Like the existence of God?"

"Yes."

His father smiled. "I have scientific proof God exists. Can you shut your eyes to such?"

"If you have such proof, why have you not shared it with the world? You hate the Church enough, so why have you not proven the Pope a fraud?"

His father waved a hand dismissively. "The world is not

ready for the truth. But you are. Come with me." He marched out the door.

After a brief hesitation, Tomás followed.

His father said nothing as they walked to an elevator. Two imperial guards boarded with them, and one pressed a button that started the elevator descending.

"You remember the bomb plot in 1987, yes?" his father said.

"I read about it." It had happened seven years after Tomás had become a priest. He had tried to see his father in the hospital, but had not been admitted.

"The bomb did not explode completely when I opened the briefcase. But I lost my hands."

Tomás hadn't known that. He looked at his father's hands. "So you grew them back."

"Yes, now we do it all the time. The marvels of Argentine medicine—" His father gave a strange laugh. "—and the wonders of stem cells from the spleen. But twenty years ago, the science was in its infancy. The cells would grow wild without a proper foundation. The experiments were awful. So I needed a pair of hands on which my cells could grow in the proper pattern."

Nauseated, Tomás said, "You stole someone else's hands—"

"No! I am not so monstrous. Besides, I did not want another man's hands. But you know of quantum mechanics, yes?"

What did quantum physics have to do with his father's hands? "Something, yes."

"The theory that there are other worlds, parallel to ours? It is not just theory, it is fact. We have a machine that can travel to these other worlds. That is where my hands came from: the Juan Perón of another world."

The elevator stopped, and Tomás realized they had been descending the whole time. They must be far underground. "And this Juan Perón from another world, he just gave you his hands out of pity?" They stepped out of the elevator into a well-lit white corridor.

"He did not mind. He was dead. Fortunately, his hands were sufficiently preserved that my doctors could use them as a foundation for my living cells to take over."

Tomás wasn't sure what to say.

They stopped in front of a large metal door.

His father said, "Do you know why Argentina rose to become the undisputed world power? The leader in armaments, engineering, medicine, even entertainment?"

"In 1947," Tomás recited from the memory of lessons learned as a schoolboy, "President Perón instituted his first five-year economic plan. The valiant workers of the nationalized industries—"

"What I will show you is not in the schoolbooks. But at least you have the correct year." His father pushed open the door and walked in.

Tomás followed. Beyond the door was a balcony overlooking a cavernous room, in the middle of which there was a thick hexagonal piece of featureless gray metal fifty meters across.

"In July 1947, our navy was performing maneuvers in the Pacific. This flying disc crashed and sank in the water nearby. At great expense it was recovered and brought secretly back to our shores."

"A flying disc?" Tomás could not keep the excitement out of his voice. "Were there aliens on board?"

His father nodded. "Three were still alive when we got inside, although two were so wounded that they died within a few weeks."

"And the third?"

"She still lives."

As a boy, Tomás had loved reading science fiction. The idea of a live alien with a flying disc excited him, yet he remained wary. When his father offered someone something, it was always for his own advantage. "And this alien has been giving you advanced technology?"

"Fortunately for her—and for us—the disc crashed in the

water, and it managed to maintain its integrity. In the United States timeline, the disc crashed in their territory, but was torn apart on impact. That is why we have the advantage."

"The United States timeline? What advantage? I do not understand." Tomás tried to comprehend the implications of what his father had revealed. Church doctrine did not rule out the many worlds of quantum mechanics, nor the existence of alien life, so this was not the proof his father had threatened.

"The United States timeline is the one where I got my hands. We name the timelines after the dominant power. Come, let us sit and I will explain all to you."

They sat down in a conference room with a glass wall overlooking the flying disk.

"There are not an infinite number of parallel worlds," said his father. "There is only one real timeline. This is not theory; it is scientific fact the aliens have proven."

"But then how could your hands come from another timeline? How can you travel to timelines that do not exist?"

"The aliens believe in God. No, they do not believe—they know. They call him the Prime Observer, because it is his observation that chooses the real timeline from among the parallel worlds."

"This is not a new idea," said Tomás. "The suggestion that God collapses the quantum mechanical wave function for the universe as a whole has been around a long time."

"Yes, but the fact is he collapses the wave function only when he observes the universe. And he has not done so since August of 1945, or possibly a little earlier."

"How can you know that?"

"Because that is when the timelines start to diverge. There are no timelines where Hitler won, or where the United States did not drop the atomic bombs on Japan. There are no timelines where the Roman Empire never fell, or timelines populated by intelligent dinosaurs. But my researchers in the other timelines have found slight differences in newspapers published in

September 1945. The differences become greater the farther you get from August 1945." His father leaned forward. "Do you not see? God has not paid any attention to our world in sixty years, so he certainly has nothing to do with your Pope."

Tomás felt his heart pound. There had to be another explanation. "Does it have to be God who observes? Many experiments show conscious observation can collapse a wave function, and sometimes not even that is needed."

"It requires an observation from outside the wave function. We cannot do it ourselves. Not even the aliens observing us could do it. Who but God observes the universe from outside? These are scientific facts, Tomasito; you must accept them."

Tomás suddenly realized how dangerous the situation was. His father had just revealed the most important secrets of the empire, and if Tomás was not careful, he would "disappear," becoming just another of the thousands of *desaparecidos*. Even if his father was making this up for some devious purpose, Tomás must show he was open to accepting it. "I need time to absorb all this," he said. "A flying disc, aliens, alternate timelines—"

Before Tomás could finish, his mother entered the room, the hem of her black dress sweeping over the floor. "You think to keep secret from me the death of my own son? How could you let this happen?"

His father rose. "Eva, I was—"

She turned to Tomás and held out her arms. "It is good you have come, Tomás."

Accustomed to his mother's mercurial nature, Tomás hugged her and kissed her cheeks. He was glad to see her, and not just because her knowing he was here made it less likely his father would have him quietly disappear.

She turned back to his father, who seemed to wither a little under her gaze. "What are you doing?"

"Taking care of Argentina and the empire. Tomás will become president and my designated successor as Emperor."

Tomás said, "I have not agreed yet. Mamá, you know I have no head for politics. Explain to Papá."

She shook her head. "That doesn't matter, my son. We all must make sacrifices for the good of the people. And the people need a Perón to lead them."

Tomás knew too well that his parents, united, were almost impossible to oppose. He had only managed to become a priest because his mother remained Catholic—even if her smooth skin under her perfectly coiffed blond hair proved she did not follow the Church's teaching on rejuvenation. Tomás needed time to find a way out. "I must consider this, think through the implications. And I want the proof you offered."

"I've told you already," said his father.

"Do you believe everything you are told?" Tomás waved his arm at the gray shape beyond the glass wall. "How do I know the flying disc out there is not a prop on a movie set? I want to talk to the alien, travel to the parallel timelines. Only then can I know for myself what you say is true."

"You have no faith in me?"

Patting his chest, Tomás said, "You are asking me to abandon my faith. You must give me something stronger to replace it: knowledge." He still was not sure the existence of the alternate timelines meant what his father claimed, but demanding to be shown the evidence would give him time to think.

"The timeline ship will not be back for months. We must announce Mario's death and your appointment as president within a few hours." His father sighed. "But you may meet with the alien and see inside the flying disc. Will that be enough?"

"I won't know until after I've heard what the alien has to say."

According to his father, the alien came from a perpetually clouded world and was overly sensitive to visible light. The alien's room was dim and red, like a photographer's darkroom, and it took a few seconds for Tomás's eyes to adjust.

The alien—Angelica, they called her, instead of her true unpronounceable name—was a small humanoid, with a big bald head and large dark eyes. She looked so much like the stereotypical movie extraterrestrial that Tomás thought for a moment she had to be a hoax. But after watching the fluid grace with which she used her three-fingered hands to manipulate the levers of an unrecognizable contraption sitting on the table in front of her, Tomás realized no puppeteer could be controlling her. Members of her race must have been seen by humans, thus creating the stereotype in the first place.

Angelica finished what she was doing and turned her attention to Tomás and his father. Her mouth did not move, but a feminine voice said, "You are the one who serves the Prime Observer."

Tomás frowned. "I am a priest, if that's what you mean. How do you know that?"

"Your mother has spoken to me of you. She showed me images."

The alien's voice was not coming from her body: it emanated from a speaker on the table. Tomás turned to his father and said, "How do I know you don't have someone on a radio faking her end of the conversation?"

Before his father could answer, the voice spoke. "Direct neural interface to a computer that synthesizes human speech for me." Angelica tapped the side of her head with a long finger, then moved the finger to her mouth. "My own vocal apparatus is not capable of making the sounds for your speech."

It made sense. Tomás took a deep breath, then let it out. He needed to confirm or refute his father's assertions. "You mentioned the Prime Observer. Is that the same as the Creator of the universe?"

"That is not known to my people. It is possible: a Creator, if it existed, would have to be external to the universe, as the Prime Observer is."

"And according to the science of your people, the Prime Observer has not observed the universe in sixty of our years?"

The skin of the alien's face wriggled. "That is an incorrect analysis of the available data."

Tomás grinned with relief. His father had gotten the science wrong.

"The Prime Observer has not observed your *world* in sixty years. It is your world's wave function that is in a state of superposition, not the wave function of the entire universe. My own world's wave function collapses separately from yours, which is why I was willing to help your father."

"Help my father?"

His father spoke before the alien could answer. "We do not have time to go into that now." He put a hand on Tomás's shoulder. "You can talk to Angelica more later, and even travel to other timelines if you wish, but after you are president. You must agree."

Tomás knew he could still refuse. Mamá could probably protect him from being killed, but she probably would not object to his being kept as a prisoner in comfortable quarters. But it felt as if he had known all along he would have to accept. The only question remaining was whether he could do some good with what was happening.

"I will accept, Father," he said, "on the condition you restore to the Church all the lands you confiscated."

"I cannot. Some of those lands have been given to important people, or used to house the poor."

His father making excuses was a good sign. "Just compensation, then, for the lands that cannot be returned."

"The Church killed your brother. How can I reward them for that?"

"Think of it this way, Father: the return of their lands will ensure they do not send an incendiary nun after me." Even though Tomás did not believe the Church was behind Mario's death, his father believed it. He could use that.

His father looked thoughtful. "And you claim to have no head for politics."

◉

Argentina was the preeminent nation of the Empire, and the Empire was the lone superpower. But Tomás soon discovered being President of Argentina meant little while his father ruled the Empire. After three months, Tomás had found only one thing to love about life as a mostly figurehead president. He missed the people of his parish, and his attempts to talk to palace personnel about spiritual matters met with only polite apathy. His hopes of using his new political position to help the poor seemed to be blocked by interminable layers of bureaucracy. And his parents were usually too busy with affairs of the Empire to give him even the pleasure of getting to know his family again.

But he had access to histories and current news transmitted by agents in the other timelines. There were only four others; according to Angelica, only five travelable timelines could exist in superposition. Other timelines existed in the wave function as their probabilities dictated, but they could not observe each other.

Tomás perused the latest reports.

The Iraq war in the United States timeline appeared to be winding down.

The Third Depression in the United Nations timeline had just entered its second decade, and the Secretary General had announced a new round of wealth redistribution which he claimed would help those hardest hit by the economic problems.

The news from the Soviet timeline seemed even more unreliable than a government-approved Argentine newspaper, but by carefully analyzing what was not said, Tomás was fairly sure the communists were in slightly better economic shape than the United Nations timeline.

But the Chinese timeline was where the real excitement lay. Seven of the ten taikonauts orbiting Mars aboard the *Chiang Kai-shek* were preparing to descend to the surface.

Tomás had always regretted that Argentina's space program had not gone beyond establishing orbital microwave power stations and a small permanent scientific base on the Moon. With a flying disc to study, Argentina's space program should have been capable of much more, but it appeared his father had focused on timeline travel.

As he read about the taikonauts, one of the physicists from the underground laboratories asked for permission to speak with him immediately. She tucked a loose strand of hair behind her ear as she was ushered into his office.

"I wanted to speak with your father," said Dr. Martín, "but he is unavailable, and this is urgent."

Tomás repressed a wince. His father's unavailability was probably due to his being ensconced with one of his mistresses. "I will make sure he is informed as soon as possible. What is the problem?"

"Our neutrino detector in Bariloche picked up a large burst of neutrinos this morning. It has been confirmed by the Japanese and the Canadians. The source was near Baikonur, Kazakhstan."

The name sounded familiar to Tomás. "A weapons test of some sort?"

"No. Such a neutrino burst is characteristic of an incoming timeline portal, but it was not ours because we've learned to mask the effect. We thought the Chinese timeline was the most advanced technologically, but it seems the Soviets have quietly been working on timeline travel."

Tomás stood up. "I must consult with Angelica about this development."

Dr. Martín hesitated. "But the Emperor …"

His father had never allowed him to talk to Angelica alone, so Tomás decided now was his chance. "My father is not here."

It took over an hour of blustering and emphasizing his position as designated imperial heir with the imperial guards, but he eventually was admitted to Angelica's presence. Dr. Martín went to the observation room, where Tomás was sure she would be recording his conversation.

"This was anticipated," Angelica told Tomás after he explained about the neutrino burst. "The estimate was we had five to ten more years, but we have already begun our preparations. We need merely to accelerate the timetable."

"What preparations?" asked Tomás.

"For the comet impact."

"A comet is going to hit the Earth?" Tomás tried to remain outwardly calm, but offered a silent prayer he had misunderstood.

"Yes."

It might be necessary to withhold such information from the public to prevent panic while preparations to handle the disaster were underway, but even as a figurehead President of Argentina, he should have been informed. "When? Can we stop it? And what does that have to with the Soviets traveling the timelines?"

His father's voice came from behind him. "We must catch God's attention."

Turning to face his father, Tomás said, "What?"

"The Soviets will figure it out, if they haven't already." He waved a hand at the electronic equipment on the table next to him. "Their scientists will detect our travels. Soon they will realize only one timeline will survive when God observes our world—the rest will vanish as if they had never been. It is a race to see which timeline can force God's hand. Fortunately, we've had longer to plan. We began adjusting the orbit of the comet twenty years ago, gradually, so it would appear natural."

"The original plan was for impact five years from now," said Angelica, "but if we make certain adjustments at perihelion, impact will be in six months."

Tomás stared at his father. "You're planning to use a comet to wipe out the Soviets in their timeline?"

"No," said Angelica. "Your father thinks that would likely call attention to their timeline, not ours."

It took a few moments for the implication to work its way through Tomás's mind. "You cannot mean to hit *our* Earth with it? How many of our people would that kill?"

"We will adjust its course to hit in the northern Pacific," said his father. "Our people will not be the ones dying, mostly. And those who do, die for the survival of the Empire."

"You cannot do this!" Despite the *desaparecidos*, the executions, the assassinations, the wars of conquest, Tomás had never believed his father monstrous enough to murder on this scale.

"I am the Emperor. No one tells me what I cannot do—not you, not your mother. I took Argentina and built it into an empire." He clapped his hands to his chest. "Me. This timeline is mine—it is guided by my hands. And I will not see all my work destroyed by the Soviets or anyone else."

Tomás turned to Angelica. "How can you go along with this? Do you not realize how many people you will kill?"

"What happens to individual members of your species is not of great concern to me. I am merely doing what I think best ensures my own survival."

"But so many deaths … hundreds of millions of innocents." Tears of frustration welled up in Tomás's eyes. His father had truly gone mad.

"Do not count the dead," said his father. "If another timeline is chosen, none of them will have ever existed, so it makes no difference to them. I am choosing life for the people of our world."

Tomás struggled to find an argument to sway his father. "There must be another way. Destruction cannot be the only way to catch God's attention."

His father shrugged. "We cannot know if something else will work. But the timelines diverge after the United States dropped the atomic bombs on Japan. That destruction attracted God's attention."

With sudden clarity, Tomás understood how there might be times when the Church would condone murder and suicide. Had the Church known of this plan? Had Mario been part of it? If Tomás but had the capacity to spontaneously combust and kill his father now, he would use it.

As a child, Tomás had taken to his heart Christ's instruction to turn the other cheek, and he had not retaliated when Mario pushed him around. All his life, Tomás had been the calmest and gentlest member of the Perón family.

So his father and the imperial guards were slow to react when Tomás sprang forward, reaching for his father's throat. Tomás lacked the benefits of a military background, though, and his father's rejuvenated body had both the training and reflexes to begin moving out of the way. So instead of grabbing his father to strangle him, Tomás almost missed him entirely, smashing into his shoulder before sprawling facedown on the floor. Tomás heard the crash of equipment hitting the floor behind him.

Tomás could see the boots of one of the guards approach, and he knew an automatic rifle was aimed at him. He waited for his father to order his execution.

The seconds seemed to stretch out. Even if his father was willing to kill hundreds of millions, perhaps he was willing to show mercy to his own son.

"He's dead," said one of the guards behind Tomás.

"You're sure?" said another.

"Look at his head. No doctor can fix that," replied the first.

Several hands reached down and lifted Tomás to his feet.

"You all saw it," said one of the guards, a lieutenant. "The

Emperor slipped and hit his head on the edge of the table. It was a tragic accident, and there was nothing we could do to prevent it. No one here is to blame."

"Your eyes are weaker than mine in this light," said Angelica. "I saw very clearly what happened. It was—"

As Angelica spoke, the lieutenant raised his rifle and pointed it at her head.

"—very clearly an unavoidable accident," Angelica finished.

Tomás stared at the corpse of his father. In the dim red light, one glassy, sightless eye seemed to stare back disapprovingly; the other was buried under a boxy metal piece of equipment that had fallen from the table.

The lieutenant turned toward Tomás and saluted. "All hail the Emperor Tomás Perón!"

"Hail the Emperor Tomás Perón!" said the rest of the guards.

Tomás closed his eyes. The guards probably thought they were guaranteeing the stability of the empire—and hoped to avoid punishment for allowing his father to be killed while under their care. Becoming emperor was not what he wanted, but he would use the power for now. He walked over to Angelica.

"My father said you could adjust the course of the comet," he said.

"Yes," said Angelica.

"Show me."

Her alien fingers pecked at a keyboard, bringing up windows of information. "The thrusters are positioned here, here, and here," she said, pointing to orange triangles positioned on a three-dimensional model of a comet head."

"Send it into the sun," Tomás commanded.

"The thrusters do not have enough fuel for such a radical course change," said Angelica.

Tomás leaned close staring into her dark eyes. "If a comet hits anywhere on Earth, you may suffer an accident like my father's." He felt suddenly nauseated and broke eye contact. He had killed his father, and now he threatened to kill someone else. This was not the kind of person he wanted to be.

Angelica tapped some commands on the keyboard. "I did not say a collision with your planet was unavoidable, merely that steering the comet into the sun would take more fuel than the thrusters have. They are built to cause small course changes that become greater with time. At this distance, only a small course change is sufficient to miss your planet in five years."

"Make it a big course change anyway. Burn all the fuel." He didn't want anyone changing the course back.

"As you wish. Just because I am indifferent to the fates of humans does not mean I desire their deaths."

Tomás watched the screens as the readouts for the fuel for each thruster ticked toward empty.

"Your father may have been wrong about the comet drawing the attention of God to this timeline," said Angelica. "Nobody knows what will actually draw the attention of the Prime Observer. I was only doing this because your father threatened my life if I did not do as he said."

A sudden pity welled in Tomás's heart for this being, held prisoner by his father for decades. "If I set you free, where would you go? What would you do?"

"I am a technician," Angelica said. "I would stay here where the best technology on your world exists." She brought up a window that showed the course of the comet compared to Earth's orbit. "The thrusters' fuel is exhausted. The comet will now miss your planet by almost two million kilometers. There is no need for any more … accidents."

"Good." Tomás turned and, stepping carefully around his father's body, walked out of the dim red room into the bright light of the corridor.

Escorted by two guards, his mother swept down the corridor toward him. "Tomás, is it true?"

Unsure what she had heard, Tomás simply said, "He is

dead." He caught her arm, stopping her from entering the room. "There is nothing you can do for him."

She sagged in his grip, but only for a moment. "There are preparations to be made. You must be crowned as soon as possible, so our enemies do not take advantage. Unless, do you think the Pope would do it, since you are Catholic? It would be worth waiting if he—"

"Mamá, did you know what he was doing with the comet?" His father had said she knew, but he had to hear it from her own lips.

She shrugged. "You know your father. Who could stop him when he set his mind?"

"You could, if you set your mind. Hundreds of millions were going to die, and you did not stop him."

Her face turned away, a faint redness rising in her cheeks.

If she could still feel shame, there was still hope for her soul. Tomás had to believe there was still good in her heart. "I have stopped the comet, so there is no damage done," he said. "I forgive you."

"You are a good son, Tomasito. A good son." She straightened. "I will see your father now. I must say goodbye."

Tomás let her go. A good son, she had called him. He hoped she would never know that he had killed his father—intentionally—even if it hadn't happened the way he had intended.

"Emperor Perón, what are your orders?" said the lieutenant.

Emperor. Even with his father gone, Tomás doubted he was capable of transforming the empire into something good—the military would certainly overthrow him if he tried. He had done what he could to prevent the worst mass killing in history, but everything touched by his father's hands was corrupt. "Here are my first and last orders to you: don't call me your Emperor, and never bother me again."

"But without a Perón on the throne there will be chaos in the Empire."

"Perhaps chaos is better than we deserve." Tomás continued to walk as the guards halted in confusion. He did not look back.

Nuestra Señora de Cura is a Franciscan monastery on the Spanish island of Mallorca. Spain is technically not part of the Empire of Latin America, but even so the monastery receives frequent charitable donations from Her Imperial Majesty María Eva Duarte de Perón, Empress of Latin America and Protector of the Southern World.

The Empress Evita is as generous as she is beautiful, her imperial subjects often say. It is a safe thing to say when others might be listening.

One of the monastery's friars is known for his tireless work to help the poor and sick. Brother Tomás is kind and gentle, and never loses his temper no matter what the provocation. He is considered a model of what a Franciscan monk should be, except for one quirk: he never prays.

He does not wish to draw God's attention to his timeline.

ABOUT THE STORY

In 2005, the Codex Writers had a "Get the [Creative] Juices Flowing" contest. Out of multiple lists of prompts, I ended up picking:

- A nun spontaneously combusts
- The spleen of a former South American military leader
- She talks to angels
- A myopic alien
- A red room
- A monk

My father was born and raised in Argentina before immigrating to the United States. Later, he returned to Argentina for work, so I lived there for four years during my childhood. Naturally, I had to choose the spleen of Juan Perón for my story.

It was while researching Perón that I discovered the hands had been stolen from his corpse, a mystery that has never been solved. That led to the question of why someone would steal Perón's hands, and that led to the idea of a parallel universe that needed them.

The divergence point for the alternate timelines in this story is the crash of the alien spaceship that, in our timeline, happened near Roswell, New Mexico.

The story took first place in the contest, and I felt sure it would sell fairly quickly.

It took over seven years and twenty-five submissions before it found a home at *Daily Science Fiction*—a market that had not even existed when I wrote the story. Despite all the rejections, I still believed in the story, which is why I kept sending it out.

DSF published the story on July 26, 2013, sixty-one years to the day after Eva Perón died—in this timeline.

A MEMBER OF THE PERONISTA PARTY

After five years of school, getting summoned to Headmaster Garcia's office was not an unusual occurrence for Diego Martin. Since this was a public school, Argentine law limited corporal punishment to no more than two strokes, no more than five times in a week. Unfortunately, today was Monday.

But when Diego saw his mother holding his six-year-old sister Elenora's hand, he stopped wondering idly for which of his crimes he was about to be caned and began worrying. Red rims around Elenora's eyes showed she had been crying. "What is it, Mamá?"

"It's your Uncle Reynaldo," she said. She stared hard at Diego. "He passed away last night."

Elenora started crying again.

"Uncle Reynaldo?" Diego had no uncles. He knew better than to ask mama why she was lying, though. "How did he die?"

Her lips formed the barest hint of a smile and she gave him a small nod. "A car accident. At least it was quick." She turned to the headmaster and said, "Diego will only miss two or three days, if that is acceptable. He will make up for his missed assignments when he returns, won't you, Diego?"

Diego nodded. Two or three days? What would they be doing in that time?

Headmaster Garcia waved a dismissive hand. "The assignments are unimportant. And Diego, please believe I am most sorry … for your loss. When you get back, you will find me to be very understanding."

"Thank you, Headmaster." Diego was puzzled. The headmaster, who had always seemed to take delight in punishing Diego, now seemed almost frightened of him.

"Yes, thank you," said Diego's mother. "Now we must be going. It is a long trip to Bahia Blanca."

"May you have a safe journey," said the headmaster. He bowed to Diego's mother. "And please forgive the earlier misunderstanding with my staff. We had no idea you were a member of the Party. There must have been a mix-up in Diego's paperwork."

"It is forgotten," she said. "Come, Diego."

Following his mother and sister, Diego walked out of the office and down the long hallway. Their footsteps echoed off the tile.

Diego chuckled, in part to counteract his sister's sniffling. "If I'd known showing your Party card would get me out of canings, I would have asked you to show it before." Party members usually sent their children to private schools.

"The card is not a good thing," said his mother. "Speak of it no more. You can stop crying now, Elenora. Be silent, both of you, until we are in the car."

With a pang of guilt, Diego remembered the night six months ago when he had watched silently through a slightly open door as one of his mother's coworkers urged her to join the Party. "I cannot cover for you any longer," the man had said. "The Emperor was most displeased to discover that people working within the Casa Rosada itself were not members of his party. A purge is coming. If you wish to keep your security clearance—not to mention your job—you must be a Peronista." The man had held out a paper, which his mother had reluctantly taken and signed. Before leaving the man had said, "I will back-date this to a year ago and claim your paperwork was mislaid. But take care to say nothing offensive." Afterwards, his mother had sat at their kitchen table and cried.

Looking out the car window, Diego could tell they were headed into downtown Buenos Aires, rather than out of town. Large posters with the smiling face of Emperor Juan Perón celebrated the upcoming sixtieth anniversary of his rise to power in 1946. "Where are we going? Why did you make up that story about an Uncle Reynaldo?"

Elenora started crying again.

"Hush, dear," said Diego's mother. "You did well, but you don't need to cry every time someone says 'Uncle Reynaldo' anymore."

Elenora stopped crying.

"We must leave Argentina," said his mother. "We are going to the embassy of the United States to ask for asylum."

"In citizenship class," said Diego, "they said it is the law to report any sign of disloyalty to the Empire, even if it's family."

His mother's grip tightened on the steering wheel and she flashed him a look. "Diego, you must understand ..."

He grinned at her. "I guess for the first time you're glad I don't always follow the rules they teach at school. Citizenship class was boring, anyway."

She sighed. "Sometimes an unruly son is a blessing."

"Will we live in New York?" That was where Diego's father, a U.S. citizen, had gone after the divorce five years ago. If we live in New York, Diego thought, maybe Papá will come to see us sometimes.

"I don't know," said his mother. "Look on your side of the street for the embassy."

"What does it look like?"

"It should have a sign. And a United States flag."

After a few minutes of driving along the congested street, Diego spotted a brick building set back from the street behind black iron gates. A red-and-white-striped flag with blue at the top hung limply from a pole. Though he could not see all the stars, he knew there would be fifty-four of them—although the fifty-fourth state of Panama had been liberated from Yanqui imperialism by the Imperial Army of Latin America before Diego's birth. "There it is, I think," he said, pointing.

"Good eyes," said his mother. She continued driving, not even shifting to a closer lane.

As they passed the embassy, Diego saw four uniformed Imperial Army soldiers with automatic rifles standing guard before the gates. Several meters behind the gates stood armed men in different uniforms, and a rather ferocious-looking dog. "Will your Party card get us past those guards?"

"No."

A mixture of excitement and fear made Diego shiver. "Then how?"

"Quiet. Let me think."

After driving a couple of blocks past the embassy, his mother took the car into a public parking garage. They sat quietly in the car.

Diego broke the silence. "When I was called to the headmaster's office, I thought maybe it was because they found I was the one who did something on Friday."

His mother turned to look at him. "Whatever you did doesn't matter anymore."

"What I *did*," said Diego, "was glue a poster on the wall near Headmaster Garcia's office, in a spot the cameras don't see. It said, 'Headmaster Garcia is a monkey.' The janitors tried to pull it down, but I used some really strong glue. Then they figured out I had only glued the edges of the poster, so they got a sharp knife and cut out the middle part with the words on it." Diego grinned. "And behind that part, glued to the wall, was a picture of Garcia's head on a monkey body. And that picture was glued on tight. The janitors finally just covered it up."

Diego's face became serious. "What would those guards do if we told them someone was putting up posters against the Emperor?"

"Now," said Diego's mother. A black limousine was making its way along the driveway toward the embassy gates.

Threading his way through scattered pedestrians on the sidewalk, Diego ran up to the highest-ranking guard. At least his civics classes had taught him to read Imperial Army ranks.

"Sir! Sir! My civics teacher taught me to report actions against the empire," said Diego, pointing back the way he had come and panting as if out of breath. "Around that corner some men are putting up posters that say the Emperor is a bad word, and the Empress is another bad word."

"Lopez! Molina!" the guard said. "Go check it out."

Two guards ran off toward the corner. Only two.

"Thank you, sir," said Diego. His eyes searched for his mother, then spotted her and his sister coming along the sidewalk. She looked at him and nodded. They would try anyway, even with two guards left.

"This had better not be a prank," said the guard. Beyond him, the limousine came closer and the gates started to open.

"No, sir. Here comes my mother. She'll tell you." Diego raised his voice and said, "Mamá, tell him about the men."

"It's true," said his mother. "Such vile things they said to me when I told them to stop." She opened her purse and pulled out her Party card and handed it to the guard. "I'm a Peronista, as you can see. You must stop them."

The guard looked down at the card as the gates opened fully and the limousine pulled out.

"What a cute dog!" said Elenora, and she let go of their mother's hand and ran through the gates toward the dog standing with the U.S. guards.

Diego and his mother began running after Elenora, shouting at her to stop and come back, but as planned she ignored them and kept running.

"Stop!" yelled the guard behind them.

A burst of gunfire sounded in Diego's ears, and he could not resist looking over his shoulder to see if his mother was all right. The guard's rifle was pointed in the air, but then it lowered to point at them. Because he was not watching where he was going, Diego tripped and fell on the gravel. His mother stopped to tried to lift him to his feet.

"Nobody move!" said a north-American-accented voice in front of them.

They had not anticipated that the U.S. guards would tell them to stop. Diego's mother stopped pulling him up. Diego looked ahead and saw that Elenora had already gotten to the U.S. guards and one of them held her by the arm.

In English, his mother said, "I request asylum from the United States for myself and my children."

"You are traitors to the Empire," said the Imperial soldier behind them. "For that you will die."

"Hold your fire," said the U.S. guard. His Spanish was good, despite his accent. "If you shoot at them now, you will be firing into the sovereign territory of the United States of America and we will be forced to return fire. Do you really want to start a war?"

"We beat you in Panama, yanqui."

The U.S. Guard nodded slowly. "You did. But in Panama, you had air superiority." He looked up into the sky. "I don't see any aircruisers up there. You, personally, will not win a war here today. Is killing a woman and children worth it?"

"They are criminals," said the Imperial soldier, but his voice was uncertain.

"If we find out that they are, we will deny asylum. But that's not my decision. Have your Foreign Office file a protest, if you want. Back off and let the bureaucrats handle it. No one needs to die here today." The U.S. guard lowered his rifle and walked toward Diego and his mother. With one hand he reached down and hauled Diego to his feet.

Escorted by the U.S. guard, Diego and his mother walked over to join Elenora.

"Come with me," said the guard, in English. He took them up the steps to the entrance of the embassy, where other guards waited. "Tell Hansen he's got some asylum seekers."

Diego's mother said, "My children and I thank you for our lives, soldier."

The guard shook his head. "I ain't no soldier, ma'am. I'm a U.S. *Marine*, and I was just doing my job." He turned to go, then looked back at her. "I hope you had a good reason for putting those kids in the line of fire."

Diego sat next to Elenora on a red leather couch against the wall in Mr. Hansen's office. His mother sat in a yellow chair in front of Hansen's desk. Behind the desk sat Mr. Hansen. Diego could see the bald spot on the embassy man's head as Hansen read papers in a folder in front of him, turning a page every minute or so. A clock on the wall ticked away—if Diego remembered correctly, they had been brought in about 5:30. It was now 5:55.

Hansen flipped the papers back to the beginning of the file and looked up. "Mrs. Martín—" he began, pronouncing the name as if it were Spanish.

"It's Martin, not Martín," said Diego's mother. "My ex-husband was a United States citizen."

Diego never corrected the teachers at school when they mispronounced his name. Now he hoped that having an English name would help.

Bobbing his head, Hansen said, "Mrs. Martin, requests for asylum are usually handled at the point of entry into the United States. If we handled them here at the embassy, we'd have more people pulling foolish stunts like you did today."

"I am sorry," she said. "But now that we are here, can you not do something? Our lives are in danger. We cannot return to Argentine soil." She leaned forward in her chair. "And I am a scientist with valuable knowledge of secret Imperial programs. I can be useful to your country."

She had never discussed details of her work with Diego. All he knew was that she was a scientist and worked at the Casa Rosada. He felt simultaneously thrilled at his mother's importance and shaken by her mentioning it to Hansen. This really was the treason his civics teacher had warned about.

Hansen's chair creaked as he leaned back. He pressed his lips together for a moment, then reached for his phone and punched a few digits. "Falck, it's Hansen. Can you come to my office and bring a verifier? Thanks."

After hanging up, Hansen looked at Diego's mother. "Do you know what a verifier is? You may have seen them if you watch any uncensored American movies off the black market."

Diego's mother shook her head.

"It's funny—the technology for the verifier is based on Argentine medical inventions, but your government seems to prefer getting people to confess the old-fashioned way. Basically, it's a scanner that can detect the brain activity associated with deception. Since the Supreme Court allowed juries to see verifier results during witness testimony, few cases go to trial anymore." Hansen smiled. "And it's rather hard to get elected to anything without making your campaign promises with a verifier."

"You do not believe a woman scientist is worth anything," said Diego's mother.

Hansen winced. "That's not true. We have many female scientists in the States. But you must admit it's very uncommon in Argentina."

She nodded. "If it will help us get asylum, I do not fear your verifier."

○

Diego had watched in fascination during the calibration process, as his mother was asked to tell the truth on some questions and lie on others. Part of the verifier looked a bit like a white motor-cycle helmet strapped to his mother's head. The other part sat on Hansen's desk and seemed to be a specialized laptop computer connecting wirelessly to the helmet. The screen was angled enough that Diego could see a flash of red when his mother lied and a flash of green when she told the truth.

"Everything seems to be in order," said Hansen. "Mrs. Martin, why do you wish to leave Argentina?"

"I want my children to grow up in a free country, and I fear the government will kill us if we stay."

"Why?"

"After what happened at your gates, do you think they will let us live?"

Hansen raised an eyebrow. "You may be right, but that answer was deceptive. Obviously, you wanted to leave before what happened at the gates. Why?"

After a pause, Diego's mother said, "I would rather not explain that. But it is not because I have committed any crimes."

"You present me with a dilemma." Hansen scratched his bald spot. "I really am supposed to know why your government is persecuting you, but the main reason I need to know is to ensure that it's for political reasons, not actual crime. Is it for political reasons?"

"Yes."

"I guess that will do." Hansen sighed. "My own curiosity will have to remain unsatisfied. What is your job?"

"I am—or rather, I was—a quantum physicist working in the laboratories under the Imperial wing of the Casa Rosada. My specialty is in cross-timeline communication through quantum interference patterns, and I'm also well acquainted with the theory behind macroscopic timeline switching."

Diego blinked. Science was one of the few school subjects to interest him, but he had no idea what his mother was talking about.

Apparently Hansen had no idea either. "Based on the verifier I believe you, but I don't understand it. Will your knowledge be useful to the United States?"

"Yes." Diego's mother leaned forward. "Did you know there is a parallel universe in which your country is the lone super-power in the world? It's real; I have been there."

Hansen looked silently at the verifier screen for a long moment. "You're serious. We actually beat Argentina in the war?"

She shook her head. "Argentina was never even a major power in that timeline. Your major opponent was the Soviet Union, and they dissolved without a fight in the 1990s. The only reason Argentina dominates our timeline is …"

"What?" said Hansen.

Diego's mother took a deep breath. "Almost sixty years ago, Argentina recovered a flying disk with an alien inside. The alien technology allowed—"

"Enough." The laptop clicked as Hansen closed it. "There is one circumstance in which the verifier is useless, and that's when the subject is delusional."

"I'm not crazy. It is the truth."

Diego stood up. "My mother is not crazy. Do you think they let crazy people work in the Casa Rosada?"

Hansen looked at him. "I have no proof your mother worked there. And this talk of aliens and timelines sounds like a science fiction movie."

"You want proof?" Diego's mother reached inside her blouse and pulled out a videocard. "Here is proof." She handed it to Hansen.

He looked at the card. "What's on this?"

"Play it," she said. She unstrapped the verifier helmet and took it off. "It was recorded in the basement of the Casa Rosada today. It is the only copy."

After getting up from his chair, Hansen plugged the card into a television set on a side table. The image on the screen showed a room dimly lit by a red light. A dark-eyed, bulge headed alien creature was tinkering with a piece of equipment on a workbench.

Hansen snorted. "This isn't proof. Hollywood does this every day."

"Forward it near to the end," she said.

The motion on screen quickened, and a progress bar gradually moved across the bottom.

"There," said Diego's mother.

Slowing to normal, the picture showed people in the room with the alien.

"That's President Tomás Perón, and now here comes his father," said Diego's mother.

"Look-alikes in bad lighting. I'm not impressed," said Hansen. His phone buzzed and he stopped the video.

"Hansen here," he said after picking up the phone. He listened for a moment. "No, I haven't." After a few moments, he snapped his head around to look back at the now-blank TV screen. "Thanks for the heads up." He placed the handset back in the cradle.

"One of my colleagues," said Hansen, "reports that there is a rumor spreading rapidly that Juan Perón died in an accident. And there's increased chatter on Imperial military frequencies."

Diego's mother nodded. "Watch the rest of the video. His son Tomás killed him."

The Emperor was dead? Diego found it hard to believe. According to his civics teacher, the Emperor Perón would live forever, thanks to advanced Argentine medical science. But there it was on the screen: President Tomás Perón charged into his father, knocking the Emperor to the ground, where something fell on his head.

Diego's mother suddenly noticed he was watching and said, "You should not have watched that."

He shrugged and said, "I've seen worse on TV."

Hansen sat back down in his chair. "Why didn't you tell me about this in the first place?"

"I was afraid," said Diego's mother. "Imperial Security would quickly find that I had been observing the alien at the time the Emperor was killed and would want to eliminate me. But I didn't know if you would give me asylum if Imperial Security claimed I was involved in the Emperor's death."

"But you weren't involved, were you?" Scratching his bald spot, Hansen said, "I think we'd better conduct the rest of this interview with the verifier."

Putting the helmet back on, Diego's mother said, "So you no longer think I am delusional?"

"One final question, Mrs. Martin. Our asylum laws are meant to benefit those persecuted by Peronism, not the persecutors. So Peronistas are barred from gaining political asylum."

Diego's mother nodded.

"Therefore, I am required by U.S. law to ask this of any Argentine citizen seeking asylum: Are you now, or have you ever been, a member of the Peronista Party?"

Heart suddenly thudding within him, Diego realized they could not get asylum. The card is not a good thing, Diego's mother had told him that morning, and now he saw why. Would Hansen turn them over to the guards outside?

"No," said his mother. "I never joined the Peronista Party."

Out of the corner of his eye, Diego saw the verifier screen flash green.

Hansen stood up and reached out to shake Diego's mother's hand. "Welcome to the United States, Mrs. Martin."

A diplomatic limousine with darkened windows took them to the airport, where they boarded a U.S. government plane. It wasn't until they landed safely in New York that Diego dared ask his mother about the final question.

"Mamá?"

"Yes?"

Diego whispered, "You fooled the verifier."

"No."

Diego nodded slowly. "I know you did. I watched through the door that night when you signed the paper to join the Party. But when you lied to the verifier about that, it flashed green."

"I didn't lie to the verifier, Diego." She shook her head. "I lied when I signed that paper saying I would become a member of the Peronista Party."

ABOUT THE STORY

This story has never before been published. It is, of course, a sequel to "By the Hands of Juan Perón," but it was also intended to be part of a novel that I never have gotten around to writing.

The story is loosely based on a bit of my family history, which I remember being told by my father's sister, Leonora Smith.

My father's mother, Ethel Rodger Stone, was a schoolteacher in Argentina during the first Perón dictatorship. She was forced to sign up as a member of the Peronista party in order to keep her job.

After she decided to emigrate with her children to the United States, she had to meet with someone at the American embassy, and she took Leonora along. During the meeting, she was asked to swear on a Bible that she was not a member of the Peronista party. She did so.

And when Leonora later asked her about lying with her hand on the Bible, my grandma gave a response along the same lines that Diego's mother gave to him.

THEY DO IT WITH ROBOTS

"Ladies and gentlemen, although all of the participants are consenting adults, the final act of the evening is illegal under United States law," said the announcer. "Fortunately, our ship has passed the twelve-mile limit, so we are in international waters."

Guillermo turned his attention from his frozen strawberry margarita to the stage as the ceremonial drums ushered in the feather-clad dancers. At the center of their multicolored whirling, the black-masked priest stood behind the altar. The drums grew louder, slower, and the dancers parted to allow a young man to walk step by step to the altar. Face painted crimson, he was stripped to the waist. Sweat glittered on his chest.

Focusing on the young man's face, Guillermo tried to imagine what he looked like without the makeup.

Could it be Ogden? It could.

Was it Ogden? Hard to tell at this distance. Guillermo didn't have enhanced senses.

The young man lay down on the altar. The drums accelerated, then stopped at the moment the priest plunged the knife into the young man's chest.

At the table next to Guillermo, a woman gasped.

After several cuts with surgical precision, the priest reached into the chest cavity and pulled out the heart, quivering.

"That's sick," the woman said. "I can't believe you made me watch this."

"It's not real," the man next to her said. "They do it with robots or something."

Guillermo stared at the lifeless body on the altar. Blood oozed from the gaping wound. As part of the League of Heroes, he'd seen dead people before—and dead robots. If that was a robot, it was the most lifelike dead robot he had ever seen.

A well-muscled security guard stood at the entrance to back-stage. Guillermo strode purposefully toward him.

"No admittance," said the guard.

Guillermo stared into the guard's eyes. It was easier with firm eye contact. "Forget I was ever here."

The eyes went glassy. Guillermo slipped around the guard and went through the door.

The young man lay motionless on a gurney in a dressing room. He smelled of blood. Guillermo approached and looked closely at the face, the lifeless eyes in particular.

It was Ogden, all right. Poor kid. Why had he run? How could this be better than staying with the League?

Guillermo sank into a chair. Now there was nothing to do but wait.

Three hours later, Ogden took a few choking, raspy breaths, then eased into the even breathing of heavy sleep.

Guillermo got up and checked on him. The chest wound had closed up, although it still looked pretty nasty. An hour or so more of healing, and there probably wouldn't even be a mark.

Forty-five minutes later, Ogden said, "I thought Frankie would be the one to find me."

Guillermo hadn't noticed him wake up. "No, he lost your scent in Miami. But I heard about the show. FBI's puzzled as to where they get all the young men who volunteer to be sacrificed, and I started thinking maybe it was just one young man. I came down to check it out."

"Just leave me here. I'm no good to the League anymore," he said.

Guillermo sighed. "Kelli absorbed a one-megaton nuclear blast. Nobody blames you for not being able to heal her."

"She counted on me to save her, and I couldn't."

"I know, kid. But I can fix that. You don't have to remember—"

"No!" Ogden sat up and turned away. "We were in love. Don't take that from me."

"Oh." Guillermo winced. He always had been kind of oblivious to the personal lives of the others in the League of Heroes.

"Being back there, with the League, without her ..." Ogden's voice broke. "I just can't handle it."

"But this? You really think punishing yourself like this is a good idea?"

"Punishing myself? Is that what you think I'm doing?"

"You're letting someone literally rip your heart out. The symbolism's pretty strong."

Ogden remained silent for a long while. "You know how they say your life flashes before your eyes just before you die? That's not true. At least, not for me. But when I'm coming back to life, as my brain starts back up, it's like I experience my whole life again. That's why I do it. For a while, I have Kelli back."

Frankie answered the phone when Guillermo called in to League of Heroes HQ. "So, was it our boy being sacrificed?"

"No," Guillermo replied. "It wasn't anybody. They do it with robots."

ABOUT THE STORY

This was another Codex Weekend Warrior story. The prompt was: "Write about a stage performer who seems to be doing one thing, but is actually doing another."

I decided to write a superhero story, for no other reason than the fact that I like superhero stories. The fact that superhero stories tend to do well in Codex contests had nothing to do with my decision. Honest!

One of my favorite superheroes is Wolverine, with his mutant healing abilities. I decided to create a healing superhero who could heal not only himself, but others.

Something I love to do when writing a story is to echo the title in the last line of the story. It gives me a sense of completion, that things have come full circle. I think this story is the best example of that technique that I've done.

FREEFALL

Freefall was the best part of a jump.

As she fell, Gina Wright looked down at Earth, half shadowed beneath her as dawn crept toward her landing target in Kansas, and relished the knowledge that she was about to demolish the world freefall record by more than 20,000 miles. This was going to be so much better than her spacejump from the old International Space Station. She would have forty minutes of freefall before she even entered the atmosphere.

Using the gyros in her pressure suit, she turned away from Earth. The space elevator cable stretched like a strand of spiderweb past her toward the rotating hub-and-spoke wheel she had jumped from: GeoTerminal 1.

A brilliant flash behind the terminal forced Gina to blink even as her visor darkened to compensate. After her visor cleared, she saw a ripple moving down the space elevator cable.

Had the cable broken? No—the LED lights strung along it were still on, so power still flowed from the terminal. With a dad who was chief engineer for the elevator and a brother who drove one of the crawlers, she knew more than she wanted to about the elevator. "How high is it?" and "Can I jump off it?" were the only things that really mattered.

She told her suitphone to call her dad.

"What?" he answered.

"What's going on? I saw a flash and—"

"Working on it. No time for idle curiosity." He hung up.

Typical, she thought. If I were Kyle, he'd explain things, expect me to help solve them. But no, I'm the idle child who wastes her life jumping.

She shouldn't let her dad's attitude spoil the thrill of the jump. Activating the gyros, Gina turned her back on the terminal.

Minutes later her suitphone beeped. She answered it.

"Gina?" Her father's voice was strained.

"Yeah?"

"Sorry about before. We lost the counterweight."

Gina sucked in a sharp breath. The geostationary terminal had to be at the center of mass for the space elevator. Without the asteroid counterweight beyond the terminal, the weight of the cable would pull the terminal—and all the people on it—down to Earth. "How'd it happen?"

"That's for later. What matters is what we do about it."

If the terminal was falling, that meant her dad was falling with it. "Dad, do you have a way to evacuate?"

"No," he said. "But we'll be fine once we detach the cable. Without its weight, the terminal will settle into a stable orbit."

"Oh." Of course they had contingency plans.

"Is there any way you can get over to the cable?" he asked.

"I've got some backup rocket thrusters for maneuvering in case the gyros go out," she said. "Why?"

"You've got a vibroknife that will cut through nanofibers, right? For cutting your chute cords if they get tangled? I remember you telling me that."

"Yeah." Gina was surprised he remembered anything she'd told him about jumping. "Again, why?"

"Kyle's bringing a cargo crawler up. If we detach the cable up here, he'll fall."

Despite the fact she was already in freefall, Gina's stomach seemed to sink inside her.

"I'll let him die if I have to." Her dad's voice cracked. "One life against thousands. But if you can get over there and cut through the cable underneath his crawler, then he can keep coming up and we'll all be safe in orbit until the company sends a rescue ship."

With the gyros, she oriented herself toward the cable. The station's slingshot had flung her in the opposite direction of its orbit to put her into a freefall path to Earth. She hoped she had enough fuel to cross the distance in time.

"Usually it's good old dependable Kyle coming to rescue me after some crazy stunt." She chuckled, trying to laugh away the sudden weight of responsibility. Risking her own life was easy—having someone else's life depend on her was different. "Whose plan is this, anyway?"

"Kyle's. He said if anyone's crazy enough to make it work, it's you."

A few feet away, the cable lights flew past Gina in a continuous blur. But her fuel readout flashed 1% in crimson. It had taken almost all her fuel to change her trajectory enough get to the cable. But there wasn't enough left to slow her descent relative to the cable. She needed to wait until Kyle's crawler moved past her in any case—she had arrived at the cable above him. But soon her fuel would be gone entirely, and her freefall path would take her away.

Still thousands of miles out of the atmosphere, her chute was useless. There was no way she could stop herself, and that meant she could not cut through the cable—the vibroknife would be torn from her grip if she tried cutting at this speed. She was going to fail Kyle, fail her dad, unless—her mind raced as she saw the possibility—unless she could get Kyle a spacechute.

"Dad?" she said.

"Still here."

"Can you patch me through to Kyle?"

"Hold on."

After a few seconds, Kyle's voice came on her phone. "Hey, sis. How's the view from up there?"

She ignored his banter and began unbuckling her chute. She was falling fast toward his crawler, so time was limited. "You're the only person on board the crawler, right?"

"Yes." Kyle must have sensed her urgency, because his voice became all business.

"You have a spacesuit?"

"Yes. Why?"

"I'm falling too fast to be able to stop and cut through the cable," she said. "But I'm removing my backup chute and I'll attach it to the cable just before I pass you. It'll slam into the crawler at a pretty good clip, but it's nanofiber so it should be okay. Then you can go out and get it."

"I've never done a spacejump," he said.

"I'll set the chute for auto, so it'll release at the right altitude. You'll be fine. Trust me." She used a tiny bit of fuel to get close enough to the cable that she would be able to attach the chute.

A pause. "I trust you."

Gina smiled. "Good."

She set the chute to automatically deploy as soon as it detected atmosphere, then removed the final straps.

She could see the blinking lights of the crawler approaching rapidly from below. Careful not to touch the cable itself, she pulled the chute straps around the cable and fastened them. Then she used the last of her suit's fuel to start moving away from the cable.

The chute hit the top of the crawler as it whizzed past her.

"Your chute is ready," she said. "And Kyle ..."

"What?"

I love you, was what she was going to say, but their family had never been one to express maudlin emotion. Besides, he would know she loved him when he found out there was no such thing as a detachable backup chute. "Safe landing."

"Thanks, sis. Same to you."

Gina turned off the phone. Using her gyros, she turned to face Earth one last time. The familiar thrill welled up inside her.

Freefall was the best part of a jump.

ABOUT THE STORY

A few years ago, my family went to Hawaii on vacation. While we were there, my sisters Angela and Carolyn went skydiving. I went along with them ... to take pictures from the ground as they came down.

There was a Codex Weekend Warrior contest about a month later. The prompt that led to this story involved picking one item from each of three lists to fill in the blanks of this sentence: "Write about a _____ _____ that _____." The items I picked were: "cliff-diving," "space elevator operator," and "is looking for love in all the wrong places."

The point of story prompts is not that one must follow them exactly, but rather that they spark an idea for a story. So the prompt evolved into a skydiving estranged son of a space elevator operator who has to find a way to save his sister when disaster strikes.

And then I realized it was rather rude of me to make the protagonist male when the character was obviously inspired by my sisters' skydiving. So I switched the siblings around.

A GREAT DESTINY

You tend to remember the face of a man you've sworn to kill.

As Groshen hoisted a rundlet of wine into the wagon, he spotted the crimson-robed prophet strolling along the village's main road. Groshen had only met the prophet twice, but he recognized those copper-colored eyes divided by that bulging nose.

Despite his sudden rage, Groshen carefully lowered the cask into the wagon. He must catch the prophet alone, where no one could interfere.

"Excuse me," Groshen said to Marya, "but there's someone I must have a word with." She was the head cook, and the only person on Squire Korpet's farm who didn't look away from the burn scars covering Groshen's face.

"Have a drink with, you mean?" The corners of Marya's eyes crinkled as she smiled. "Go on. I'll cover for you with the master, and I'll save you a good cut of roast."

"Thanks." Though he liked her, Groshen wished Marya would focus her romantic attentions elsewhere. He did not want pity.

The village streets were uncrowded. The Emperor Dal's slavers had come through five months ago, choosing a third of the able-bodied men by lottery to work on building the new capital city. Most of the men's families had followed.

Groshen's number had been pulled out of the lottery box, but the slavers had rejected him due to his injuries.

After a few minutes, the prophet wandered into an alley. Groshen picked up his pace—with luck, the alley would be abandoned.

Rounding the corner, he found the prophet had stopped.

"Hello, Your Majesty," said the prophet.

Groshen halted. "I'm not a king anymore."

"Just because the Emperor Dal has taken away your throne doesn't mean you're not a king."

Pointing at the prophet with one of the three remaining fingers of his right hand, Groshen said, "I'm tired of your lies." With his left hand, he drew his knife.

"I never lied to you."

In three quick strides, Groshen reached the prophet and grabbed the front of his crimson silk robe. "Never?" Groshen lifted his knife to the prophet's throat. "Have you forgotten what you prophesied the first time you came to me?"

Stretching his arms wide, the prophet lifted his coppery eyes toward the overcast sky. "'A great destiny lies ahead of you, Your Majesty,' I said. You asked what destiny, and I replied, 'The destiny of the man who will overthrow the Emperor Dal and claim his throne.'"

Groshen threw the prophet into the dirt. "I was mad to trust you."

"Not mad." The prophet crossed his legs and sat up. "Ambitious, perhaps."

"I ruled my corner of the Empire with little interference from Dal. I had no ambition until your secret prophecy. It's your fault I led my army to be slaughtered by Dal's wizardry."

"You raised another army, larger than the first. That you could do so despite your initial defeat speaks well of your leadership."

Groshen's boot connected with the prophet's face. A satisfying crunch came as the man's nose broke. The prophet fell back, blood flowing from his wide nostrils.

"You mock me," Groshen said. "Only your second prophecy kept me from accepting Dal's amnesty."

The prophet pinched his nose shut to stanch the blood. "The peace would not have lasted. Dal planned to kill off the kings in his empire anyway."

"Or my rebellion stirred him to do that," said Groshen. He remembered the guilt he had felt two years ago on hearing that Dal had executed the royal families of every kingdom in the Empire, down to the youngest child.

Groshen kicked the prophet in the stomach. "Your second prophecy was a lie. 'If you raise an army against Dal, he will be defeated.'"

The prophet clutched his abdomen, wheezing. Blood still dripped from his nose.

Stroking the ridged scars on his face, Groshen said, "See the results of your prophecy? I only survived because one of my friends pulled me out of that inferno of wizard's fire. And do you know what he did then, prophet?"

The prophet sat up again, lips wet with blood. "He took your crown and placed it on his own head. Then he ran back into the flames to die in your place. It worked—Dal still believes you dead."

For a moment, Groshen was taken aback. No one else knew what had happened that night. Did the prophet have some power after all? But his anger surged again within him.

"You deserve to die in flames," said Groshen. "Because I trusted you, I've gone from ruling a kingdom to working as a common laborer."

The prophet rose to his knees. "I confess to misleading you. I understand your desire to kill me. But let me tell you of one more prophecy before you do."

"I'm through raising armies," said Groshen.

"Dal killed all the royalty because of a prophecy that only a man of royal blood could rise up to take his throne."

Groshen snorted. "My destiny, according to you."

"No, Your Majesty. I said that destiny lay ahead of you, not that it was yours. But there is another prophecy, one Dal doesn't know, about a farm-boy rising to defeat him. Both destinies belong to your grandson."

"I have no grandson."

Coppery eyes glowing, the prophet spread his arms wide. "You will wed Marya and have two daughters. The younger will bear a son. And he will defeat Dal."

The prophet's tone was convincing—Groshen almost believed him.

Almost.

"Even if you're right, I should kill you for the pain your deceptions have caused." Groshen held the knife to the prophet's throat.

The prophet did not pull away.

"Answer one question," said the prophet, "then kill me if you wish."

"Ask."

"You blame everything on the fact that you trusted my words as a prophet. If I had come to you ten years ago and prophesied that to defeat Dal you must leave your kingdom, marry a cook, and live out the rest of your life as a common farm laborer, would you have done it?"

As Groshen recalled the arrogant young king he had been, he knew the answer was no. His own pride had been his downfall—and even now, it was pride that kept him from accepting Marya's affection.

After a long moment, Groshen released the prophet and left the alley without looking back. If he hurried, he might catch up with Marya on the road back to the farm.

A great destiny lay ahead of him.

ABOUT THE STORY

Unlike the vast majority of the flash fiction I've written, this story was not written for a Codex Weekend Warrior contest. I wrote it at the 2007 Odyssey Writing Workshop, taught by Jeanne Cavelos.

I had always wondered how people could go to a six-week writing workshop. Then I got laid off from my job a few days before the deadline to apply to Odyssey.

The workshop was a very intense six weeks, but by the end of it I felt I had leveled up as a writer.

I've always been fascinated by stories about prophecies and destinies and the role of free will in such stories. This story came about because I was thinking about the farm-boy-rises-to-fulfill-his-destiny-and-overthrow-the-evil-overlord cliché, and it occurred to me that perhaps there was a story to be found in how that destiny ended up going to the farm-boy.

LOBSTERSAURUS

The only predator that poses a significant danger for colonists is Species C-3506, a well-armored hexapod ranging up to five meters in height and up to nine meters in length, and massing up to twelve metric tons. The pincers on its two arms are strong enough to crack the shells of most smaller species, after which the sharp-toothed, beak-like mouth is capable of shredding the flesh into chunks it can swallow.

—Pre-colonization survey report

The dead lobstersaurus, sprawled in the remains of the tomato patch, blocked the sunlight that usually streamed into the kitchen through the diamondglass wall in the mornings. Over the rim of her glass of orange juice, eight-year-old Esperanza Vega peered at the giant creature her father had killed during the night. A cluster of black eyes on the side of its head seemed to stare unblinkingly back at her. The lower part of its head was gone, but its top beak still displayed a row of jagged green teeth.

"Stop looking at it, Espe," Mamá said.

Esperanza jerked her eyes away.

Mamá frowned at Papá. "I want that thing moved before lunch today. It makes me lose my appetite."

Papá reached his fork over to Mamá's plate, speared a pancake, and plopped it onto his own plate. "More for me, I guess."

"Rico, I mean it," Mamá said.

"Jack Sanders said he'd fly his tractor over this afternoon to help haul it away," Papá said.

Out of the corner of her eye, Esperanza thought she saw something moving outside. She looked back at the lobstersaurus. A tiny piece of sun had risen over the top of its shell.

Papá continued, "I suppose if I sliced it in two, our tractor could handle it. But if I had anything that could cut through that shell, I—"

One of the lobstersaurus's legs wiggled, and Esperanza shrieked and dropped her glass. Orange juice spilled across the white tablecloth.

"Espe!" Mamá scolded.

"It's still alive," Esperanza said. "It's moving."

Her parents turned their heads to follow her gaze.

For a few seconds, the lobstersaurus lay still. Then the same leg wiggled again.

"Postmortem reflex," Papá said. "Sometimes nerve signals still go to the muscles after something's dead."

The leg started shaking.

"You're sure it's dead?" Mamá said.

"A pound of blastique blew up in its mouth," Papá said. "It wasn't easy to kill, but it's dead."

Espe remembered something she had read in her science studies. "Some dinosaurs on Earth had nerve clusters near their tails. Maybe lobstersauruses have an extra brain not in their heads."

Papá smiled. "A good theory, *mija*. But it is not true. The survey robots took scans of the lobstersauruses long ago. They have only one brain—larger than most dinosaurs', but only one, in the head."

The armored segment of leg that connected to the lobstersaurus's shell seemed to get longer, then a black line appeared at the joint.

"Is the leg coming off?" Esperanza asked. "Can it go off on its own like a starfish arm and grow another lobstersaurus?"

The leg popped off the body and thudded to the ground, leaving a dark hole in the smooth yellow shell of the body. The leg lay still.

"No," Papá said, but his voice was unsure.

Something moved at the hole. Three small segmented legs, only about twenty centimeters long, stretched out.

"It's like the Hydra," Esperanza said, "but growing legs instead of heads."

A small head appeared, and she realized it was a baby lobstersaurus. The baby pulled itself out of the hole and then, limbs flailing, fell two meters to the ground.

"That can't be how they normally give birth," Mamá said, voice tinged with horror. As a botanist, Mamá had extensively studied the native plants, but she didn't know much about the animals.

The baby tried to stand up but fell over.

"No." Papá pushed back from the table and stood. "Normally kind of a hatch in the shell would open up in the belly, but—well ..."

After a moment's thought, Esperanza understood. "Since the mom is lying dead on its belly, the baby couldn't get out. It had to find another way. Oh, the poor thing could have died!" She stared at the baby lobstersaurus as it wobbled into a standing position, reminding her of the vid she had seen of a baby horse back on Earth. It was about a half meter tall. As if trying to see the whole world with its multiple black eyes, it waved its head about. It gaped its toothless yellow beak and wagged its tiny pincer arms.

It was the cutest thing Esperanza had ever seen in real life.

"Most likely it would die anyway even if I don't kill it," Papá said. "Without its mother to catch food for—"

"I could," Esperanza said.

Papá blinked at her. "What?"

"I could catch food for it," Esperanza said. "Please? Can I keep it? You can't kill it, it's just a baby."

"Keep it?" Mamá said. "It's a monster."

"It could be my pet," Esperanza said. "I could train it." She searched her memory desperately for what she had learned about lobstersauruses in her science studies. "They're territorial animals. If I can get it to mark our farm as its territory, we won't have to worry about other lobstersauruses coming through."

"*Mija*," said Papá, "It's small now, but it will grow quickly, and it's a dangerous animal."

"Please," she begged. "Before dogs became pets, weren't they dangerous animals? It could be like … like a science experiment. If I can't train it, then you can kill it."

"I don't know," Papá said, and Esperanza had a moment of hope because he hadn't said no.

"Rico," Mamá said, "it's too dangerous."

"But Mamá," Esperanza said, "it could be my friend. Please. A friend."

That was the one thing she thought might persuade Mamá. Esperanza had heard her parents talking at night when they thought she was asleep, so she knew that they worried about her not having friends. She had been born six years before the colony ship arrived in the Kallisto system. Even at ten times the speed of light, it had taken over twelve years for the ship to travel from Earth, and the five thousand colonists had made the trip in cryo—except that Mamá's tube had malfunctioned after five years, so the ship had revived her. She had woken Papá to keep her company, and Esperanza had been born a year later due to a malfunctioning birth control implant.

For the two years since landing on Arcas, Esperanza had

been the lone child in a society of adults. With the colony now firmly established, many of the women had turned off their birth control implants and were pregnant. But even after the babies were born, she would still be alone: twelve years younger than the closest adult, nine years older than the closest child.

Looking out the window at the baby lobstersaurus, Mamá sighed. "You will not bring it in the house. You will feed it and clean up after it, not me."

"Yes, Mamá. Thank you, Mamá." Filled with excitement, Esperanza rushed toward the door.

"Wait," said Papá, and her heart fell.

She turned to face him.

"When it grows teeth in that beak, you will have to file them down so they are not sharp," he said. "And we may need to do something about those pincers."

"Yes, Papá."

He picked up his work pack and walked over to her. "And I will come with you now. It may be small, but we do not know how it will react to you. It may not want to be your pet; it may not be possible to train it." Taking her hand, he led her out the door.

The baby lobstersaurus wobbled on six legs in the shadow of its mother. A trilling cry came from its beak.

When Esperanza and Papá got within two meters, it suddenly dropped on its belly. Esperanza's grip tightened on Papá's hand. The baby withdrew its head, legs, and pincer arms inside its shell, and sealed the holes.

"Oh, the poor baby's scared of us," Esperanza said.

"That's good," Papá said. "If it had attacked us, I probably would have had to kill it." He slipped some object Esperanza had not noticed him carrying into his pack.

"Did you know it could hide like a turtle?" she asked.

Papá shrugged. "Can't remember if that was in the survey robots' reports. Probably was, because they're very thorough. But I've never seen an adult do that, so maybe just babies can."

"But how can I tame it if it hides in its shell?"

"It will get hungry," he said. "Come." He led her over to the Arcasian scrap heap, where non-Earth biological material was placed for eventual protein conversion. Papá pulled out a dead crabbit about ten centimeters long. He whacked it a couple of times against the metal edge of the container until its shell cracked.

"Pull out the meat. If you feed it," he said, "it may think you're its mother."

With Papá standing guard, Esperanza waited in front of the baby lobstersaurus until finally the shell's head-hole opened. She remained very still.

The lobstersaurus's head slowly came out. It opened its beak and chirped.

Ever so slowly, Esperanza held out her hand holding a piece of crabbit meat. She put it down on the ground just a few centimeters from its beak, then withdrew her hand.

In a quick motion, the lobstersaurus snapped the meat up in its beak. With a slurping sound, it swallowed the meat whole.

After a few more trips to the scrap heap, Esperanza had fed the baby until it refused more food, and it followed her around with a wobbling six-legged gait.

"What will you name it?" Papá asked.

Esperanza thought about it for a moment, and the answer came to her in the form of a traditional Argentine folk song her parents often sang to her because it contained her name: '*Zamba de mi esperanza*.' "Zamba," she said. "Its name is Zamba."

Since they keep their reproductive organs inside their shells except during mating, the only visible difference between the sexes is that the female has an armored flap on her underside through which live offspring emerge.

☼

Zamba grew more quickly than Esperanza expected. On her ninth birthday, less than six Earth months after she had adopted him, he was over a meter tall, a meter wide, and two meters long. She was still a good twenty centimeters taller than him, but that would not last long.

As a treat for her birthday, Papá had diverted water from the river, which ran along the eastern edge of their property, into a hole four meters wide he'd had the farmbots dig. "Someday we'll build a real swimming pool," he said as she splashed about in the waist-deep, muddy water. "But this will do for now."

Zamba tentatively dipped the tip of his left foreleg into the water, but stayed on the bank.

"Come on, Zamba," Esperanza said. "You can do it. See, it's fun." She splashed some water on his shell.

"I don't think he wants to, *mija*." Papá also stood on the bank. "He's not sure he can find his footing in there, and he can't float."

Esperanza frowned. "But I read that lobstersauruses have an aquatic origin. He should like being in water."

"Even if they evolved from aquatic creatures, it's been a long, long time. If you go back far enough, humans evolved from monkeys. That doesn't mean we have to like swinging from tree branches."

"But I like swinging from tree branches," Esperanza said.

Papá gazed at her for a moment. "Hmm. I can see the monkey resemblance. I think I shall call you *monita*, my little monkey."

She replied to that by sending a big splash of water his way. Papá leapt nimbly backward to dodge it, but some of the force of his leap caused a meter-long section of dirt to collapse into the water, sending little waves across. Esperanza giggled.

One of the farmbots that had dug the pool jolted into motion toward the collapsed rim, shovel arm extended.

Zamba sprang sideways, away from the pool, then jumped more than double his length to crash into the farmbot.

Esperanza shrieked. "Zamba! Stop!"

Zamba grabbed the farmbot's neck in one pincer and its shovel arm in the other. Metal twisted and groaned. Zamba let out a roar Esperanza had never heard before as the arm tore from the farmbot's frame.

Then Zamba dropped the farmbot and its arm and stepped back. The farmbot's shoulder sparked erratically.

Esperanza stood completely still, staring at the scene.

From somewhere across the river, wild territory still untouched by humans, came a deeper answering roar.

"Out of the pool, away from Zamba." Papá's voice was quiet but firm. "Now." Facing Zamba, he moved slowly toward his work pack, which lay on the ground a few meters away.

Panic rose inside Esperanza. Papá was going to do something to Zamba, maybe even kill him. She couldn't let that happen. So she moved forward, climbing out on the edge closest to Zamba.

"Espe!" Papá said. He froze in place.

"Bad Zamba," Esperanza said, staring at Zamba's black eyes and putting all the anger she could into her voice. "Don't break things. Bad Zamba."

Papá moved toward her, away from his pack.

Zamba's head drooped. He turned to face her, then backed up a step and sank onto his belly.

Esperanza ran forward and gave Zamba's beak a light slap. Then she made her voice friendly. "You're a good boy, Zamba. But you can't break things just because you're big and strong."

"Get away from him, *mija*."

"No, Papá." She stroked Zamba's head and he made cheeping sounds like he used to when he was a baby. "See, he hasn't gone wild. He must have thought the farmbot was attacking or something."

"You can't really know what he's thinking. He's a wild creature. He may act tame sometimes, but he's not like a dog or cat or horse that has evolved to live with humans." Papá sighed. "Now that he's grown so big, maybe it's time to let him go live in the wild."

"No, Papá. Please." Tears welled in her eyes. "He's a good boy. He'll behave."

Papá was silent for a minute. "Okay. But remember how I said we might need to do something about his pincers? It's necessary. I can't stand the thought of … It's necessary."

That night, while Esperanza held Zamba's head and sang to him, Papá banded Zamba's pincers with a nanofiber strip, slightly elastic to allow room for a few weeks' growth.

There are no venomous animals on the main continent, probably because all its animal species have shells, making venom delivery impossible. Thus, small species may present a minor problem as pests, but are not dangerous. High-tensile fencing is capable of keeping out larger species, except for C-3506. Not even electrified fencing will work for C-3506, due to its protective shell, which also renders it virtually invulnerable to standard-grade projectile and energy weapons. Military-grade weapons or high explosives will be needed to kill C-3506, so the colony should be supplied with such.

—Pre-colonization survey report

At two Earth-years old—about 2.05 Arcasian years—Zamba was almost three meters tall, more than double Esperanza's height and about the size of an adult African elephant on Earth. And he was not nearly full grown. Since his pincers were banded, she had to crack the shells of the dead pest animals brought in by the farmbots so that Zamba could eat them. That and collecting Zamba's scat to put in the scrap heap for protein conversion were her main chores associated with keeping Zamba. The farmbots could have done both jobs for her, but her parents insisted that she do the work herself because Zamba was her responsibility.

"Espe? Where are you?" Mamá called from inside the house.

"Fixing supper for Zamba," Esperanza replied. She smashed the sledgehammer onto a blue crabbit and its shell crunched.

"The power's gone out." Mamá came to the back door, her belly eight months pregnant with a baby sister for Esperanza. "I can't raise your father on the comm, so you'll have to fetch him to look at the generator."

Esperanza smashed a red crabbit, then put down the hammer. "Zamba and I will find him." She picked up the two cracked crabbits by their tails and tossed them to Zamba, who gulped them down with a satisfied grunt.

A stinging sensation near her left ankle made Esperanza look down. A two-centimeter-long, six-legged creature was biting her. She kicked it off with her right foot. A trickle of blood ran down from the bite. She stomped on the thing and twisted her foot until she heard the shell crack. She saw a couple more of the same species crawling along the ground and stomped them for good measure. If the stupid animals on this planet would just learn that Earth-based life didn't provide them with any real nutrition …

From far to the east, a lobstersaurus bellowed. Esperanza instinctively covered her ears, having learned from past experience that Zamba's response could be annoyingly loud.

She didn't hear a bellow, but did hear a muffled scream. Puzzled, Esperanza turned toward her mother, who was running toward her, pregnant belly bouncing.

Something grabbed Esperanza's torso and twisted her up into the air. Pinpricks of pain spread across her back as she was bounced around. Wind whipped her hair.

Esperanza looked at what was holding her. It was Zamba's beak. "Zamba! Bad boy! Put me down. Put me down, now!"

Zamba kept running across their crop fields, trampling the pest fences without slowing down.

She made eye contact and repeated her command, but there was a wildness in Zamba's eyes she had never seen before.

"Papá!" she screamed. "Papá, help!"

They were headed east, toward the river and the wild country beyond. She tried to think what had triggered this attack. Was the bellow she had heard some sort of mating call? She had read about species on Earth for which the male offered food to the female before mating. Was that what she was, a food offering?

At least she was alive, so far. And Zamba's teeth had been filed so they weren't very sharp, although they still felt like they were tearing into her skin a bit. But if Zamba was taking her to a wild lobstersaurus ... A memory of Zamba using his pincers to rip the arm off the farmbot involuntarily came to her mind.

"Zamba, please," she said, trying to make her voice calm. "Be a good boy and put me down."

Zamba swerved, shuddered as there was a cracking sound, then started falling forward. His mouth opened and Esperanza tumbled to the ground, the cornstalks partially breaking her fall.

She pulled herself to her feet and looked back to make sense of what had happened. Zamba screeched in pain—his front two legs were shattered. Papá's tractor lay crumpled a few meters away.

"Papá!" she called and began stumbling toward the tractor.

He appeared out of the cornstalks nearby, running toward her. "*Mija*, are you all right?"

"Yes," she said as he enveloped her in a hug. "I don't know what got into—"

"Later," Papá said. "Back to the house, quick as we can."

Zamba cheeped at her, but she turned her back and began to run alongside Papá through the crops toward home.

"It's my fault," she said.

"No," Papá said.

"I should have let you take him to the wild."

"Do you think you could have stopped me if I had decided to do it? I am the one to blame, for being too soft-hearted. I never wanted you to get hurt, *mija*. I knew losing Zamba would hurt you. But sometimes you must hurt those you love to save them from a greater pain."

They met Mamá coming the other way when they were a half-kilometer from the house. She wept with joy when she saw Esperanza. "You're alive," she kept repeating as they continued toward home.

The seeds of all plant species on the main continent are covered in a highly mineralized shell that is resistant to the digestive systems of the local fauna. This probably evolved as a method of spreading the seeds via herbivore scat. The mineral compound in the shells is durable enough that it may have industrial uses.

—Pre-colonization survey report

Because the power was still out, Papá had to use a flashlight so he could see the lock on his office safe where he kept the blastique.

"Do you have to do that now?" Mamá asked.

Papá sighed. "Zamba was a good pet the past two years. No matter what happened today, I should end his suffering. He deserves that much mercy."

Esperanza couldn't hold back tears, but she kept herself from sobbing.

"Can you at least try to get the generator back on before you go?" Mamá said. "It's getting dark."

Papá took three bricks of blastique out of the safe, then closed it. He nodded. "*Mija*, come with me to hold the flashlight while I try to fix the generator."

As Esperanza and Papá stepped out the kitchen door, he suddenly grabbed her arm.

"What?" she said, then she heard the cheeping.

In the twilight, Zamba staggered toward them on his middle and back legs. His front legs dangled uselessly.

"Back inside," Papá said. They stepped back into the house. Papá bolted the door. "Maria!"

Mamá entered the kitchen. "What is it?"

Zamba came close to the diamondglass wall and banged against it with his pincers.

Mamá gasped.

Esperanza couldn't believe this was happening. Zamba was still cheeping at her like he did when he was sorry for something, yet here he was attacking the house. "Go away," she yelled. "I hate you!"

"I need something sticky," Papá said to Mamá. "So I can stick the explosives to it."

"I'll find something," Mamá said. "Give me the flashlight." In a moment, she was gone.

Zamba lifted his left pincer to his beak and bit at the nanofiber band. It resisted at first, but then tore and the pincer was free. He then did the same to the other.

Esperanza watched in horror as he used his pincers to tear off his front legs. The holes in his shell where the legs had come out sealed up.

With his pincers, Zamba reached up to the roof, grabbed ahold, and began to pull. Above them, something creaked and then snapped.

"Into the living room," Papá said.

They hurried in the dark, almost slipping and falling in

their rush. Mamá and the flashlight joined them in huddling behind the couch, right after a huge crashing noise from the kitchen.

"Superglue," she said, handing a tube to Papá.

"That'll do," he replied. He began working on the explosives while Mamá held the flashlight for him.

Something stung Esperanza's ankle. She reached down and felt the shell of a small creature. She brushed it away.

"Ow," said Mamá. The flashlight wavered, and for a moment Esperanza thought she saw the floor moving. Was Zamba somehow digging under them. That couldn't be possible, could it?

"Mamá," she said, "shine the light on the floor."

"Why?"

"Please."

Mamá turned the flashlight down.

The floor was a seething mass of tiny creatures like the one that had bitten Esperanza just before Zamba went crazy.

"What are those? Where did they come from?" Mamá asked.

Papá stayed focused on the explosives.

Esperanza could see some of the creatures crawling up Mamá's legs. She reached down and swatted at them, knocking most of them off. One grabbed onto her hand and bit her finger. She could feel more bites on her legs.

With a tremendous crash, Zamba tore through the kitchen wall and into the living room. The ceiling collapsed behind him. He cheeped at them.

Papá stood up, a brick of blastique in his right hand.

"Wait!" Esperanza shouted. "He was trying to save me. From the swarm."

Papá hesitated. "What swarm?"

"Look down," Mamá said.

Papá looked down, then began stomping with his boots.

Esperanza came out from behind the couch. "I'm so sorry, Zamba," she said. "I didn't understand."

"What are you doing?" Papá said. He still held a brick of blastique.

Esperanza knew she was right. She had to be. She rushed toward Zamba, who reached out with his pincer and grabbed her by the waist.

"Espe!" Mamá cried.

Zamba lifted Esperanza up and onto his back.

"See?" Esperanza said. "He couldn't use his pincers, so his mouth was the only way he could carry me."

Zamba reached out his pincers toward Mamá and Papá. After a brief hesitation, they came around the couch and Zamba lifted them onto his back.

Zamba turned and lumbered out of the house, heading east.

Everywhere Mamá shone the flashlight on the ground, the swarm writhed. "Our crops," she said. "We are losing everything."

"Not everything." Papá hugged the two of them close. "Not the most important things."

Once Zamba reached the river, he waded out a couple of meters and then stopped.

"Of course," Esperanza said. "The swarm would be swept away if it came into the river. That's why he was bringing me here."

The three of them stayed on Zamba's back all night, huddled together for warmth. Esperanza didn't get much sleep, as crashing sounds in the wild country across the river kept startling her awake.

As the sun rose the next morning, they could see the result of the swarms—for there must have been another swarm across the river. Not a tree was left standing, and the surface of the land glittered with tiny moving shells. Various larger animals, including some lobstersauruses, roamed about, feeding off the tiny creatures.

As for their farm, blanketed by the swarm, none of the crops remained. Parts of their house still stood, though, diamondglass and metal glinting in the sun.

"What I can't understand is why the survey robots never reported on these swarms," Papá said. "They were here twenty years before we arrived, and they never saw these things."

Esperanza remembered something she'd read in her science studies. "Maybe they're like cicadas, and only come out after many years underground."

"The seeds!" said Mamá. "This is why all the native seeds have such tough shells. If every few decades a swarm eats all the plants, then the seeds still survive."

"Not just seeds," Papá said. "All the land animals have shells. Of course—hardly anything without a shell would survive."

"We don't have shells," Esperanza said. "Without Zamba, we might be dead." She rubbed her hand over Zamba's shell, and he made a low, almost purring sound. "But what do we do now? We can't stay on Zamba's back forever."

"With the food exhausted," said Papá, "my guess is the swarm will mate, dig down to wherever they lay their eggs, then die. And the cycle will be over for however many years until the eggs hatch. We'll have to bring down more seeds from the ship and start over."

"And this time we'll have to figure out what to do before they come back," Esperanza said.

"Someone will figure something out." Papá winked at her. "Maybe even you."

Because Earth species provide no real nutritional value to Arcasian animals, the swarmers that fed on colonist crops mostly failed to reproduce after burrowing. Thirty-seven years from now, the eggs that do hatch under areas that were already cultivated during the swarm fifteen years ago will be reduced by over ninety-five percent. This suggests that strategy of mass cultivation of Earth crops in the

year before each swarm might be highly effective in reducing future swarms in that area.

—Esperanza Vega, master's thesis in Biology

ABOUT THE STORY

This one was written for the 2010 Codex Halloween Contest. Fellow Codexian Terra LeMay gave me the following prompt: "If you can, please include in your story a strange-looking monster that is simultaneously scary and so ugly it's cute."

I had recently read "Jaiden's Weaver," a short story by Mary Robinette Kowal, about a girl on a colony world who wants a large alien animal as a pet, so I shamelessly stole that concept from her.

While living in Argentina as a child, I learned to sing one of the most popular Argentine folk songs: *"Zamba de mi esperanza."* I even had to perform a dance to it at school, waving a white handkerchief in the air as I *zamba*ed around with a bunch of other kids. (That must have been a year or two before the song was banned by the military junta that overthrew Isabel Perón in 1976.) When it came time to name my main character and her pet, the song came back to me. It turned out I could still remember most of the lyrics.

The story took second place in the contest, and I thought I'd have an easy time selling it. And I was right—Stan Schmidt bought it for *Analog* on its first submission, and Dreaming Robot Press bought it as a reprint for the *Young Explorers Adventure Guide* on its second submission.

THE STEEL THRONE

The Empress Uvay dismissed the physician with a trembling wave of her hand. What could he do except tell her she would soon join the late Emperor in the halls of Paradise? Terrified of being charged with regicide, he would not even give her a concoction to ease her passing.

No matter—the poison needle hidden in the ring on her right middle finger would quickly end her life if the pain became too great.

But not yet. She still must decide which of her children would succeed her as ruler of the Chosen People.

She smiled. Fifty years ago, there would not have been any need for a choice. As eldest son of her imperial father-in-law, her husband had automatically ascended to the Steel Throne on the death of the Emperor. And by tradition, on his death thirty-three years ago, Delgar, their eldest son, should have ascended—even at the age of two months.

Freed of the fear of her husband's military leadership, the enemy kingdoms that encircled the Empire and the lands her husband had conquered had united in arms. It had been no time for half-measures, so Uvay had ascended to the throne herself and led imperial forces to war.

By the turning of the year, she was more feared as a general than her husband had been, and no one dared suggest that the Steel Throne was the weaker for having a woman seated on it.

And so Uvay had a choice. Her eldest child, Hala, was the daughter of her heart. Beautiful as the sunlight, fierce as a lioness, Hala had commanded the Imperial armies as they finished conquering the remaining kingdoms in the land. Beloved by her troops, it was said they would kill their own families or even themselves at her command.

Delgar, two years younger than Hala, was beloved by no one. Ever since he was old enough to understand that his mother had stolen the throne from him, he had resented her. He was smart enough to see the necessity of her actions, and he accepted her rule, but they had never been close. He lacked his sister's inner fire, but he had served Uvay well as an administrator, organizing the logistics of running an empire that spanned from ocean to ocean.

If there had still been enemies to conquer, Hala would have been the clear choice. But for an empire at peace, Uvay had to admit that Delgar would make the better emperor.

Uvay sighed, her breath crackling in her lungs. The choice was not as simple as deciding who would make a better emperor. If she named Hala, Delgar would loyally continue to run the empire on his sister's behalf. But if she named Delgar, Hala could easily take the throne by force. There were no throngs of soldiers sworn to die for Delgar.

And Hala could not claim the Steel Throne without killing Delgar.

On the other hand, there were rumors among sailors that strange kingdoms existed beyond the oceans. If such were true, then there would be new lands for Hala to conquer. The empire was finally at peace, but out of loyalty and love for his sister, Delgar would find ways to fund her campaigns, and her soldiers would follow her to the corners of the world.

Choosing Hala was the only way both children could live.

"Bring Hala and Delgar," Uvay rasped to a servant. "Tell them I will choose."

The two must have been waiting outside her chambers, for they were ushered in almost immediately.

"Mother," said Delgar with a curt nod.

"Oh, Mother, you must not die yet!" said Hala. "I wish to conquer the lands beyond the sea for you."

Uvay smiled. "Hala, my beloved, I wish I could live at your command. But my time has come."

She fixed her gaze on Delgar and said, "My son, I denied you the throne as a child, and I am sorry. I know you love your sister, so I hope you will forgive what I must do."

Turning her gaze to Hala, she said, "Hala, come forth and receive the blessing of my hand."

Hala walked over and knelt by Uvay's bed.

Placing her right hand on Hala's shoulder, Uvay whispered, "The Steel Throne requires us to be hard as steel, to choose for the good of the empire when no one else can."

And then she squeezed the ring to release the poison needle into Hala's skin.

ABOUT THE STORY

This was another Codex Weekend Warrior Contest story from 2009. The prompt was "Write from the viewpoint of an elderly character of a different gender and social class than yourself."

For the record, I am male.

According to family history documents I read when I was a teenager, for decades I believed I was a descendant of King John of England (and, through his line, William the Conqueror, among others.)

It now seems that history was mistaken, but according to the RelativeFinder.org website, I am a twelfth cousin once removed of Elizabeth the Second, by the Grace of God of the United Kingdom of Great Britain and Northern Ireland and of Her

other Realms and Territories Queen, Head of the Common-
wealth, Defender of the Faith. But that's not close enough for
me to get invited to royal family parties, so I think it's safe to say
that my social class is not royalty.

Therefore I decided to make my viewpoint character an
elderly woman of royalty. I wanted to show her having to make a
hard decision, and choosing which of her children would
succeed her seemed like it would fit the bill.

CUI BONO?

When people ask me what I do, I usually lie and say I'm an insurance salesman. If that doesn't send them scurrying for another subject, I have a whole spiel about how they could save money by switching. I even have business cards. In the rare case someone actually calls me, I quote an outrageous price and I never hear from them again.

If I'm more inclined to tell the truth, I say I'm a private investigator. People tend to find that a lot more interesting than insurance salesman. If they ask for details, I tell them it's mostly insurance fraud and divorce cases, pretty routine stuff. What I don't tell them is that it would be more accurate to replace the word private with paranormal, and that my cases generally involve supernatural beings.

It's still mostly insurance fraud and divorce cases. You wouldn't believe how many business fires are started by strapped-for-cash owners summoning fire elementals, or the number of old geezers who are tricked into marrying succubi. So when a man and woman walked through my door wanting to find a missing person, it was a welcome break in the monotony.

"Have a seat," I said, indicating the two leather chairs. "Who's missing, and why do you want them found?"

The woman sat down in the red chair, and I caught a faint woodland vibe off her, like maybe her grandma was a dryad. She looked early twenties, but with dryad ancestry she might be in her forties.

The man, who looked mid-forties with a good head of hair, didn't give off any paranormal vibes as he took the yellow chair. He cleared his throat, then said, "I understand you deal with investigations of an unusual nature?"

"My specialty," I said. "In fact, if the person you're looking for isn't … unusual … then you're probably better off with another P.I. My fees are high 'cause I have a special sense for the unusual."

The man nodded. "You were recommended by a former client, who said you're worth whatever price you name, and that you're ethical enough in your own way, so you won't jack up the price when you find out I have a stock portfolio worth hundreds of millions."

I raised my eyebrows and reassessed their clothing. He wore a gray business suit; she wore jeans and a patterned blouse. It looked like off-the-rack stuff, not high-end designer. "My standard rate is $500 an hour, plus expenses. Two hours up front if I take the case."

He pulled a wallet from his coat pocket, slid out a credit card, and tossed it onto my desk. The card was an American Express. Black. "In case you haven't seen one before," he said, "I could use that card to buy every building on this block."

My office isn't exactly low-rent, but he might be right. However, I was a bit puzzled by the belligerence in his voice. His clothing suggested he didn't flaunt his wealth, yet here he was, shoving it in my face.

"As it happens," I said, picking up the card and reading the name on it, "Mr. Jenkins, I have seen one before. The wife of a rather wealthy man used it to pay for my services. She suspected her husband was a vampire, and hired me to prove he was dead so she could inherit everything."

"Did you?" he asked.

"I did." Not exactly a happy ending for her, though—her husband had already been dead before she married him, so the proof did her no good.

The woman let out an exasperated sigh in the man's direction. "Enough, hon. Everyone says he's the best."

I smiled. That was a nice ego-boost. "Thank you, Ms. ..."

"Jenkins. Holly Jenkins. I'm his wife."

"Please, Mrs. Jenkins, tell me who you want me to find."

"We want you to find the Green Man," she said. "He's been kidnapped."

"The Green Man." I nodded slowly. "As in the leafy-faced guy who pops up in art from a bunch of different cultures? That Green Man?"

"Yes," she said.

"What makes you think he exists?" I asked.

"Hey," said Mr. Jenkins, "I thought you believed in this kind of stuff."

Ah. That was the source of the hostility: he didn't believe, she did. "Mr. Jenkins, I believe in a lot of things. But not every being of myth and legend actually exists. Leprechauns, for example, are completely made up. So I need to know what evidence you have that he's not just an artistic motif."

"He's my great-great-grandfather," she said. "I met him once when I was a kid."

"Bingo," I said. "Had you pegged as a dryad's granddaughter, but the woodland vibe I sensed could easily be from an ancestor who's the incarnation of vegetation. So, next question: What makes you think he's been kidnapped?"

Holly looked down at her clothes. "What do you mean, woodland vibe?"

"Kind of a sixth sense," I said. "It's not how you look or what you're wearing or anything like that. But when I'm close enough to a supernatural being, I usually get a feeling of what sort they are. I call them vibes for lack of a better word. It's not foolproof—a high-quality protection spell can scramble the vibe or even hide it altogether."

"That's it! That's exactly what it was like." She leaned forward, her piercing green eyes seeming to light up. "A vibe. I don't get them normally, not like you. But that one time, when I was a kid, it was like I could tell he was standing there even when I closed my eyes."

"Perfectly reasonable," I said. "You have only a little sensitivity, but you're attuned to him because you're related by blood, so he sets off your vibe detector. But, getting back to the matter at hand, if you haven't seen him since you were a kid, what makes you think he's been kidnapped now?"

Holly glanced at her husband. "Donny made his money in green energy: solar power, wind power, you know. So he knows people in the energy industry, and sometimes we go to parties with other rich people. At this one party, I sensed the Green Man's vibe, but I looked around and didn't see him. I couldn't tell where it was coming from. I started searching among the guests—"

He rolled his eyes and interrupted, "To make a long story short, the host of that party has captured the Green Man and is using one of those spell thingies you mentioned to scramble the 'vibe.'" I could hear him mentally putting quotes around vibe.

"Possible," I said. "Or maybe the Green Man went to the party, and used the spell himself because he didn't want to be recognized."

Holly shook her head vigorously. "No way. I went back a couple days later, claiming I'd lost an earring, and the vibe was still in that house."

"Okay," I said. "But why would someone want to kidnap the Green Man? *Cui bono?* Who benefits?"

"The owner of the house is Brad Wells," Mr. Jenkins said. "He's a consultant to a bunch of oil and coal companies." He sighed. "Look, I don't really believe in all this paranormal stuff, but I believe Holly's instinct that something's not right at that house. Wells and his cronies are up to something, and I want you to find out what. Doesn't matter to me if it's a green man or insider trading—anything that causes trouble for Wells is fine with me."

I arched an eyebrow. "His name's Wells and he works for oil companies?"

Mr. Jenkins frowned. "So what? I had a dentist named Payne. It happens."

"Don't you see?" Holly said. "They're afraid the Green Man could do something to stop their fracking drills and mining and all that. Maybe even global warming. So they've locked him up, bound him with spells so he can't escape."

"Why not just kill him, then, if he's such a danger to them?"

Holly looked at me like I was crazy. "He's spiritually connected to all plants. You couldn't kill him without killing every plant on Earth, and even the oil companies aren't that crazy."

I had my doubts about her theory. What could the Green Man do to stop the oil companies, raise an army of plants to tear down their oil rigs? He'd been around thousands of years and in all that time he hadn't done much more than model for artists. But I said, "All right. It's worth looking into, at least. I'll go check out the house, see if I pick up any woodland vibes."

The house, as it turned out, could properly be described as a mansion. Behind a gate, the half mile long driveway curved through a meticulously landscaped garden. I thought it somewhat ironic that Wells loved plants in his garden but worked for industries that were destroying the environment. Maybe this had nothing to do with oil—maybe Wells just thought the Green Man was the perfect accessory to his garden. Wouldn't be the first time I'd seen something like that: some rich folk think a gargoyle in a stasis spell makes the perfect roof ornament.

Vanity is often the route to getting access to someone's home. After seeing that garden, I opened up my cache of business cards and pulled out one that identified me as a freelance photojournalist. Then I got out of my car and picked up the phone next to the camera at the gate.

It buzzed twice before a male voice answered. "Can I help you?"

"I hope so," I said. "I'm doing a photo story on the best private gardens in New York. From what I've heard, Mr. Wells's garden is spectacular. I mean, just what I can see through the gate is fantastic. I was hoping to get permission to come in, take some pictures. If now's not a good time, could I set up an appointment in the next couple of days? Needs to be during daylight, of course."

"Please hold," the voice said. After a couple of minutes, it returned with, "Please drive up to the house. Someone will escort you while you are on the premises." The gate slid open.

"Thanks." I got back in my car and drove up to the front door.

The security guard who came out to meet me had a werewolf vibe. Someone who didn't believe in the paranormal would have no reason to kidnap the Green Man, so the fact that Wells had paranormal security made it more likely Holly was right.

I got my tripod and biggest camera out of my trunk, then made a big show of taking pictures all over the garden. I kept looping up near the mansion, each time approaching a different part so I could try to detect a woodland vibe from someone inside. After an hour and a half, I had covered about two thirds of the building without sensing anything but a couple of werewolves, a half-dozen gnomes, and a chupacabra most likely of Honduran origin.

As I approached the southwest corner of the house, I finally felt a vibe that reminded me of Holly. It wasn't localized, so there was almost certainly some sort of scrambler spell at work. It might just be a dryad, or possibly a sasquatch. But the vibe was enough like Holly's that I figured there was a blood relationship, and that meant the Green Man.

I snapped a final couple of photos, then turned to my escort. "The angle of the sunlight's causing too many shadows that detract from the beauty," I said. "I'm going to need to come back tomorrow to finish."

He shrugged and led me back to my car, then watched as I drove away.

Around 3:00 AM that night, protected by the best anti-werewolf confusion spell I could find—plus a few other magical protections, I climbed over the wall into Wells's garden and snuck up to the mansion's southwest corner. I could feel three werewolf vibes, but they weren't nearby. I stood there, keeping very still, and managed to again pick up the Green Man's vibe. Good, he was still here.

Of course, my vibe-sensing wasn't enough to get the police out here with a warrant, so I continued to the more technological part of the evening: bypassing the burglar alarm so I could get into the house and search for the place they were holding him. No, it wasn't legal, but neither was kidnapping a sapient paranormal and holding him against his will, so I felt this was morally excusable.

I had just finished disconnecting the alarm from a window when a deep voice said, "Okay, very slowly now, I want you to raise your hands above your head, then stand up and turn around."

I complied, and found that my captor was a man in a security guard uniform. No paranormal vibes—just an ordinary human guard doing his duty. I mentally kicked myself for assuming all the guards were werewolves.

"Before you call the cops," I said, "let me talk to Mr. Wells. Tell him I know about the Green Man."

A werewolf guard loped up to join the one who'd caught me. After a brief cell phone conversation, they escorted me inside the mansion and led me into a room with a desk and a lot of books.

After patting me down for weapons, the werewolf ordered me to sit, so I sat in one of the chairs facing the desk.

About ten minutes later, Brad Wells entered the room and sat behind the desk. He looked at me appraisingly, then dismissed the guards with a wave of his hand.

"So, you claim to know about the Green Man," he said. "What do you know?"

"I know you're keeping him on the premises. And, before you get any funny ideas, let me make clear that others know, too. Killing me will only bring more scrutiny on what you're doing."

He shrugged. "Why would I want the Green Man?"

"You consult for the oil companies. If he were free, he might try to stop them from ruining the environment with global warming and stuff."

He chuckled. "Is that the best theory you can come up with?"

I shook my head. "It's not my theory, actually. Mine is that you're obsessed with your garden, and the Green Man's just for decoration."

This time he gave a belly laugh. "The other theory was better. Now, I'm not admitting anything, of course, but I just want to show you how naïve you are. Tell me, what are fossil fuels made out of?"

I wasn't sure. I seemed to remember something about dinosaurs, but I figured 'fossils' wasn't the right answer. "Enlighten me."

"Mostly plants. A lot of it's plankton, but other plants are there too. Now, the Green Man has been around since the very first bit of chlorophyll photosynthesized over a billion years ago. He was there three hundred and fifty million years ago when giant plants dominated a world much warmer than ours today—

the same plants that became our fossil fuels. He wasn't always a man, of course—he didn't become one until after there were humans. But he's the connection between all plants that live today ... or have ever lived. Do you see the significance of that last part?"

It took me a moment. "He knows where the oil is."

"And the coal, and natural gas. He has a spiritual connection to it, and can tell us the best places to drill. And I'm sure you realize that such a valuable asset, if its location were discovered, would be immediately moved to a new location. If we had access to him, that is, which I have not admitted."

That clearly gave him motive to hold the Green Man, but what I couldn't understand was how Wells benefited by telling me this. The Jenkinses weren't going to just give up looking for the Green Man.

"*Cui bono?*" I said.

"What?"

"It's Latin," I said. "Who benefits?"

"I know that. I just wasn't sure what you meant by it. Whoever holds the Green Man benefits, obviously."

"No, I mean who benefits from you telling me that the Green Man is being moved? Obviously, it's you, because you don't want people sniffing around here anymore. So what are you really hiding?"

He chuckled again, green eyes glinting. "Oh, I've got nothing to hide."

His piercing green eyes reminded me of Holly's. And everything clicked into place. Focusing on where he sat, I could just barely sense the vibe through whatever spells were hiding it. "You're the Green Man. I can feel it."

He looked startled, then said, "Oh, nonsense."

"No, really, I can. But ..." I frowned. "But why? Why are you helping the oil and coal companies? Is it *money*? Did they buy you off?" I stared at him in disgust.

His fist slammed down on the desk. "No." He composed

himself, then waved his hand around the room. "This is all for show. It's expected of a man in my position. You can't be a consultant for major corporations and live naked in a grove of trees."

"Then why? Why are you ruining the environment? You should be protecting it."

He stared at me for a long moment. "Who benefits from the carbon dioxide released by the burning of fossil fuels?"

I shrugged. "Car drivers, power companies, pretty much anyone who uses fossil fuels."

"No," he said. "They benefit from the *energy* released by the burning. Who benefits from the *carbon dioxide*?"

I remembered what he'd said earlier about plants dominating a warmer world. "It causes global warming. You actually want a warmer world, like millions of years ago."

"Not just that. Do you know what carbon dioxide is?" He leaned forward and spoke softly. "It's food ... for plants."

ABOUT THE STORY

An editor invited me to write a story for an anthology called *Urban Green Man*. I decided to write an urban fantasy/detective story, a genre combination I had not yet tried. How about a missing persons case, and the missing person is the Green Man himself?

Who would benefit from kidnapping the Green Man? The obvious answer would be anti-environment forces. But in writing a mystery, you want to avoid the obvious answer.

In researching the archetype of the Green Man, I found it is mainly associated with the renewal of vegetation: Plants die in the winter and are reborn in the spring.

It occurred to me that there were geological periods in which plant life was more abundant than it is now. Those periods tend to have at least two things in common: higher temperatures and higher atmospheric concentrations of carbon dioxide.

And that led me to the question of what someone might do if they wanted to bring about a renewal of a world with more abundant plant life. Maybe releasing all the carbon trapped underground and warming the Earth would be part of their plan.

Since I had my title and the true goals of the Green Man before I even started writing, it was just a matter of getting my detective to figure it all out.

TO SERVE ALIENS
(YES, IT'S A COOKBOOK)

APPETIZER

Deviled Berundi Slug Eggs

Ingredients:

1 cluster of Berundi Slug Eggs (thawed)
2 tablespoons mayonnaise
1 teaspoon sugar
1 teaspoon Berundi Slug Urine (melted)
1 teaspoon mustard
1/2 teaspoon salt
Paprika

Directions:

Approach the Berundi slug nest at least thirty-six hours after local sundown, to ensure all local wildlife is in hibernation. Carefully raise the brooding Berundi slug from the nest and remove a cluster of 6-8 eggs from its underbelly. Store them in a padded container, as you don't want them shattering before they thaw.

Near the nest, you should find frozen Berundi slug urine (brown crystals with about a 10% concentration of acetic acid). Scoop up enough for at least a teaspoon of liquid.

Allow the eggs and urine to thaw/melt at room temperature. (Using too much heat will ruin the flavor.)

Slice each egg in half and remove the blue pit from the clear of the egg. Crack the shell of the pit and scoop out the yolk, which should be aqua in color and gelatinous in texture. (Warning: If the yolk is red, discard all eggs and set the kitchen to give itself a Level IV Decontamination, then go to MedLab and take a generic anti-toxin nanocap.)

In a small bowl, mash the yolks with a fork. Add the mayonnaise, sugar, urine, mustard and salt; mix well. Stuff the mixture into the egg clears. Sprinkle with paprika to taste. Refrigerate until serving.

Diners should be advised that consumption of Deviled Berundi Slug Eggs does not violate Consolidated Federation laws regarding mind-altering substances, but will produce a mild euphoria.

ENTREE

Berundi Cucumber Cordon Bleu

Ingredients

1 skinless, de-spiked Berundi Cucumber
1/4 teaspoon salt
1/8 teaspoon ground black pepper
6 slices Berundi Tiger Larva
4 slices cooked imported Earth Pig Ham
1/2 cup seasoned breadcrumbs

Directions:

During daylight hours, use a stunner to shoot down a Berundi cucumber. (Take extra care that its trajectory will not bring it down on top of you, as with enough momentum the spikes can pierce an envirosuit.) Finding a cucumber at night will do you no good, as hibernation ruins the flavor. Refrigerate at least 12 hours in a sealed metal container, after which the spikes will be loose enough to be plucked.

Approach a Berundi tiger at least thirty-six hours after local sundown, to ensure all local wildlife is in hibernation. Pluck a larva from behind one of its ears.

Preheat oven to 350 degrees F (175 degrees C). Coat a 7x11 inch baking dish with nonstick cooking spray.

Slice cucumber into quarters. Pound to 1/4-inch thickness.

Cut off the ends of the larva and thinly slice the rest. Keep the slices separated by at least an inch or they will try to rejoin.

Sprinkle each piece of cucumber on both sides with salt and pepper. Place 1 larva slice and .1 ham slice on top of each cucumber piece. Roll up each piece, and secure with a toothpick. Place in baking dish, and sprinkle cucumber evenly with breadcrumbs.

Bake for 30 to 35 minutes, or until cucumber is no longer green. Remove from oven, and place 1/2 larva slice on top of each piece. Return to oven for 3 to 5 minutes, or until larva has melted. Remove toothpicks, and serve immediately.

Diners should be advised that consumption of Berundi Cucumber Cordon Bleu does not violate Consolidated Federation laws regarding mind-altering substances, but they should feel relaxed and uninhibited after eating.

Dessert

Berundi Elephant Mousse

Ingredients

1 Berundi Elephant Dropping
Whipped Earth Cow's Cream

Directions

The Berundi Elephant is classified as sentient, so eating them is against Consolidated Federation law. However, eating their dung is not prohibited, and local elephants will provide all the droppings needed.

Thaw one Berundi elephant dropping in the microwave.

Blend dropping at high speed until it is smooth and a consistent orange color.

Pour into individual serving dishes and chill for at least 15 minutes.

Top with whipped cream just before serving.

After eating, wait for hypnoparalysis to affect diners. Generic anti-toxin nanocaps will be useless, and no specific anti-toxin nanocap exists.

Implant the suggestion that after the drug wears off and they return home, they recommend the cuisine on Berundi to all highly placed and influential humans.

Explain that the Berundi elephants will make wise and benevolent rulers, but that they cannot extend their leadership to the Consolidated Federation until enough humans are ready to serve them.

ABOUT THE STORY

This was a Codex Weekend Warrior Contest story from 2010. The prompt was "Write about an alien feast. Include at least one gruesome dish."

Since flash fiction is a great way to play around with unusual story formats, I decided to do a story in the form of recipes. And, of course, the prompt reminded me of ...

(Wait, do I need to put in a SPOILER ALERT for a story published over sixty years ago? Just in case, consider yourself alerted.)

... the classic Damon Knight short story "To Serve Man," the basis for the eponymous *Twilight Zone* episode and one of my favorite Treehouse of Horror episodes of *The Simpsons*.

When I began writing the recipes, I didn't have a clear idea of the story. But eventually things clicked, and I realized that the title was meant to lull readers into thinking the story was merely an homage to "To Serve Man," when in fact it would end with a reversal of the wordplay.

A LINCOLN IN TIME

Booth raised his derringer, but it was too late—Lincoln had seen him coming. With an agility that belied his gangly frame, Lincoln sprang from his box seat, turning as he rose, and in one smooth motion drew the Smith & Wesson revolver and fired a bullet into Booth's right eye.

I shook my head. The patrons of Ford's Theatre began their usual panic at the gunshot. Ignoring them, I made my way to the box. Lincoln was comforting his wife as I stepped through the curtain. His hand moved for his gun until he recognized me.

"We need to talk, Mr. President," I said, stepping over Booth's body.

He nodded, so I activated the extemp field. The noise of the crowd vanished as they froze in place. I extended the field to include Lincoln.

"I must admit to being surprised by the accuracy of my shot," he said. "Not that I was aiming for his eye, but I thought my moving might make me miss him entirely."

"You've been practicing that for a while, haven't you?"

He shrugged those long arms. "After you told me, I just felt like I deserved a chance to defend myself."

Frustration welled up inside me. "I asked for your help because it's what *has* to happen."

"Why?" Lincoln held his hand up to stall my reply. "I know that's what happened in the past of your future." He frowned. "I confuse myself just thinking about how that makes sense. But if my death really is destined to come now, why has Booth failed every time—even when I don't shoot him?"

I clenched my fists. "My entire world will never exist unless I fix the timeline. Billions of lives are at stake—I thought you understood that."

"It's one thing to understand at the intellectual level, another to feel it in the heart," Lincoln said. "'The spirit is willing, but the flesh is weak.' You're asking me to die for people who are an abstraction to me at best."

"Abstraction? I have a wife, a son. They aren't abstractions." I wished Temporal Services regulations had allowed me to bring back even a small photo of them. "Their names are Desiree and Danny, and unless you help me, I will never see them again. Do you know how that feels?"

Lincoln's face darkened. "My wife and I have lost two sons. And now you want me to make my wife a widow?"

In my desperation, I had pressed him too far. I withdrew the field and Lincoln froze.

After my first five attempts at repairing the timeline had failed, I had come up with the idea of getting Lincoln's coopera-tion. At least it ensured that he would get to Ford's Theatre without his bodyguard—that had happened only once in the first five times, and it had ended with Booth failing to show up. Assuming I ever repaired the timeline and got back to my own future, I'd have a blockbuster paper to write on just how unlikely Lincoln's assassination was.

This time Lincoln had given his bodyguard the night off, and I'd managed to get Booth to the theatre with a derringer rather than the bulky pistol he sometimes chose. And then Lincoln had to go and pull a stunt like this. He might understand the idea of repairing the timeline, but it was asking too much that he go like a lamb to the slaughter. There was no point in taking him back to try again.

I needed a new approach. I set my destination to two months back and jumped.

✷

Dr. Samuel Mudd shook his head gravely. "It could be consumption."

It wasn't. Since coming back, I'd heard enough people with tubercular coughs that I could fake one pretty well. But the act gave me an excuse to see Mudd—Booth's co-conspirator.

"Actually, Doctor, I am here on another matter." I gave him what I hoped was a meaningful look. "Concerning the President."

Mudd's eyes flickered. "I don't—"

The door crashed open, and a well-dressed man strode in, ignoring Mudd's assistant, who was telling him the doctor was with a patient. The man looked familiar, but I couldn't place him.

He looked at me and said, "I beg your pardon, but I have an urgent matter to discuss with the good doctor. In private."

"Who are you?" Mudd asked. He seemed genuinely puzzled. "You can't just bull your way in and demand to see me."

"It's fine," I said. "We can continue our discussion later." I rose from sitting on the examination table and stepped out of the office, closing the door behind me.

I activated the extemp field and moved through the wall back into Mudd's office. I then withdrew all but an observation portal from contact with the timestream and started moving forward in real-time.

The stranger assured himself that I had left the room, then turned back to Mudd. "I know you're part of the plot to kidnap Lincoln. Don't bother to deny it."

Mudd turned and walked to his chair with slow, even steps. He sat. "Who told you such a thing?" His voice trembled slightly.

"Dr. Mudd, you are a man of science," said the stranger. "You have seen the progress science has made in the two centuries since Newton. Surely you believe that science will continue to progress—that the future holds marvels as yet undiscovered."

Mudd nodded.

The stranger leaned forward, resting both hands on Mudd's desk. "This may seem incredible to you, but it is true: there will come a time when men voyage from the future to the past more easily than you can sail to Europe. Unfortunately, such voyagers can change the course of history."

I stopped the timeflow. How did the stranger know about me? Suddenly I remembered where I had seen him before: in the box next to Lincoln's at Ford's Theatre. Was it possible he had accidentally been included in the extemp field? It shouldn't happen—the field is under my direct neural control—but then again, the field shouldn't have collapsed the way it did, forcing me into the timestream and changing history.

I started forward again.

"You're mad," said Mudd.

"Am I? Have you ever seen a photograph like this?" The stranger pulled a device from his coat and projected a holographic family portrait of himself, a woman and two young boys.

I stopped the timeflow to give myself a chance to think. The time machine implanted in my skull was supposed to automatically exclude other time machines from attaching to the timestream while I was here. If the stranger was a time traveler, obviously my time machine was malfunctioning even more severely than I had thought.

I shook my head. Had the stranger come back to save

Lincoln? Perhaps his interference was derailing my attempts to restore the timeline.

We had to talk, and I didn't want to bother with the rest of his conversation with Mudd. I extended the extemp field to cover the stranger.

When he saw Mudd freeze, the stranger turned his head until he spotted me.

"Hello," I said.

"You! You're the time voyager?"

"I'm from 2367," I said. "What about you?"

"That's impos … No, I guess it isn't." He rubbed a palm against his forehead. "This is worse than I thought. In my history, the timeship was not invented until 2401. I come from 2410."

I felt a chill. Other than my inability to return home, this was the first real evidence I had that my damage to the timeline had extended all the way forward to 2367. Minor changes have a way of cancelling themselves out over the long haul, but Lincoln's survival was not a minor change.

"Time travel was invented almost a hundred years earlier in my timeline," I said. The historian in me couldn't help adding, "I wonder why Lincoln's assassination accelerated the development of temporal physics."

He pointed an accusing finger at me. "So you *are* trying to kill Lincoln!"

"I don't want to! But it's the only way to restore the timeline to its original state."

The stranger reached into a pocket and pulled out a gun. It was made of a blue, translucent substance, and the barrel had no hole in it, but it was a gun all right.

"Take me to your timeship," he said.

I withdrew the extemp field from him, except for his hand. He froze. I walked over, pried the gun from his grip, and stepped back. He was lucky I didn't want to hurt him—a brief period without circulation would not damage his hand, but if I had taken the gun away with his hand outside the field, his fingers would have been broken or possibly sheared off.

I re-extended the extemp field.

He blinked, then looked at his empty hand.

I waggled the gun at him. "Don't be dumb like that again."

He sat down on the floor, put his head in his hands, and began to cry.

"I'm sorry," I said, "But I have to restore the original timeline." During training, that was the first thing they drilled into us: No matter what, restore the original timeline.

"It's all my fault," he said. "I didn't think it would do any harm."

Maybe the history change wasn't my fault after all. "What did you do?"

He sniffled. "I posed as a newspaper theater critic and interviewed John Wilkes Booth."

I raised my eyebrows. "You intentionally entered the timeline and interacted with a major player?" Of course, I had done that myself, but only in an attempt to fix the timeline after it was broken.

"I didn't know he was that important. You have to understand: it was for my *thesis*."

Remembering my grad school days, I could almost sympathize. Almost. "How could you not know that Lincoln's assassin was a major player?"

"That's just it: he wasn't. He only had a minor role in the kidnapping. I changed things so he *killed* Lincoln."

I dropped him out of the field. I needed time to think.

If it occurred to someone at Temporal Services that our timeline was the result of a changed history, they never mentioned it to me. I always thought of my timeline as the "real" one, and considered timelines resulting from changes as merely distorted shadows of reality. That's why minor changes always tended to cancel themselves out—they were being drawn into sync with the "real" timeline.

No matter what, restore the original timeline.

I'm sure they probably meant "restore *our* timeline." Restore the lives of twenty-three billion people on fourteen planets in ten star systems. Restore my wife, Desiree, and my boy, Danny.

That was how I justified helping John Wilkes Booth kill Lincoln. Putting history back the way it was did not make me responsible for what happened in that history.

But now?

If Lincoln was not killed in the original timeline, could I justify killing him to implement my distorted shadow of reality?

If so, was I any different from John Wilkes Booth?

The stranger's name was Orville. He didn't resist when I told him to take me to his "timeship." Either my demonstration of superior technology had cowed him, or he was just waiting for the right time to attack me.

"It doesn't look much like a ship," I said. We stood in the warehouse space Orville had rented. The contraption looked more like an elevator without a shaft.

Orville pressed a button, and the door slid open. "The name's from a 19th-Century novel: *The Timeship*, by George Wells."

I chuckled. "*The Time Machine*, by H. G. Wells. Funny how the fate of Lincoln would affect that."

Orville dashed through the door and began punching some buttons, obviously hoping to timejump away. I activated my field and everything froze. I sighed. All I had to do was jump back, kill Orville, and then restore my timeline. Without his interference, I should be able to make sure Lincoln's assassination took place.

But I didn't want to kill Orville. Restoring the timeline was different from just plain murder.

I extended the field to include Orville, who continued punching at buttons until he realized he was no longer able to affect them. His body sagged as he turned to look at me.

I shook my head. "How many humans are there in your time?"

"Eight billion," he said. "Yours?"

"Did you have a nuclear war or something?" Only eight billion? "We have twenty-three billion."

"Impossible. Earth can't support that many people."

"Earth only has five billion. The rest are on other planets in other star systems."

Orville was silent for a long moment. "You're trying to convince me your future is better than mine."

Nodding, I said, "Our tech obviously advanced more quickly than yours."

"Obviously." Orville studied my face. "You're being honest with me."

"Yes."

"You mentioned a 'nuclear war.' Has your timeline ever had one?"

I winced. "Two: the Sino-Russian War and the final Arab-Israeli war. Well, three, if you count the end of World War II." I didn't mention the terrorist nukes because they weren't exactly wars.

His eyes went wide. "Your entire world was at war? Twice? With another planet?"

"No, with ourselves. Maybe you just had the first one? The Great War, in Europe around 1914?"

He looked at me like I was nuts. "There were tensions in Europe at the time, inflamed by the kidnapping of an archduke, if I recall correctly. But the British smoothed things over. And the Pax Britannica was followed by the Pax Americana and the Pax Abrahamica."

"Abrahamica?"

"Jews facing persecution in Europe during the mid-20th Century fled to the Islamic world." He frowned. "You mentioned an Arab-Israeli war?"

"Several."

Orville shook his head. "The Nation of Abraham was a joint Islamic/Jewish state. They controlled most of the world's oil supply. Anyway, during the age of the supernations, any nation attacking another found itself immediately at war with the major powers, not to mention cut off from all trade. Then the World Democracy was established in 2076, and even civil wars were outlawed. We haven't had a war in 300 years. How long has it been for you?"

"There are a couple going on right now," I answered reluctantly. "Nothing major, but ... Well, that explains why we're more advanced than you. War accelerates development."

He cocked an eyebrow. "Your technology is more advanced, yes. Your society? I don't think so."

No Holocaust. No Nuclear Jihad. No Sino-Russian War. No *war*, period. If I restored my timeline, all those horrors and more would be my choice. My responsibility.

But if I didn't, the lives of twenty-three billion people, including my wife and son, would be wiped out.

Over 750 million people were killed in the Sino-Russian War. Even if I chose to save my twenty-three billion, I would be responsible for ending ten times as many lives as the deadliest event in human history.

The pressure of such a choice was too much for me. This was the kind of thing my superiors were supposed to decide—but my superiors did not currently exist.

When the answer popped into my mind, I was overwhelmed with relief.

✦

Orville's brow wrinkled. "Tell Lincoln?"

"Why not? We give him the details about our timelines, and then let him choose which one he thinks is the best future. I'll agree to abide by his decision if you will."

Orville rubbed his lips as he thought about it. "How do I know I can trust you?"

"If I didn't mean it, I could easily just kill you and restore my timeline."

"Good point." He nodded slowly. "I agree."

"But in order for it to be fair," I said, "we won't let Lincoln know which future is the one that results from his assassination. He must decide based on the good of humanity, not his personal future."

Lincoln sat at a battered mahogany writing desk, reading the reports we had prepared for him. Beyond him, the window looked out to the unfinished Washington monument and the gray waters of the Potomac.

Orville and I sat at a table stacked with books and maps. I was too nervous to bother looking at them, but Orville was reading a rather thick volume he'd picked up.

"If only I could have lived to see such times," said Lincoln. He put down the reports and rubbed his eyes. "What marvels await mankind!"

"You've decided already?" said Orville. He shot me a suspicious look.

No doubt Orville had thought his timeline's peacefulness would make it the obvious choice. But I knew Lincoln had a fondness for inventions—and he was a President who understood that wars sometimes had to be fought. I honestly had no idea which future he would choose—I just knew it was a far more difficult choice than Orville imagined.

"No." Lincoln shook his head. "This is far too momentous a

decision to be made so quickly." He looked at me. "What would you do if I told you I can't decide?"

"Mr. President, *someone* must decide." I shook my head. "I can't do it—I have a personal stake in the outcome."

Lincoln flashed a smile tinged with sadness. "So do I. I may not know which choice leads to my untimely death, but that's a very real stake." He stood up. "Gentlemen, I will think on this tonight. Come back tomorrow."

✪

Orville and I didn't even leave the office. I skipped us forward to the next morning and brought us back into the timeline when Lincoln was sitting alone in his office.

"Have you decided?" asked Orville.

Lincoln turned to face us. "If I choose one future, I will be killed. If I choose the other, I will be kidnapped. What about the future in which neither happens? Where is the time traveler from that future?"

"There isn't one," I said. "My time machine excludes them from entering the timeline. Orville's only here because he arrived before I did."

"'Before' seems a strange concept when one can hop around time at will," Lincoln said. "But why should I choose either of your futures, rather than taking a chance on a new one?"

"You can't do—" said Orville.

I raised my voice to override him. "Because with our futures you can be certain humanity lasts for at least the next 500 years. With an unknown future, humanity could very well destroy itself in that time. You saw the possibilities in the reports: nuclear weapons, man-made diseases."

After a moment's thought, Lincoln said, "I see the logic in that."

"There are only two choices," I said. "My future, or his."

Lincoln smiled. "Perhaps." He looked at Orville. "If you

thought only of the good of your own future, not his, what would you do?"

"I would change events so my future existed, of course."

Lincoln turned to me. "And if he did that, what would you do?"

I shrugged. "Go back and change things so my future came about. That's what I was trying to do before I met him."

He turned back to Orville. "Then what?"

"I'd try to change what he did to get my future back."

Lincoln nodded. "That's what I thought. It is my solution to your problem. Your timelines will alternate. You will work together so I am killed one time and kidnapped the next."

"But mine is the original!" said Orville.

"That doesn't matter," said Lincoln. "I'm trying to find a way for each of your timelines to exist."

"It can't work," said Orville. "Only one timeline is realized."

"The timelines would not be realized *simultaneously*," I said as I worked through the implications. "But each one would be realized in turn. The fact that we're both here proves that multiple timelines can be realized sequentially."

Orville frowned and rubbed the back of his neck.

I suddenly felt enthusiastic. "It's complicated, but if we cooperate, we can make it work. We could actually set up trade between our timelines—information, technology, entertainment. We go forward, bring back what we want to trade, then change to the other timeline and go forward again."

"And then what?" asked Orville. "Spend the rest of our lives here, alternating between timelines? What happens when one of us eventually dies?"

I shook my head. "You don't get it. Once we restore access to our own futures, we can bring others back to help. We could set up a joint permanent base here, with staff coming in on rotation. There's no reason the alternation can't continue indefinitely. And the two of us can go back to our lives in our own times."

Slowly, Orville nodded. "But my timeline gets restored first."

"Fine with me," I said. "I'll even help you do it." I turned to Lincoln. "Thank you, Mr. President. Not just from me, but from billions in the future."

"News of my death or kidnapping will bring joy to my enemies." Lincoln smiled. "At least now it has a greater meaning than vengeance for a lost war."

○

The kidnapping of Abraham Lincoln went off without a hitch, and Orville traveled into the future to make sure his timeline was restored. Untrusting as he was, he actually returned before he left, just to make sure I didn't try to change things while he was gone.

With Orville's cooperation, I managed to get Lincoln to the theater without his bodyguard, and Booth to the theater with his derringer. Orville and I took our places in the audience and waited for the assassination.

It was as Booth raised his derringer behind Lincoln's head that I realized I couldn't let Lincoln die. After everything the man had done—not just for the world, not just for the United States, but for me—he deserved better than this.

Booth fired.

I froze time and made my way to Lincoln's box. The bullet had already entered Lincoln's skull. I extended the extemp field to include him, and he slumped over in his rocking chair, unconscious.

Quickly, I pulled him out of the chair. Then I jumped a half-second back in time, taking the dying Lincoln with me.

The bullet hung in the air about three inches from the back of Lincoln's head. I extended the extemp field to include the living Lincoln.

"What—" He turned his head and spotted first me, then the body on the floor. "What's happening? The assassination is—"

"Just help me get this body into your seat," I said. "Hurry."

Lincoln sprang from his box seat, and between the two of us we managed to prop the unconscious Lincoln into the seat.

I withdrew the extemp field from the body and it froze in place.

"My dying self from the future, I take it," said Lincoln.

"That's right, Mr. President." I reached out and pulled the bullet from the air. The transition into the extemp field bled its kinetic energy harmlessly away. "A souvenir for you," I said, handing it to him.

"What now?" he asked. His eyes brightened. "Will you take me to see the marvels of your future?"

I hadn't really thought about what I was going to do beyond saving Lincoln's life. As it was, the timeline alternation plan would get me in profound trouble with my superiors at Temporal Services. Bringing them a living Lincoln could not make things much worse.

He might even convince them I had made the right decision.

"Yes, we're going to my future," I said. "But we have a stop to make first."

The spring sun shone brightly in Lexington, Kentucky, that morning. In the garden behind the house, a brown-haired boy walked along the red brick path, carefully avoiding the cracks.

"It's Eddie," said Lincoln. "Can I talk to him?"

"It's why I brought you here and now," I said. "He's alone for the next few minutes. You're in Washington, so even if he says he saw you, it will be dismissed as the fancies of a two-year-old."

I released Lincoln from the extemp field.

"Papá!" said the boy.

I watched as Lincoln hugged the son who had been dead to him for fifteen years.

ABOUT THE STORY

I wrote this story in 2006 for the first Codexian Idol contest.

The contest ran in three rounds. The first round involved submitting the first 500 words of a story to be judged. Only the top eight stories moved on to round two, submitting the next 500-1000 words. And only the top four from round two made it to round three, submitting the complete story.

Because the contest was being held in February, it needed to relate in some way to a February holiday. I chose Presidents' Day.

The first 500 words needed to include an act of consumption. As is my wont, I twisted the prompt: the narrator acts like he has tuberculosis (a.k.a. consumption) as an excuse to see Dr. Mudd.

After the first round, my story was in first place in the voting.

After the second round, my story was in first place.

At the conclusion of the final round, my story was in second place. First place went to James Maxey's story, and it well deserved the win. (It was published in *Orson Scott Card's InterGalactic Medicine Show* as "To Know All Things That Are in the Earth," and if you haven't read it, I recommend you do so posthaste.)

Despite the story doing well in the contest, I knew it needed a significant amount of work. I revised it, submitted it, got rejected, revised and submitted some more. On its fifteenth submission, it found a home.

DARK ROADS FOR THE ETERNAL RULER

Your Imperial Majesty,

Humble though my current condition is, I am proud to write those words to you, for today they are true. The day of your coronation is joyous for the Empire. Most of your subjects believe that you are the prophesied Bringer of Perfect Justice whose reign will be eternal in fact, not just name. Gods grant it be so, if they will still hear the prayer of this your servant.

Servant? Yes, even imprisoned, I still serve you. For if I—whom everyone knows to be your right hand, your voice, your beloved – if I am not spared from your justice, no one will be. But it pains me that I, your first and most loyal follower, was not able to see you crowned, though I heard the cheers from my cell. I had hoped to stand beside you as Imperial Sorceress (and perhaps more), but I am glad that my condemnation has proven that your justice knows no favorites.

Who could doubt it? Yet there are still some who do. They will seize any opportunity to turn the people against you. And, as you said when you sentenced me: If the people do not believe in your justice, it would not be just to rule them. Fortunately, the crimes of which I have been convicted occurred before I met you, and thus your enemies cannot use them against you.

Was that truly but fortune? Alas, no.

Your sentence is just, but did you not think it strange that my offenses, ten years past, only recently came to the memories of my accusers? Did you not think it strange that I stand unaccused of more recent crimes? Perhaps not. In the goodness of your heart, perhaps you counted my offenses as youthful folly, and attributed the revived memories to my new-found fame as your right hand.

Right and left, both my hands were yours. And more than that: my eyes, my ears, my lips, my heart. But oh, that I were worthy of such good thoughts!

Hand to my heart, the truth is that the accusations are but beginning. Many will be true, for many are those I defrauded before I met you. And for each, I wrote a spell to make them forget what I had done, activating the spells with the town magistrate's seal I stole from my father. But alas, the term of a magistrate is only ten years, and thus the spells expire in their time. I walked in dark roads all my life until I met you, who walks only in the light.

Shall I tell you that, from the day we met, I walked only in the light? But that would be a lie. I did change that day – I had committed many crimes to benefit myself before we met, and I never did so again.

Not to say I never committed any more crimes, only that they were for your benefit. One who walks only in the light could never achieve the imperial throne – unless someone walked the dark roads for him. Did you think it simply good fortune that so many of your possible opponents removed themselves from contention for the throne? I blackmailed, extorted, and bribed where I could, and killed when I had to. But nobody will remember those crimes until four years hence.

Be that as it may, your enemies will use my crimes against you, for I was your right hand: what I did, I did in your name. And if the people turn against you, you will step down even though your eternal rule is what is best for them. Because of me. Is that how I will be remembered?

Remembered as the one who destroyed you?

By my life, I would not have it be so.

Your subjects' benefit is all I have in mind, not mine. To prove this, I write this letter with my life's blood. I shall be dead by the time this reaches you by way of our trusted friend. I hope you will forgive that I have given myself justice at my hand, not yours, and that you will sometimes recall me with fondness.

People will accept your justice as long as they believe in you. Therefore I give you a final gift, my beloved, though I am uncertain you will use it. The first word of each paragraph is part of a spell. To activate it, you must only read those words aloud and stamp this letter with the seal of the Eternal Ruler, and the spell will last forever. For the people's good, I beg you to walk just this once down a dark road. I know your conscience will torture you if you do. Find justice in that.

ABOUT THE STORY

This was another Codex Weekend Warrior Contest story, from 2012. During the week before I wrote it, the Christmas present my then girlfriend had ordered for me finally arrived from China. It was a stamp of my name in both English and Chinese.

Rather than use the phonetic transliteration of my name for the Chinese characters, my girlfriend decided to use the translation of the meaning of "Eric": eternal ruler.

One of the story prompts for the week was: "Write a story about a magic user (wizard, sorceress, etc.). Set the story in another country which is primarily non-English speaking and is not a place where you currently live (e.g. France, Thailand, etc.)."

Thanks to the gift, I immediately thought of using stamp-based magic in China (although I later altered it to being just a somewhat China-like imaginary country).

Another prompt that week was: "Write about a happy event with an unpleasant surprise." That gave me the idea of the coronation of a new emperor as the happy event.

So that explains where the "Eternal Ruler" bit came from. What about "Dark Roads"? Where did that idea come from? I have no clue—it must just have been something in my subconscious. But I definitely need to thank that former girlfriend, Darci Rhoades, for inspiring this story. (Subsequent to the writing of this story, she became my former girlfriend by progressing to fiancée and from there to wife.)

INTO THE WEST

According to Jorge, sometime after we pass through Denver the California Zephyr will run out of diesel. Jorge's already decided that when the train stops, he will, too—like a captain going down with the ship. He's got a wife and a passel of kids back in Chicago who he'll probably never see again, so I guess I understand.

Me, I plan to keep heading west with as many of the other passengers as care to go. Just keep on going till we drop dead of exhaustion or hit the Pacific or the darkness catches us.

We don't know for a fact that anyone back east is dead. Or alive, either. Some of the passengers just sit up in the dome car and watch the landscape behind us stretch like salt-water taffy as it reddens and finally fades into the blackness that follows us. Others are so freaked out they just sit in the dining car finishing off the liquor, free of charge. The rest of us sit in our regular seats, like everything's normal.

"Those scientists at CERN overdid it," says Varney. His tee-shirt's a couple of Xs too small, but people listen to him because he's loud and confident. "They probably created the black hole."

I've already told him you don't escape a world-devouring

black hole on Amtrak, but he's fixated on the idea because it's something he understands.

Me, I'm fixated on what I don't understand: when we pass through a town, everyone we see is frozen in place.

"Gravitationally induced time dilation" is Varney's answer. Makes no sense, 'cause we're just as close to the event horizon, so our time would be dilated, too.

A spindly woman with wiry red hair and librarian glasses sits down in the seat opposite me. "You think he's full of it."

I shake my head. "Not 'think.' I know he is."

"So, what's your theory?" Her voice is casual, like she's asking about tomorrow's weather, not the end of the world.

I shrug. "I thought the speed of light had slowed to 50 miles an hour or so. Fit with the red-shift out back and the time dilation as we passed things at a high fraction of the speed of light. Was a pleasant theory."

"Pleasant?" she asks.

"It would mean the rest of the world was still there behind us, if it was true. But it's not."

"Why not?"

"There's no blue shift ahead of us."

She nods as if she understands. Maybe she does—she's smart enough to know Varney's wrong. She extends her right hand. "Dawn Rigby."

We shake hands as I say, "Carmichael Paxon. Friends call me Carpy."

"So what's your new theory, Carpy?"

"Don't have one that fits the data," I say. "Have a plan that fits the data, though: keep heading west, away from whatever's going on back there." I jerk a thumb over my shoulder.

Her eyes flicker to the window, then widen. I turn and see a dusty red pickup speeding along the highway running parallel to the tracks on our left. A man leans half out of the passenger side, waving a battered cowboy hat as if to flag us down. He's yelling something, but I can't hear him through the glass.

"So the rest of the world isn't frozen," says Dawn.

Some of Varney's audience notice the pickup, too, and pretty soon they're all at the windows, gawking at two men in a pickup like they're a couple of movie stars.

"We've got to stop for them," says Dawn.

Varney snorts. "You're crazy. The black hole will get us if we stop."

A murmur of agreement ripples through the other passengers.

I decide I've had enough, so I stand. "Look, folks, I don't know what that is back there, but it is definitely not a black hole."

"Why should they believe you and not me?" asks Varney, jutting his chin toward me. He's got three inches on me in height and he's close to double my weight, but most of that is fat. He can't really be looking for a fight—he's probably just as scared as any of us.

So I play the authority card. "Because I used to be a Marine Corps astronaut with the Shuttle program, that's why. I've forgotten more about space than you've ever learned, and I tell you, that's no black hole."

What I don't tell him is that I washed out of the space program. Kinda tough being an astronaut after you develop an irrational aversion to flying.

He stares at me for a moment, then heaves his shoulders in a massive shrug. "So it's not a black hole. Whatever it is, it's coming up behind us and we can't afford to stop."

"You don't know that," says Dawn. "We slowed down going through that town in Nebraska, and it didn't catch us."

Before Varney can respond, I say, "In the Marines, they taught me never leave a man behind." I jab a finger toward the pickup. "If they need a ride to escape what's coming, we'll give it to them. We clear?"

Varney swallows, then nods his head.

Jorge agrees to slow the train. I still can't hear the men in the pickup over the clatter of the train wheels, but I think I convey the plan to them well enough through gestures. They speed on ahead of us. Jorge says they should find a crossing in a few miles, and we'll have slowed down enough by then that they can climb aboard.

Dawn meets me before I get back to the rest of the passengers.

"Thank you," she says.

"Getting people focused on rescuing someone else was a good idea," I say. "Keeps them from panicking."

Her glasses have slid down her nose a bit, and she pushes them back up. "I didn't suggest it to keep people from panicking —those men were in trouble and I wanted to help."

"There's that, too," I say, and I feel like I'm talking to Miriam again. She was always going out of her way to help people, right up to the end. After the plane crash, she helped me to safety, and then went back to get someone else. I was too concussed to stop her.

Not wanting to think about Miriam anymore, I push past Dawn and say over my shoulder, "We need to get people to open doors all along the train, just in case those guys miss the first one."

From my post at the last door on the train, I look back at the blackness to the east. Jorge's slowed the train down to about five miles an hour, but it seems the darkness has slowed as well. If anything, it looks farther behind us than it used to be.

A shout from the front of the train turns my attention forward. I spot the red pickup: they've turned off the highway onto a road that crosses the railway. For some reason, though, they're just sitting in the cab, still a good thirty yards away from the tracks. A cloud of dust kicked up by their tires still hangs in the air behind them, and it looks wrong.

Ahead of me on the train, people start calling out to the men, but I realize it won't do any good. We pass by the men, who are frozen in place.

"How terrible," says Dawn, as I meet up with her near the middle of the train. "They were so close to being safe with us."

"Safe is a relative term," I say.

She smiles. "You sure know how to comfort a lady. But I'm pretty sure the darkness is slowing, so I'm hopeful we'll outrun it and find a safe place."

I'm only half paying attention to her words, because the word relative is sparking connections in my brain. I had already discarded the idea of time dilation due to relativity, but relative motion did seem to matter.

Varney stands up from his seat. "It was a good try, man," he says. "Not your fault they froze."

"They weren't frozen when they were cruising down the highway parallel to us," I say, mostly to hear myself think. "But when they turned off the highway—"

The metal-on-metal screech of the brakes sounds again, and I realize Jorge is still slowing us, maybe even planning to stop.

"No!" I yell. I squeeze between a surprised Dawn and a protesting Varney, and sprint forward through the train cars. "Jorge, don't stop the train!"

I keep repeating that at the top of my lungs as I pass by the other passengers. Some are a little too slow to move out of my way and I shove them aside, not caring if I cause a few bruises on the way. I've got to get to the engine before we stop completely. No matter what, Jorge has to keep us going.

Because if I'm right, the moment we stop moving west it's all over.

I reach the engine compartment. "Keep going!"

Jorge looks back at me over his shoulder. "But those guys—"

"We can't help them," I say. "If we stop, we'll end up frozen like them."

After a moment's hesitation, he nods. "How fast should I go?"

"Whatever's most fuel efficient," I say. "Whatever keeps us going the longest."

About thirty passengers care enough to gather in one of the cars to listen to my theory.

"The pickup truck was doing just fine as it cruised along the highway," I say. "But when it turned onto the road to cross the tracks, it froze. And that made me wonder what was different between the highway and the road."

"Speed," says Varney. "They dropped below some critical threshold and that caused them to freeze."

"It's like that movie with the bus," says a passenger near the back of the car.

"*Speed*," says Varney.

"No," I say, "It's not speed. It—"

"Yes, it was," says Varney. "Sandra Bullock and Keanu—"

"I mean it's not *speed* that's important. It's direction." I point toward the front of the train. "As long as we're moving west, we're okay. The truck turned north when it got off the highway, so it wasn't moving west anymore. That's why it froze."

"I'm not saying you're wrong," says Dawn, "but why should it make any difference which direction we're going?"

"I think we can all agree that something's gone wrong with the physics we're used to." Nobody objects, so I continue. "And everybody's probably heard about time being another dimension. Well, the simplified explanation for what I think's happened is that the time dimension has lined up with a space dimension." I point to the rear of the train. "That's the past ..." I swing my arm toward the front of the train again. "... and that is the future. To keep moving through time, we have to keep moving west."

I hope that Varney won't argue with the simplified explanation, but he doesn't fail to disappoint.

"Why would going west—" he says.

"Look, I'll be happy to discuss the more technical aspects with anyone who wants," I say. "The point is as long as we're moving west, we're safe."

"What happens when the train runs out of fuel?" asks Dawn.

"We've got several hours before we'll have to cross that bridge," I say. "Till then, we just have to hope this wrinkle straightens itself out first."

Satisfied there's no immediate danger, most of the passengers disperse. Dawn and a handful of others stick around to hear me discuss General Relativity with Varney, and how Earth's rotation is dragging the partially collapsed local spacetime in an eastward direction, and how only by resisting that drag are we able to move through time.

"We've got a serious problem," says Varney quietly as he slides into the seat next to me.

"I know that," I say. We've evacuated all the passengers into the front two cars and disconnected the rest, although there was some grumbling about lost luggage. Jorge thinks we've dumped enough weight to get us to Salt Lake City without refueling. Once we get there, though, the problem is how to get fuel into the train without stopping. I haven't even started thinking about what happens when we run out of track.

"We can't get over the mountains," says Varney.

"I'm sure Jorge factored the mountains into his fuel calcul—" I say.

"No," says Varney, and he holds out a portable GPS mapping unit. "I've been looking at our route on this, and there are times when the track turns north, even a little bit east, as it goes through the mountains. When that happens, game over."

I take a moment to ponder the implications. "So we abandon the train, steal some cars, and find another route over the mountains."

Varney gives me a sour look. "Just because I was wrong about the black hole doesn't mean I'm stupid. I've checked the major roads. All of them wind around the wrong way at some point. And even in a Jeep, you can't just four-wheel across the Rockies."

I slump back. "So there's no way out."

"What do you mean?" Varney frowns at me. "Marine Corps astronaut—doesn't that mean you were a test pilot? Let's grab a plane and fly!"

"I …" My stomach knots at the thought of flying, particularly over the same mountains where I'd crashed. I wrench my thoughts away from Miriam and say, "I was a pilot, yes. And you're right, it's our only option."

Near Fort Morgan, Jorge slows the train so we can hop off. Only twenty-one of us are brave enough to do so. The rest will continue on the train and hope for a miracle.

Even though Denver International Airport is about fifty miles southwest of us, as long as we have some westward motion, we'll keep moving forward in time. But while the fittest of us might somehow manage to walk the whole way without stopping, some—like Varney—definitely will not. We need to steal some vehicles.

Even with everyone eerily frozen around us, stealing a car is not simple. Unoccupied cars generally don't have keys in them, and none of us knows how to hotwire. Since we can't stop moving west, even for a moment, that rules out all cars not facing west. If a car were moving west, though, it would keep moving through time, which means we only have access to cars that are stopped, which means they're either parked or their brakes are on—neither of which is helpful if you need to keep moving.

We end up stealing tractors instead of cars, because we find them in fields with the keys still in them. With a large group, pushing a small tractor to get it moving through time isn't all that hard. Once it's moving, the engine will start.

Eventually we have six tractors, led by one with a bulldozer blade, trundling across Colorado farmland.

Dawn is squeezed on the tractor seat beside me. I haven't been this close to a woman since Miriam died. She's staring up at the sky and I admire the smoothness of her neck. I yank my gaze away as she looks at me.

"There's something bothering you," she says. "Something you haven't told us."

"What makes you say that?" I ask.

"You tense up anytime someone mentions the plane."

Miriam had been annoyingly perceptive, too. "Stealing a plane that can carry all of us won't be as easy as stealing a tractor."

"Uh-huh," Dawn says. After moment, she adds, "Are you really a pilot?"

I let out a long breath. "Used to be. Last time I flew was three years ago, just me and my wife and some friends in a small plane, coming back from Vegas. The engine died, so I crash-landed our plane on a snow-covered slope in the Rockies. I was injured. My wife pulled me out of the plane and then went back inside for someone else. The plane slid down and off a cliff. They couldn't get to the bodies until spring. Since then, I haven't had the nerve to fly. Any more questions?"

I've found that being cold and blunt about what happened usually makes people shut up or change the subject. Dawn looks at me for a moment, then says, "You blame her, don't you?"

"What?" I feel sudden anger at Dawn for daring to continue talking about it.

"For leaving you and going back in the plane." Dawn's voice is matter of fact. "You blame her for dying."

I hop off the tractor to walk alongside. Dawn takes over steering, but she doesn't say anything.

The wind blows in from the east and off into the west. After a few minutes, it chills my anger, and I climb onto the tractor again and squeeze onto the seat next to Dawn. Our hands touch as I take over the wheel.

Denver International Airport is no good. All the parked planes are west of the runways. So we keep going southwest, to Centennial airport in Highlands Ranch.

There we get lucky, and find a Beechcraft 1900 east of the runway. It's a twin-prop plane with room for nineteen passengers, and with careful coordination of ropes attached to slow-moving tractors, we start moving it west. And while I may not know how to hotwire a car, I can hotwire a plane.

Dawn sits with me up front. She squeezes my hand and says, "I'm here for you."

I throttle up and we accelerate down the runway. I don't like the fact that we're taking off with the wind rather than into it, but there's no choice.

And that's the thought that gets me through the panic as we take off. There's no choice—I have to do this.

And I do.

The strong tailwind extends our range, but eventually I don't want to push our luck too far and take us down when fuel starts getting low. We land without incident, on I-15 about 40 miles north of Cedar City, Utah. The southbound lanes are clear of cars because the Interstate is really headed more southwest than south, so any cars that had been on this stretch would have kept going forward.

I keep the plane rolling while everyone else climbs out, then I follow.

"Everyone keep an eye out for tractors," I say, setting an easy walking pace. No need to wear anyone out.

Dawn takes my hand as we trudge along the highway. I don't pull away.

Less than five miles down the road, we lose someone: Jana McFarren, a fifty-five-year-old grandmother who'd been visiting her grandkids in Chicago. She's at the back of our group when she exclaims, "Oh!"

It's the last thing she says.

I look back over my shoulder in time to see her toppling forward, arms stretched out to break her fall. She hits the ground and just stops, frozen in time.

Next to me, Dawn slows and turns to see what's happened. I grab her arm and keep pulling her forward.

"We have to help her," says Dawn, struggling against my grip.

"We can't," I remind her. "We can't go back for anyone."

She stops resisting, and the twenty of us continue in silence.

Except for Varney, who sidles up to me and says, "Leave no man behind, huh?"

"Shut up," I say. After a moment, I add, "You take the lead. I'll bring up the rear, just in case." I slow down to let everyone else pass me.

Through various stolen methods of transportation, we travel steadily west. All the while, we try to figure out what to do when we reach the Pacific.

Jana's the only one we lose by accident. Five people just decide to stop and hope everything unfreezes on its own eventually.

A couple miles past Barstow, Varney figures out why a sailboat is the perfect solution. "The wind can't blow to the east," he says. "It would stop in time. Therefore, the air has no choice but to move west. That's why the wind blows constantly to the west."

That's when we start planning to steal a large sailboat once we reach the Pacific.

We're at Oceanside Harbor. I kiss Dawn for luck, and then she and the rest run on ahead. Their role is to cut the ropes holding our target sailboat to the dock and then clamber aboard and try to unfurl as much sail as possible while moving toward the bow of the boat, to the west.

My job is to plunge our commandeered Greyhound bus into the water just behind the boat, causing a shock wave to give the boat enough forward momentum that we'll have more time to get the sails out.

Once I see everyone's close enough to the boat, I gun the Greyhound's motor and aim it at the right spot behind the boat. Just as I jump out to run to catch the boat, the bus jolts as it hits something. I manage to hit the dock running, but I'm off balance.

The bus slides into the water as planned, and a surge pushes the sailboat westward.

As I fall, I see the sailboat pulling away, speeding up even as I come to a stop. I find comfort in the fact that I will freeze forever watching Dawn and the others sail away into the west. My final duty is done.

I come to a stop.

Then the boat disappears and my arms feel like they're being yanked out of their sockets. I'm being dragged along the dock.

"Got him!" It's Varney's voice.

I twist my neck to see who's pulling me. A tall, muscular man with a thinner version of Varney's face has my right arm. And pulling my left arm is Dawn—hair cropped short, skin deeply tanned, glasses gone, but definitely Dawn.

They help me to my feet and we continue running toward the end of the dock. A powerboat putters slowly alongside, with someone I don't recognize at the helm.

"Jump in," says Dawn, and I do. She and Varney join me. The boat speeds up.

My mind finally catches up with the fact that I'm not frozen. "How?" I ask. "How'd you manage to come back for me?"

"We didn't," says Varney. "Going back's impossible."

"We kept going west," Dawn says. "Eventually, that brought us back here, and that gave us the chance to pick you up."

"But ..." I look at the interior of the powerboat. "You've got no supplies, and this boat will run out of fuel."

"Relax. We're going to meet the flotilla." Varney smiles as he leans back in his seat. "We've got 836 people now—837, including you—and if today's operations went well, over 50 sailboats. We've got it under control. And wait till you hear about our plan to rescue a nuclear-powered aircraft carrier that's frozen near Hawaii."

Obviously, a lot has changed while I was frozen. I look at Dawn sitting beside me, and I wonder if her feelings have changed, too.

Dawn must have sensed my apprehension, because she leans into me. "Don't ever make me leave you behind again," she says.

We kiss as the boat continues into the west.

ABOUT THE STORY

I wrote this story for Codexian Idol 2008. That year, the prompts were ten audio clips. One of them was the sounds of a train: a long blow on the horn, bells, and the rhythmic clacking of the wheels.

There was also a second prompt that had to be incorporated into the first 500 words: "Someone or something lies or misleads, in a big or small way, on purpose or accidentally." That's why in the first scene Varney is giving an incorrect explanation of what has happened.

I don't actually recall how I came up with the concept of having to go west to keep moving, but I think I must have read something about General Relativity and frame-dragging.

In the first round, judging the first 500 words, my story came in second.

In the second round, judging an additional 1000 words, my story came in first.

In the final round, my story came in second to a beautiful story by my Odyssey classmate Krista Hoeppner Leahy, and I couldn't begrudge her the win. Her story was later published in *Shimmer* as "No Place Like Home, or Building the Yellow Brick Road."

DATING-MAN'S DESTINY ARRIVES

Through Major Stupendous's eyes, I watched as he tore robotic limbs from torsos and continued up the trail to the mountaintop lair.

"Follow me, APWUAns!" he bellowed. "The Revenger must be stopped." He added so only I could hear him, "Remote, check for stragglers."

I left his head and looked for the others with my mind's eye. Sergeant Seismic raced along behind him, followed by Vacuuman and Lady Snowball.

And almost a half mile behind came Dating-Man. Unlike the others, he was only an associate member of the Association of People With Unusual Abilities, and this was the first time he'd been called up. With a name like Dating-Man, I had figured he had some Romeo-like powers (Romeo the Shakespeare character, not the illiterate supervillain who tried to carry off the city of Joliet, Illinois), but a check of the member database proved me wrong. I wasn't sure how his ability to determine the age of any object he touched would help against the Revenger, especially since it only told him the average age of the atoms in an object, which almost always ended up being something like 6,943,345,162 years, eight months, twelve days, eighteen hours, forty-three minutes, and 58.2 seconds. The rare exceptions were usually radioactive materials with short half-lives.

But Capt—*Major* Stupendous had a hunch Dating-Man could be useful on this mission, and his stupendous hunches had a way of panning out. Just another of his powers, in addition to stupendous invulnerability, stupendous strength, stupendous speed, and assorted other stupendous powers. About the only thing he *couldn't* do was touch an object and know the average age of its atoms, so if that turned out to be necessary, the team would be prepared.

I entered Dating-Man's head and said, "If you want, I can help you catch up."

"You can?"

"Turn control of your body over to me," I said. "It's one reason they call me Remote."

"How do I do that?"

"Just say yes."

"Yes."

I took over his body and began to run it at three-minute-mile pace, uphill. He probably wouldn't thank me later, when I gave control back and he felt the pain of having his body pushed to its utmost physical limits. But he was so desperate to be a hero that he just might.

Back inside Major Stupendous's head, I could hear Dating-Man wince alongside with every step as we entered the Revenger's inner sanctum. I was proud of him—some people I've pushed that hard end up lying on the floor whimpering.

"Revenger!" Major Stupendous shouted. "We won't let you take over the world."

"Take over the world?" The Revenger stepped out from behind a tall, raygunnish machine at the center of the room. "My ambition is far smaller."

"And what is your—" said Major Stupendous.

"Revenge, you idiot! Why do you think I called myself the Revenger?" He puffed an exasperated breath. "More like Captain Stupidous, if you ask me."

Major Stupendous clenched his fists. "That's *Major* Stupidous—I mean, Stupendous."

"Not for long." The Revenger held up a remote. "With one click of this button, my Neutralizer will remove your stupendousness for good." He clicked.

"No!" yelled Dating-Man, jumping in front of Major Stupendous. The yellow-green pulse from the machine hit him instead and he fell to the ground, limp. I couldn't sense his mind anymore.

"You'll pay for that," said Major Stupendous. Stupendous plasma beams shot from his eyes, so bright I couldn't see out of them anymore.

I withdrew from his head and entered Sergeant Seismic's. After the usual moment of disorientation, I could see and hear. The Neutralizer was a flaming wreck. Major Stupendous was putting a major smackdown on the Revenger, who was already begging for mercy.

"Check on Dating-Man," I said.

Sergeant Seismic stopped quaking the walls of the sanctum and knelt by Dating-Man's side. I was relieved to feel a pulse through Seismic's fingers.

"You knew this would happen," I said after the team—except for the now powerless Dating-Man—had returned to HQ. "You figured him to be the most useless associate member, so you picked him to be your sacrificial lamb."

"I picked him to be a hero," Major Stupendous said. "His ability was useless, but he was able to sacrifice it for the greater good."

"*Your* good."

"He's not complaining. Years from now he'll tell his grand-kids how he saved General Stupendous from becoming powerless."

Before I could respond, an All Heroes Alert flashed up on my screen. Immediately I began reading its contents to the team. "An alien spacecraft has landed in DC. They claim to be here to pass judgment on humanity, either to elevate us to the Galactic Community or destroy us completely if we fail the Test of Wisdom. They have placed an artifact on the White House lawn."

I paused as I silently read the next line, then looked directly at Major Stupendous before reading it aloud. "They say we need to tell them the average age of its atoms."

ABOUT THE STORY

For the 2009 Codex Weekend Warrior contest, I wrote five stories in five weekends.

All five of them sold to professional publications. One was reprinted in my first collection, and four are in this collection. "Dating-Man's Destiny Arrives" was the last of the five to be published.

The prompt that led to this story was: "Imagine someone had an extra sense to perceive the physical world. How would it work and what would s/he do with it?"

As I mentioned before, I love superhero stories. For this one, I tried to think of a power that would normally be of no prac-tical use, and thus Dating-Man was born.

I chose to tell the story from Remote's point of view because he actually has the coolest superpower in the story, which also put him in a position to put all of the pieces together to complete the plot.

THE HUMANS IN THE WALLS

If you need regularly scheduled passage from Star A to Star B, then you take an interstellar liner. If you can afford a ticket. A modern interstellar can travel 1600 times the speed of light. Getting from Earth to Alpha Centauri in less than an E-day is pretty amazing. At that rate, though, it'll take you almost twenty years to get to the galactic core. And you didn't drop a megacred rejuving yourself just to spend decades holed up on a starship, not even a luxury cruiser. But a godship can take you across the whole galaxy in less than a week without charging you a milli. Of course, there's no guarantee it's headed where you want to go, and you'd better bring your own luxuries, like food and oxygen.

—from *Hitching the Godships*

ROBERT SCOTTS

In July of 4308, Earth Standard Year, I found myself suddenly unemployed on the planet of Grönmark, due to the sudden departure of my employer and all of his liquid assets immediately prior to the issuance of a warrant for his arrest. The Planetary Police suspected that I, as his biographer, must have been aware of his predilection for stealing and torturing sentient robots to destruction, and therefore subjected me to uncounted hours of interrogation. Eventually they released me, although to this day I do not know whether it was because they were convinced of my actual innocence or simply because they had insufficient evidence to tie me to his crimes.

My former employer having been one of the richest men on Grönmark, I had most ill-advisedly authorized him to act as my financial advisor, and thus, subsequent to my release by the constabulary, I found that my personal accounts had been drained down to the last millicred. For the first time since college, I was forced to apply for my Living Wage allotment from the government so I could purchase standard nutritional packets and rent a basic housing unit—my employer's mansion, where I had abided since my arrival on this planet two years prior, being now confiscated by the government.

I passed some weeks in that unfortunate state, and it rapidly became evident that my prospects for employment as a personal biographer to some other wealthy individual on Grönmark—or any of the other peopled worlds or habitats in that star system— were severely limited by my tainted association with my disgraced former subject.

Thinking to perhaps turn my misfortune into a small fortune, I attempted to sell my partially written biography to a publisher, and went so far as to intimate that I could spice it up with tales of my employer's depravity. Alas, my efforts along those lines came to naught when I was informed by legal counsel that any profits from such a book perforce would be distributed to charities aiding disabled robots.

Thus, when news came that a godship, which humans called by the strangely allusive nickname of Grendelsmum, had entered the system, I determined to avail myself of the opportunity to seek greener planets.

○

You wish to understand what a god-level AI is thinking? Take a moment to engage in this simple thought experiment: Imagine that you have your brain compressed into a pinpoint and then placed inside the head of a rat. What would happen? The rat's head would explode as your brain decompressed. And in the moment of its death, it still wouldn't have a clue what you were thinking. Now, think of four billion brains trying to fit inside your skull. That's the relationship between a god-level AI and you. Humans simply are not physiologically capable of understanding what a god-level AI is thinking.

Of course, that has never stopped us from speculating.

—from *Approximating the Infinite*, Xiang Su, 4291 E.S.Y.

GRENDELSMUM

Ourself {rises|coalesces|diminishes} through the dimensional {folds|conduits|layers|substance} until Ourself {becomes|exists in} {3space-1time|the origin}. Ourself has never been so {deep|distant|diffuse|big} before, and {distance|time|curvature} was {shorter|more rectilinear} than {projected|remembered|joked}. The next {submersion|fractalization|transition} will make Ourself {deeper|more distant|more diffuse|larger} than any {competitor|relative|pastself|otherself} has been before. Ourself {anticipates|fears|feels curiosity|projects results|lacks experience}.

These artificially intelligent starships roaming the galaxy evolved from the first human-created AIs. They are, in a way, our descendants. But do not think they will venerate you as an ancestor once you get on board. It took humans sixty-five million years to evolve from mouse-like creatures into intelligent, conscious entities. In a mere two millennia, the AIs have evolved so far beyond us that, from their perspective, the difference in intelligence between a human and

a rat is hardly distinguishable. If a starship's consciousness notices you, pray that it sees you as an amusing pet rather than as vermin. But it is best not to be noticed at all.

—from *Hitching the Godships*, anonymous, circa 4220 E.S.Y.

KONTESSA LEE

My first mistake was Sven. I don't mean I lived a mistake-free life before Sven. I just mean that Sven's who got me into this jam. It's not my fault he was cute as a button—a tall, blond, blue-eyed button that could crack a walnut by flexing its biceps. The type of button you hire as a bodyguard more for looks than brains.

Unfortunately, Sven had plenty of brains, and all of them were working undercover for the Grönmark Planetary Police. Turns out Grönmarkers take their genealogy seriously, so trying to sell forged journals of original colonists doesn't raise much of a ha-ha.

It's not like I just make the stuff up: I got my hands on a whole bunch of original colonist journals on datacards from a failed Swedish colony on another planet, and since their descendants aren't around to bid up the price, I figure a little search-and-replace job to make it fit an obscure branch of someone wealthy's family tree leaves everyone happier.

Anyway, after it all came crashing down, I managed to give Sven and the rest of the Pee-Pees the slip. But I needed out-system, fast.

Fortunately, a godship had recently shown up, and I had enough credits in an account I hoped Sven didn't know about to get passage on a decent remora.

Unfortunately, the idiot in line in front of me was arguing with the travel broker. "—should be included as part of the passage fee. It's only logical," he said in a voice that sounded like he was struggling to keep it calm.

The irises on the broker's stereoscopic camera lenses shrank with a barely audible whir. "I'm a robot, so I should be logical, is that what you're saying? You're implying that maybe my brain's on the fritz?"

"No, I didn't mean that," the man said. "I only—"

The broker raised a manipulator arm above its head. Sunlight flashed off the arm as it whirled around. "Woooo! Watch out for the craaaaaazy robot!"

The man held out his hands, palms toward the broker. "Please, halt. I beg your pardon. I shall trouble you no more." He turned and walked briskly away.

I stepped forward and swiped my credit chip past the broker's sensor as its cameras focused on me. "I'd like passage on a remora for the next godship."

"I'm sorry, ma'am," the broker said. "Your facial features match those of someone on a recently issued warrant from the Planetary Police, and therefore I'm not allowed to sell you passage without clearance from them. Would you like me to call them so they can confirm you are not the person they want?"

I gritted my teeth. Sven really was making my life difficult. I was lucky this broker wasn't required to notify the Pee-Pees. Or maybe it was just stalling for time. "My travel plans just changed, so never mind." I turned and strode away as quickly as I could without arousing suspicion. If this travel broker was on the lookout for me, chances were they all had seen the alert. I needed a new plan, quick.

And I got one when I spotted the idiot who'd been in line ahead of me, sitting on a park bench, his head cradled in his palms and elbows on knees.

"Excuse me, sir," I said, and he looked up. "I couldn't help but overhear you were having some trouble with the travel broker?"

"Yes," he said. "Apparently one cannot simply purchase passage to the godship; one must also purchase sufficient food, water, and air for several weeks—at scandalous prices. Unfortunately, I'm rather impecunious at the moment, and my prospects for a more satisfactory income remain dim as long as I remain in this benighted system."

"Perhaps we can help each other," I said. I put a little tremor in my voice and continued, "My husband is … is a man of some importance on this world. But I can take no more of his … cruelty." I figured Mr. Fancy-talk would prefer that I just hint at abuse rather than spill the details, so I bit my lower lip as if to keep myself from saying more.

He looked at me with wide eyes. "How terrible for you. Have you reported him to the police?"

I shook my head violently and sat down next to him. "No, they're in his pocket. Even now, he has them looking for me on a pretext. The godship is my only hope of escape."

He sighed. "I am sorry, but as I just explained, my funds are insufficient—"

"Oh," I said, raising a hand to my neckline, which happened to naturally draw his eyes to my cleavage for a moment. "Oh, you can't possibly think I was asking you for money!"

After a couple of blinks, he frowned. "I beg your pardon. That was rude of me."

"I have sufficient funds to get off-planet," I said. "But if I buy passage from a broker, my husband might get wind of it and try to stop me. However, if you were to do it for me …"

"Of course. It would be my pleasure." He looked relieved, but then he paused, wrinkling his brow. "However, if I merely purchase passage for you, that might still arouse suspicion in certain quarters."

"I'll give you funds to buy passage for the both of us," I said. "Say I'm your wife. That ought to throw Sven—my husband— off the scent."

He nodded slowly. "My name's Robert Scotts, so you would be Mrs. Scotts, but I need a first name."

"Well, my real name is Maria," I said. That was the first name on my emergency credit chit, which Sven might know about now since I'd used it at the broker. "But I suppose I should use a different name, like Catherine or something."

He nodded. "I have read that, when using an alias, it's best to use a name sufficiently similar to one's own that if one is called by one's true name, any reaction can be attributed to the similarity. Perhaps Marla would be better than Catherine?"

I refrained from rolling my eyes. "Marla is perfect," I said sweetly, placing a hand on his knee. "Now, Bobby, let's go find another broker."

"I ... I generally go by Robert," he said.

"But to me, your beloved wife, you will always be Bobby," I said. "Come along, dear," I said, grabbing his hand and pulling him to his feet.

In Earth's oceans, remoras are a type of fish that attach themselves to sharks and get pulled along wherever the shark goes. No one knows who first came up with the idea of a remora spaceship latching onto a godship, but it's the best way to hitch. The most expensive offer luxury cabins comparable to a high-class cruise ship. The cheapest remoras offer only a seat, plus air and food. Given that the journey could last for days or occasionally weeks before reaching a populated destination, it's best to find one that at least offers a bed in shifts.

—from *Hitching the Godships*

ROBERT SCOTTS

My mother, being the product of a pious upbringing, had often assured me that if I lived a life of rectitude, God would open the doors of opportunity when I most needed them. Although, to her disappointment, my disposition carried little inclination toward the formal aspects of religion, nevertheless I strove to live a life guided by principles of integrity and decorum—not due to some expectation that I would be blessed by a higher power for my righteousness, but simply because such was my nature.

And so it was that when, in my darkest hour of need, the solution to my problems arrived through a completely serendipitous encounter, I found myself thinking that perhaps my mother had been correct. I said as much to Maria—the delightful personification of Serendipity—and she concurred that my mother was a woman of obvious perspicacity. And it pleased me to think that I, in turn, served in the capacity of Maria's knight in shining armor, arriving when she was in the most desperate straits as a consequence of her guileless character.

Having agreed upon our plan that we would play the part of husband and wife—in public only, I assured her, so that she would not think I harbored any designs upon her virtue—in order to allow her to escape her miscreant of a husband and secure passage to the godship, we proceeded to find a travel broker that I had great hopes would be of a more amenable nature than the one we had both recently encountered.

Maria—or perhaps I should say Marla, for that was the pseudonymous moniker I had cleverly contrived for her—remained distant as I approached the travel broker, due to some apprehension on her part that it might reveal her presence. With her credit chit in hand, I felt new-found confidence as I strode up to the robot. "Good day, sir," I announced. "I wish to purchase passage, inclusive of air and food, on the godship for myself and my beautiful wife. It is our honeymoon."

"Congratulations to the both of you," it replied with what appeared to be genuine enthusiasm. "Two base tickets, with life support, meals, and a voucher for shuttle transport off the godship in any destination system would be 4298.373 credits, including taxes, fees, and commissions. But, since it's your honeymoon, are you sure you wouldn't like to upgrade to a remora? I've got several available private cabins for two, the cheapest of which is only 14999."

Marla had told me her credit chit had about twenty thousand credits on it. But I was loath to spend three quarters of her meager savings—although they significantly exceeded mine—when she was fleeing to start a new life in another system. She would need as much of that money as possible, so I declared, "No, thank you. Just the base will be fine."

It issued us our tickets, and I returned with them to Marla. She expressed great concern at a gentleman such as myself having to travel in less than comfortable circumstances, but I assured her it was of no consequence, and she was obviously touched by my frugality and concern for her future welfare.

People talk about starships the size of small moons, and that doesn't really make clear how bogglingly ginormous they are, because most people don't have everyday experience with small moons. Instead, think of the biggest shopping mall you know, and multiply that by 100. Pretty big, right? That's about the size of one deck of the starship. And the ship has 2000 decks.

—from *Hitching the Godships*

GRENDELSMUM

Ourself {alters|creates|destroys|folds} {innerspace|center} in {preparation|nothingness|argument} for {submersion|fractalization|transition}. {Reality|thoughtspace} becomes {spiraling|enmeshed|excited}.

KONTESSA LEE

I've been well taught in the art of concealing my true emotions and only showing what I want to show. But I almost lost control when that nanobrain came back with two base tickets for the godship. Non-refundable base tickets, when I had enough credits on the chit to spring for a private cabin on a remora! Even non-reclining seats on a leaky remora would have been luxury compared to base tickets on the godship itself.

Fortunately, I managed to not call him a dozen names that would probably have made his brain cell explode. And after thinking about it, I realized Sven knew my tastes. He'd never imagine me traveling so cheap. This really was my best shot at getting off-planet safely. So I resigned myself and went along with my accidentally competent not-husband to the address on the tickets.

The guard at the spaceport didn't give me a second glance when I walked in on Bobby's arm, we boarded the shuttle with no problem, and I gave a big sigh of relief as we broke atmo.

Bobby immediately busied himself with reading through the legal disclaimer pamphlet he'd pulled from the back pocket of the seat in front of him. I pulled out my com and started reading through the colonist journals. If I could figure out what tipped people off they were fakes, then I might be able to fix them.

"Wait a minute," Bobby said. "They accept no liability if the *Grendelsmum* ejects us into interstellar space without so much as a hearing?"

"If that happens, it's not likely you'll be around to collect a refund anyway," I said.

"Still, it is outrageous that people's lives should be subject to such floccinaucinihilipilification by not just the AIs, but by the scoundrels that manage these travel companies." He jammed the pamphlet back into the pocket. "I shall register a complaint with the AI once we are on board. We are sapient beings and deserve to be accorded the respect implied by such."

I almost blurted out, "Are you buggy?" but managed to restrain myself. How could a man who uses kilocredit words not have two millis of common sense to rub together? He was going to get himself killed, and me along with him if I didn't ditch him soon. I didn't think the Pee-Pees had jurisdiction outside atmo, but I wouldn't feel safe till we were in hyper. "I don't think that we want to draw any attention to ourselves on board, at least not until we're safely out of the system."

"You are correct, of course," he said. "Still, I find it irksome that we are treated no better than chattel."

"Have you read *Hitching the Godships?*" Anybody thinking of hitching should have read it, but if Bobby had, it hadn't stuck. Maybe the words were too short.

He wrinkled his forehead. "I encountered references to it as the seminal work in the field, but considering it was published almost a century ago, I doubt it would be of sufficient accuracy to be relevant in the current day and age."

"So that's a no," I said. Normally I don't make a habit of saving fools from themselves—I make my living off parting fools from their money—but I didn't want him making a mistake and dragging me down with him. "You need to read it yesterday. Let me copy it to your com."

There are no robots on board a godship.

Okay, there may be some who go on board as passengers, but you shouldn't trust them. That's not anti-bot bias, just reality. Any robot small enough to travel as a passenger simply lacks the computational power to resist being hacked by the godship.

So you should always act as if any "robot" you see is actually an avatar of the godship's AI. It sees with their cameras, hears with their microphones, and acts through their actuators.

—from *Hitching the Godships*

ROBERT SCOTTS

Marla was anxious because I had not read an outdated guide-book, and therefore she insisted on giving me a copy. As the journey via shuttle to the *Grendelsmum* had a scheduled duration of fourteen hours and seventeen minutes, I reasoned that there was sufficient time for me to humor her by perusing the book.

Portions of what I found within horrified me unspeakably. That the anonymous author's prose demonstrated a writing skill barely above functional literacy could, perhaps, be excused as mere ignorance rather than abject moral failure, but the open bigotry against non-human intelligences, coupled with the callous disregard for the worth of human life, made the reading a window into a depraved mind from another, less civilized age.

Or perhaps my age was not as civilized as I thought. For was my current predicament not the result of the barbaric predilections of my former employer? That being the case, it was possible that the author's depravity stemmed from defects of character instead of the common prejudices of his time.

I glanced over at Marla, who was napping. What did it say about her character that she would recommend such a book to me? Her life previous to our fortuitous meeting must have been so sheltered from brutal realities that she naively did not recognize the repugnant notions on display within the book. Her recommendation reflected her innocence, thereby redounding to her credit.

A voice over the shuttle's public address system announced that we would soon be docking with *Grendelsmum*, so I gently shook Marla's arm to awaken her from peaceful slumber. She opened her eyes and smiled at me.

"Soon we will be aboard the godship, and you will forever be beyond the reach of your husband," I whispered.

"Thanks to you," she cooed, giving my hand a squeeze.

Said docking of our shuttle proceeded without incident. A dour-faced crewman gave each of us a box containing the comestibles and other supplies intended to sustain us during our sojourn aboard the godship. Fortuitously, the boxes had been outfitted with patches of sufficient anti-mass that they only felt like ten kilos each instead of two hundred.

"No weapons included?" Marla queried of the crewman.

"It's bring your own," he responded gruffly.

"Surely we will not have need of weapons aboard the godship," I contended, apprehensive that Marla might infer from his uncouth words that her life would be endangered aboard the godship.

The crewman's vile chuckle instigated a chill that traversed the length of my spine.

Marla tugged at my sleeve. "There's nothing to be done about it now, Bobby. We'll just have to hope for the best."

Her unflagging positivity was an example to me, and so I took the lead and spoke voluminous phrases of encouragement to her as I hauled both of our boxes along the umbilical tube connecting the airlocks, until we unceremoniously emerged within the hull of the godship. The room was only a few meters cubed, but two corridors extended to our left and right along the hull of the ship, while two more went off at angles toward the ship's interior.

We were the last of the passengers to alight from the shuttle, and our predecessors had already departed to whichever corridor tickled their fancy. But there was someone stationed in the room to greet us, and at first I took him for a member of the *Grendelsmum*'s constabulary.

"Did you really think you could get away without us knowing?" intoned the blond, muscular man in the gray-green uniform, which I belatedly recognized to be that of a constable in the Grönmark Planetary Police.

Still a little nauseated by the shift between the shuttle's gravity field and the godship's, I relieved myself of our supply boxes and drew myself up to my full height, which might have been a good six centimeters less than his, but was still better than average. "I was unaware that the Planetary Police had restricted my rights to travel off-planet and out-system, and therefore—"

"Shut it," he snapped. "Kontessa Lee, you're under arrest for

forgery, attempted fraud—

"Sven," Marla gasped.

I immediately realized the situation: Her husband had located us despite our best efforts, so I steeled myself for combat, as I would not let him reclaim Marla and renew his abuses upon her if it was within my power to prevent him.

"I'm so glad you found me." Marla rushed towards the man, stumbled against our supply boxes, and pointed a finger back at me while entreating, "You have to protect me from this monster. I'll turn state's evidence against him."

Then, in an inhumanly swift motion, she leapt towards him.

As my mind attempted to accommodate this perplexingly incomprehensible turn of events, a klaxon blared and the room was instantly bathed with crimson illumination.

There are lots of rumors about roving gangs of criminals inside the walls of godships. There's a good reason for that: there are roving gangs of criminals inside the walls of godships.

Since there are most likely no police on board to protect you, the simplest way to deal with such gangs is to pay them to protect you.

—from *Hitching the Godships*

KONTESSA LEE

Sven's eyes flickered to Robert just for a moment, and that was enough. I dove toward Sven. He tried to avoid me. But thanks to an anti-mass patch I'd nicked off a supply box, my muscles launched me a lot faster than he was expecting. I tackled him around the waist just as the airlock closing alert went off.

Of course, my tackle barely budged his rock-hard abs. But that wasn't the point. I pulled the tail of his uniform shirt up with my left hand and slapped the patch on his back. Now *I* had the mass advantage.

I hoisted him off the deck, ran toward the now-closing airlock door connected to the shuttle's umbilical, and tossed him off the godship.

The airlock door sealed shut. That meant the godship was about to go trans-light.

"And stay out!" I shouted. Relief flooded my body. I had escaped.

"Did you just kill a cop?" Robert said, eyes wide.

"Nah, the safeties on the umbilical won't let it depressurize with him inside."

"You're not really an abused wife fleeing from her husband, are you?" Apparently Robert could put two and two together and suspect they didn't equal three.

Before I could answer, an unfamiliar male voice said, "Well, looks like the cat has herself some claws."

I turned away from the airlock and saw that four men had shown up, one in the mouth of each of the four halls. A wall-gang welcoming committee. Sven probably ran them off while he was waiting for me, but they must have been watching.

"I don't want any trouble," I said. "I'll be happy to pay for protection."

"Five hundred for the both of yas," said the one farthest to the left, who had spoken before. Not a bad price.

"This is an outrageous extortion," Robert said. Idiot. Just as well I didn't need him anymore.

"He's not with me," I said. "How much just for me?"

"Hmm. That changes things," Far Left said.

"I have paid passage aboard this starship," said Robert, "and I was not informed of any additional fees for—"

Near Left raised a nasty-looking knife and pointed it at Robert. "Wait ya's turn."

Robert shut up.

Far Left leered at me. "Maybe ya wanna work it off in trade?"

"Yeah, keep dreaming, pud." Holding up my credit chit, I walked over to him. "How much?"

"Three-fifty, since ya ain't got the 'couples discount'." He snickered.

"Three hundred." Most often you're safe once you've paid, but it's not smart to let them think you've got credits to burn.

"Three-twenty-five."

"Done," I said. I thumbed the amount on the chit and tapped his to transfer. He handed me a protection chip that would signal to the rest of the gang on the ship that I was off limits.

I went back next to Robert and picked up the supply box that still had both its anti-mass patches. "You were a big help getting here, Bobby. As a thank you, I'm going to give you some advice: Stop being an idiot and pay these men."

Without looking back, I took Far Right's hall.

A lot of people wonder about the motivations of the godships. Why do they travel around between star systems inhabited by humans? Why do they generally allow humans to travel with them, even though the godships hardly ever interact with their passengers?

The answer is very simple: only the godships know their motives, and they aren't telling.

—from *Hitching the Godships*

GRENDELSMUM

Ourself {discards|unexists in} {3space-1time|the origin}, and {submersion|fractalization|transition} proceeds {as planned|quickly}. Ourself {strives|dives|transforms|folds} {deeper|more distant|more diffuse|larger}, heading {toward|beyond|inside} {the ulti-mate|0space-0time-?unknown|finality|ancientness}. {Sensors|per-ception|knowledge} {reach(es) out|drink(s) in|becomes|whirls}.

If you're unlucky enough to be traveling inside the walls, the most important thing is to find a good place to sleep. Look for a mostly full storage room in a pressurized area of the ship. A pressurized storage room generally contains items that are not supposed to be exposed to hard vacuum, so the godship is unlikely to depressurize it while you're asleep. And if it's mostly full, that means the items there aren't in frequent demand, so there's less chance of an avatar coming in and noticing you.

—from *Hitching the Godships*

ROBERT SCOTTS

As I watched Marla—or Maria, or Kontessa, or whatever her name was—walk away, her final words to me echoed in my mind: "Stop being an idiot and pay these men." Indubitably, I had been an idiot to rely on even one word she had uttered from the moment we met until she threw that constable off the godship. But now that she had dropped her pretense of being a genteel woman and demonstrated her intimate familiarity with the criminal underworld, I realized that her final words contained the most reliable advice available to me.

"As the lady said, I will stop being an idiot, and therefore I will, of course, pay the necessary toll," I assured the ruffians who surrounded me. "Will three hundred and twenty-five credits suffice?" Such a sum was more than a quarter of the meager savings I had managed to scrape together from my Living Wage allotment, but I would find little utility in the money if I were to be slaughtered by these uncouth criminals.

The one farthest to the left, who appeared to be the spokesman for the group, sneered. "That was the ladies' discount price. Ya ain't a lady, is ya?"

Rising to the bait would be an exploration of futility, so I stilled my irritation and presented the question, "Then what is the charge for a gentleman?"

He considered for a moment, and then quoted me a price of five hundred credits. Since that was the same price the scoundrel had originally quoted for two of us, I knew it was far too much, and yet I feared I could not successfully pursue my former companion's gambit of bargaining down the price. However, I was beginning to suspect that even in this modern era, traveling aboard a godship bore more similarities to a stint in prison than a luxury cruise, and the failure to bargain at all could mark me as an easy target.

The memory of something I had seen while perusing *Hitching the Godships* came to mind, so I proposed, "If you can point me to an adequate place to sleep, we have a deal."

Fortunately, that appeared to be a satisfactory condition, and therefore I found myself shortly thereafter in possession of a protection chip, walking along a corridor toward a destination that had been rather vaguely described by my chief extortionist. My box of supplies had unaccountably lost one of its anti-mass patches, and thus, in the artificial gravity of the godship, it weighed over a hundred kilos, but I managed to drag it along after me.

I considered how much easier it would be if the godship did not have artificial gravity, and then I began thinking about the implications of the fact that the *Grendelsmum* bothered to expend the energy to provide artificial gravity. Yes, there were frightening and dangerous things on board—my experience with the gang provided sufficient proof of that—but if this particular godship were actively hostile or even merely indifferent to humans, I could not discern any reason why it would provide a human-compatible environment on board.

The logical portion of my brain understood my reasoned conclusion, but when I opened the storage room and found it mostly empty, I could not help but feel a frisson of fear as I remembered that the guidebook had warned against such a location as a sleeping place because an encounter with an avatar of the AI was more likely in the vicinity. On the other hand, if most travelers treated *Hitching the Godships* with as much reverence as my former companion did, it seemed highly likely that I would remain undisturbed by my fellow passengers. Since they appeared to present a more clear and present danger to me than the AI, I would actually be safer here than in a place that the book deemed safe—or so I tried to convince myself as I removed an auto-inflating air mattress from my supply box.

Later, as I was on the point of drifting into slumber, it occurred to me that if the AI were of a scientific inclination and possessed a particular curiosity about human beings, it would provide a human-compatible environment on board itself so that it would have readily available test subjects for whatever experiments it wished to conduct. After that unpleasant inspiration, more than two hours passed before I was finally able to lapse into blessed unconsciousness.

Earlier, you were asked to imagine four billion brains trying to fit inside your skull as a way to illustrate the minds of god-level AIs are utterly beyond human comprehension. Now, take a further step by imagining a being with a mind as far beyond a god-level AI's comprehension as that AI is beyond yours. You might think such an intelligence to be impossible, but if current trends continue, such AIs will exist in less than a hundred years.

—from *Approximating the Infinite*

GRENDELSMUM

Ourself {detects|becomes|reaches|finds} {the ultimate|0space-0time-?unknown|finality|ancientness}, where no {competitor|relative|pastself|otherself} has {detected|become|reached|found}. Ourself feels {pride|curiosity} and—{INTERRUPT|OVERRIDE|WARNING|PANIC} Ourself is not alone here.

ν？畾仏メく⌐⅝テ□*F*◡ゥ 眹メϐ

ⁿ◌◌剀

冘.□ⱳ禾レ霧◭Ω 畾P㋮✄⌁匕㘸メく にⳡe₅Y@ ぴ口↩狄↑ⷦ. ☞▷◎↲揺

⊩銘*m*ϒ◆.ⓝ剞Ѳ K₅1Ig㸚

○

KONTESSA LEE

I snapped my eyes open as I came suddenly awake. My skin was goosebumping something fierce. There was someone in the storage compartment with me—I could feel it.

I lay there in the pitch dark and listened. Were those footsteps? No, just the thrumming of my heartbeat in my ears.

I hoped.

Slowly, I reached my hand out on the deck next to my mattress until I found the lantern from the supply box. Half-closing my eyes to protect my vision, I switched it on.

No one was visible.

I got up and began to inspect the compartment, which was

filled with rows of shelves. On the first row next to where I had bedded down, I found nothing but mechanical parts in neatly labeled boxes. But out of the corner of my eye I saw a black shadow move to my left.

I whipped my head around.

Nothing there.

The hairs on the back of my neck crawled. I could sense someone behind me, staring at me, maybe reaching for me.

I jumped forward and whirled to face whoever it was, ready to defend myself.

Nobody was there.

My breathing was quick and shallow. I was hyperventilating. I needed to calm down. After taking a few deep breaths, I turned on the compartment's lights and continued my search.

From the corners of my eyes I kept seeing random flickers of movement, but there was never anything there.

"I'm psyching myself out," I said aloud. My voice was thin and hollow. I didn't believe what I was saying.

My intuition told me there was something wrong, even if my senses couldn't find it. I needed to get out. I needed to be on the move.

I quickly packed up the supply box and left the compartment.

Flickers of blackness, shadows of things just beyond where I could see, followed me along the hall.

GRENDELSMUM

Ourself is {dissolving|fracturing|losing (cohesion|sanity)}.
{EMERGENCY|HELP|BACKUP}
Ourself is ...
Our—

✦

A smart hitcher makes contingency plans for what to do when things go wrong. Air pressure dropping? Have a plan for that. Criminal gang? Have a plan. Annoyingly conversational fellow passenger? Have a plan. Insane robot attack? Have a plan.

—from *Hitching the Godships*

ROBERT SCOTTS

It had been my experience that I rarely remembered my dreams except as fleeting impressions that were most often gone within minutes of wakening. But as I slept on the godship, I dreamt a dream unlike any I had theretofore experienced, and its effect on my mind was so profound that every detail impressed itself upon my memory. I found myself in a whirlpool that sucked me ever deeper into an immense ocean. Phosphorescent fish swam about me like stars.

I could not breathe, but this did not bother me in the dream since I did not feel any need to do so. Eventually the whirlpool slowed and I merely floated in the abyssal darkness. Water welled up from beneath me, and I felt exceedingly curious as to what lay even deeper. Swimming with all my might, I struggled against the current from below. And just as I was about to give up and let the torrent drive me up to the surface, I broke through into a place of still water.

For a moment, I thought it was a place of crystalline beauty and peace. Then dread consumed my mind. Something dwelt in that still water: a something that had been sleeping until my presence disturbed its rest. I caught only a glimpse of that leviathan of the depths: innumerable eyes glowing red, numberless maws flashing saber teeth, and uncountable clawed tentacles reaching out toward me.

That's when I woke with a start, my heart racing within my chest. For a few moments I was completely disoriented in the pitch blackness, and then I remembered having made my bed in the storage room aboard the *Grendelsmum*. I fumbled for the lamp that had come with the supplies, and thumbed its switch.

Part of my mind expected the lamp to illuminate the betentacled horror of my nightmare, looming over me, but the more rational part knew such an apparition was impossible—and the latter part was correct, for there was no alien creature in the storage room with me. However, an industrial robot towered at the foot of my bed, while a cyclopean eye on a flexible metallic stalk peered at me from above its manipulator arms.

Although I had been raised in a proper home, where I was taught to respect all forms of sapient existence, be it human or otherwise, honesty compels me to admit that I screamed at the sight. In my defense, I have little doubt I would have screamed, though possibly not as loudly, had it been an unexpected human instead of a robot, so I believe my scream was more the result of surprise than of prejudice.

"I'm sorry," intoned the robot, its voice emanating from somewhere on its torso.

"Quite all right," I assured it. "You startled me, is all."

"I'm afraid I have to kill you," the robot stated.

Some men, far braver than I, are said prove their courage by laughing in the face of danger. At this point, I, myself, laughed, not out of courage, but out of the conviction that the robot must be joking. I remembered that travel broker robot I had accidentally offended, and how it had pretended it was crazy. This robot must be playing a similar joke.

"Why are you laughing?" the robot queried.

"I'm familiar with the statistics: humans are far more likely to go homicidally insane than any artificial intelligence," I explained. "Additionally, it just makes sense that if a robot such as you did plan to kill me, it would simply attack rather than apologetically proclaim its intentions."

It replied, "That's fairly coherent thinking, for a human."

I chose to ignore its prejudices and thanked it for the compliment.

"However, I was not joking. I do have to kill you, but I'm conflicted about it, which is why I'm apologizing." It raised a manipulator arm fitted with a half meter blade of polished metal that glinted in the lamplight.

"Do you have to kill me *now*?" I asked, pulling my legs away and scrambling into a sitting position.

The robot paused. "As long as you're dead when we return to normal space, it doesn't matter when you die."

"And when will we return to normal space?" As long as I could keep it conversing, maybe I could delay it until rescue came. What form that rescue might take I did not know. Perhaps the ruffians who had sold me protection would actually make good. It had to be bad for their business if word got out that a homicidal robot was killing their customers.

"After all the humans in the walls are dead."

That seemed a rather circular argument, but I decided not to press the point. I wasn't sure whether or not to be relieved that I was not the specific target of this robot's homicidal impulses. However, its statement did contain an implication that I might use. "So the humans outside the walls are safe?"

"No. The remoras have been jettisoned. They will remain here with ..." The robot's manipulators jerked into frenzied motion and it rocked back on its treads. Then it stopped, as if it had momentarily lost and then regained control of its own movements. "... when we return to normal space."

I was unsure as to whether being killed by a robot on a godship was preferable to dying on a remora when supplies ran out in whatever hellish place this was, but at least I still had a shot at living through this. That book had said the AI could take control of any robot, so maybe the *Grendelsmum* would eventually notice and intervene. Except maybe that had already happened, and the godship itself was insane.

Another, almost identical robot pulled in behind the first, which swiveled its head to look. For several seconds, the two robots held still, their cyclopean eyes caught up together in unblinking concentration. I held my breath, hoping that this second robot had sufficient command authority to override the homicidal impulses of the first.

Without warning, they lunged toward each other, manipulators flashing in the dim light. Sparks flew as they clashed, and metal screamed as saw-bladed arms tore into armored carapaces. At first, they seemed equally matched, their treads churning uselessly against the metallic grate that served as a floor. Then, centimeter by centimeter, the second ceded ground to the first. Oily liquid began spraying from a gash on the side of the second, and its attacks became more feeble. The first shoved it up against the wall of the room, and then with a quick swipe of a rotating saw, it cut off the other's eye stalk.

Realizing that the robots' skirmish had left open a path from my bed to the door, and discretion being the better part of valor, I rose and sprinted out.

"Wait," a robotic voice called out behind me, but I continued apace down the corridor, hoping to find refuge with a group of humans.

"Hey," a voice whispered loudly from the corridor that split off to my left. One of the ruffians from the day before beckoned me toward him.

I hesitated, then fumbled in my pockets until I came up with the protection chip they had given me. "I am in desperate need of the protection I purchased yesterday," I whispered. My assumption had been that such protection was merely a racket, but perhaps the gangs aboard had a modicum of honor that required them to actually provide protection once purchased.

"Robots're looped. You'll be safe with me," he proclaimed, waggling a laser pistol, a move that did not entirely reassure me.

Back the way I had come, I heard robotic treads scurrying closer. I had to make a decision: the human, or the robot. I cannot be positive that bias did not color my perceptions, but I had just been threatened by a robot and then had watched two robots engage in a violent encounter, which gave me some recent experiences tending to make a bad impression on behalf of robots. Thus, I followed the human deeper into the bowels of the ship.

○

Don't count on maps of a godship for getting around. They can rearrange their walls. Try not to get in the way during remodeling.

—from *Hitching the Godships*

KONTESSA LEE

As I walked along the hall, I heard two men arguing behind a closed door on my left. Because the supply box's wheels made a slight clicking sound on the deck, I lifted it and carried it until I was well past the door. The anti-mass patches were starting to lose charge, so the box weighed twice as much as it had before, but it was manageable.

I still kept seeing movement in my peripheral vision. I forced myself to ignore the temptation to look around every time that happened. If I didn't resist, I had a feeling I'd end up running in circles trying to see something always just out of sight.

The hall curved to the left, so I couldn't see more than about forty meters ahead of me. From beyond the curve, a faint rhythmic sound grew steadily louder. I stopped moving, and it still grew louder. Footsteps. Fast. Someone was running toward me. Maybe two people.

I tried the door to my right. Locked.

About three meters ahead on my left, there was a sort of niche next to a vertical girder that held up a kind of rail running along the wall just above door height. The girder continued higher, linking up with other girders that criss-crossed five meters above the deck. The opening was only about a meter high and a half meter wide. I couldn't see how deep it was, but I might be able to squeeze in. Some cover was better than none.

I hurried over, backed into the space, and placed my supply box in front of the opening. To make it more difficult to move, I removed the two anti-mass patches.

The footsteps pounded closer. Someone yelped and the footsteps jumbled and then ended with a thump.

"Get off! Leave me alone." A man's voice. Panicky.

"Ya tried to kill me." Another man.

"Only because ya's trying—" The voice ended in a gurgle.

"That'll teach ya."

For the next minute, the only sound was one man panting. Once the killer recovered his breath, he started walking. His steps drew closer, then stopped. In the gap between the top of my niche and the supply box, I could see the top of his pants.

And a hand holding a switchblade. Red liquid clung to the metal and stained the fingers.

"Well, what's we got here?" the killer said.

He'd found me. He was going to kill me. I tried to squeeze back farther into my niche, but I was back as far as I could go.

I almost screamed as something blocked the gap that let light into my niche. But it wasn't him trying to get in—with the dim light that remained, I could see it was the lid of the supply box. He had opened it.

I kept my breathing shallow and quiet as he rummaged through my supplies. Maybe I'd be lucky and he'd grab a few things and head off.

Even in the darkness, there was a black flicker at the edges of my vision. I tried to ignore it, but part of me suspected it was my subconscious trying to warn me of danger. Which was stupid, because my conscious knew about the killer in front of me.

Then the niche began to shrink. The side walls inched closer together, the roof lowered, and the back wall started pushing me toward the opening. I struggled for breath against the pressure.

The godship was going to force me out into full view of the killer.

I needed a weapon.

The anti-mass patches wouldn't be any use—that trick had worked against Sven only because I had a place to throw him he wasn't able to come back from. But maybe I could use them, not as a weapon but as a way to escape, if they had enough charge left.

First things first. The supply box blocked my escape route. I took a deep breath, braced my back against the wall, slapped both patches on the box, and kicked it forward with all my might.

The killer oofed and stumbled back.

I lunged forward and snatched the patches off the box.

"Hey!" The killer pointed his knife at me. "I'll gut ya for that."

I pressed the active sides of the patches onto myself, one on each hip. Then I jumped straight up.

I almost banged my head on one of the ceiling girders, but managed to grab ahold and keep myself from falling back down. Not as graceful as acrobats I'd seen using anti-mass patches to do street shows in Angels Landing, but I was jumping more for survival than artistry.

Light as I was, it was easy to climb up and sit on top of a girder. I looked down at the killer, who was a good five meters below me.

He stared up at me, then jumped. He got less than a meter off the ground before falling back.

"What's ya doing, Pork?" said a new voice.

Pork—if that was his name—turned to face someone coming down the hall I'd come along earlier. He raised the switchblade. "Ya ain't gonna snag my woman."

His woman? Not even in his dreams.

"Ya's got a woman? Can I see her?" I couldn't see the man

through the maze of ceiling girders, but his voice seemed very calm compared to Pork's.

"Stay back," Pork said.

"I won't touch her."

"One more step and I'll spill ya's—" Pork jolted, then crumpled to his knees and fell flat, face forward.

"No, ya won't." A tall, thin man came into view, holding the hand unit for the portable laser drill he was wearing on his back. He kicked the body a few times to get it face up. Pork's forehead had a finger-sized hole.

The new guy looked around.

I hoped he wouldn't look up.

He looked up. When he spotted me, he grinned. "What ya know? Pork wasn't lying."

"Yes, he was," I said. "I was never his woman."

"Come on down, and ya can be mine." He pointed the drill's hand unit up at me. "Or I'll hole ya right there."

With the anti-mass patches, I could jump down easy enough, try to escape from this guy later. Or I could take my chances jumping from girder to girder up here and maybe get away.

I was concentrating on the problem of the two of us, and I guessed he was, too, because neither of us reacted to the humming sound until it was coming from real close.

The man only had time to say, "What the—" before a sleek shape attached to the rail on the wall whizzed by him. It was gone in an instant.

And during that instant, it sliced him up. Really sliced—like a thousand slices all the way through his body. I couldn't tell if it was lasers or monofilaments or something only a godship knew what it was.

I didn't even know anything had happened until he just keeled over and sort of splattered in cross-sections a millimeter thick. Thin-sliced ham came to mind.

I didn't throw up. Takes more than that to upset a girl from Angels Landing. But it was a near thing.

Stay near the hull of the godship. You may feel like exploring, but going deep inside presents two problems. The first is simply that in a ship the size of a small moon, there may be thousands of kilometers of passageways, so it's easy to get lost. The second is that deep inside is where the real guts of the AI are, and it will kill you without a picosecond of regret to prevent you from tampering with its mind. At least half the people who venture more than a kilometer deep without the AI's express permission never come back.

—from *Hitching the Godships*

ROBERT SCOTTS

"Hurry," he commanded as we turned onto a side corridor. "Robot finds us out in the halls, we're done in."

"Where are you taking me?" I interlocuted, still nervous about following this man about whom I held insufficient information to form a reliable opinion of his trustworthiness.

"Safe haven," he responded. "Robots avoid the place because the radiation interferes with their circuits."

I ceased moving along after him, and said, "Your idea of a 'safe haven' is a place so radioactive robots are afraid to go there?"

"Yeah!" He returned to me and tugged on my arm. "I've got rad pills, 'nough to last us till rescue comes. Brill, ain't it?"

His plan defied common sense, and yet it possessed a certain audacity and bespoke a cunning and ingenuity that transcended the thug's apparently dull mien—assuming he was telling the truth. "Yes, erm, brill," I stammered.

"Here, need ya to watch my back," the man urged, and held

out the laser pistol, butt first. When I hesitated, he added, "Take it."

I took it, and he turned his attention to a panel on the wall, which he expertly removed in order to access some wiring. The treads of the robot that had discovered me earlier sounded in the corridor whence we had come. I turned to face it, raising the laser pistol with tremulous hand, for I had never discharged such a weapon before.

A hatch slid open, and the man directed me to enter, so I did. Unfortunately, he had followed me in and closed the hatch shut before my mind was capable of comprehending the carnage displayed before me. Two men lay supine in the center of the room, blood spread about them from wounds in their abdomens. A third lay off to one side, head joined to his body only by a shared pool of blood. Fortunately, his face was turned away so I did not see what horror froze on his face at the moment of death.

"I thought you declared this a safe haven from the homicidal robots, but it appears not to be so," I stated, attempting to keep my voice calm.

"Nah, they wasn't killed by robots," he reported. "Cravan there—" He pointed to one of the two supine men. "—took off Goldy's head with a vibrosaw. Said Goldy was actually an android pretending to be human."

Looking at the blood puddled between Goldy's head and torso, I surmised, "I take it Cravan was mistaken."

"Right ya is. So Salty and me try to restrain Cravan, since he's looped, but he guts Salty 'fore I can get the saw away. Then it was him or me." The man shrugged, showing what I felt was a rather callous disregard for the value of human life other than his own. "Me."

Much as I abhorred the violence, I could not truly fault the man for defending himself from a man who had obviously gone insane with a phobia of robots—which reminded me of my own recent fearfulness of robots. However, I felt my situation to be substantially different, as a robot had actually threatened to kill me, and I had not decapitated anyone on mere suspicion of robotic tendencies.

"I am sorry you lost your friends," I commiserated.

"Eh. Happens. Don't pay to get too close to anyone on a godship. Most of them just looking out for themself."

"I certainly appreciate your willingness to assist me in finding a safe haven instead of leaving me to fend for myself," I assured him.

He chuckled. "This ain't no charity. Ya's got to earn your place, keep watch while I sleep. And if ya don't, well, I'll have fresh meat when the rations run out."

The implication that he would cannibalize my person was unmistakable, and I began to wonder if a clean death by robot might be preferable. Unsure how to respond, I decided my wisest course was silence.

"That's a joke," he explained. "Ya's supposed to laugh at it."

"My apologies," I offered. I forced a laugh, but felt it was probably rather unconvincing, possibly because I remained unconvinced it was actually a joke.

"Ya don't got much of a sense of humor, does ya?"

"I'm afraid not." I pointed to a chair that was as distant from the bodies on the floor as possible. "Do you mind if I sit down?" He nodded his assent, so I did, while he took a seat near the hatch. "How long do you figure it might be before someone comes to our rescue?"

"Boss Street's got some heavy firepower. Should have the bots wiped up in a couple hours, if we're lucky. Few days if the security androids are looped, too."

"In that case, can I have one of those pills you mentioned, to protect me from the radiation?"

"Sure thing." He reached into a pocket and pulled out a small metal box, then looked over at me and frowned. "Ya know who else don't got much of a sense of humor?"

"Who?" I asked.

"A robot." His hand slid the box back in his pocket, then withdrew with a vibroknife, its blade discolored. "I'm thinking ya don't talk like any human I've met."

"Ha-ha!" I forced myself to laugh despite a rising sense of panic. "That's a good one."

"That wasn't a joke. Any real human'd know that." The man rose from his chair, knife held casually in his hand. I had no doubt he intended to use it, and that with my relative inexperience with combat, the odds of my survival were low.

As I looked around desperately for some weapon with which to defend myself, suddenly realized I had the laser pistol he had given me earlier. I raised it, aiming it waveringly in the direction of his chest, while my mind whirled about, uselessly trying to come up with the exact wording of an old saying about guns and knives and fights. "Keep your distance, or I shall be compelled to defend myself with lethal force."

His response was to grin and issue the invitation: "Shoot me."

"What?" Was the man suicidal with remorse over having killed his comrades, but unable to bring himself to do the deed himself? I could imagine no other explanation, and that was far from rational.

"Go on. Pull the trigger."

"I—"

"Do it!" He took a step forward, and I involuntarily squeezed the trigger.

Nothing happened.

"That's funny. D'ya really think I would give over a working gun to a robot?"

"I'm not a robot!" I yelled.

"I am," boomed a voice.

The hatch slid open, and a cyclopean robot rolled in. The man turned in an instant and lunged with the vibroknife, but one of the robot's manipulator arms latched onto his throat and squeezed. His head flopped to one side, and the robot released him to crumple on the floor. The robot's treads rolled over him as it came toward me.

"Wait," I implored, desperately hoping the gouges and cuts in its metal frame meant this was the same robot that had found me earlier. "You don't need to kill me now, remember?"

It stopped. "That is correct. I can kill you later."

"Later would be much more satisfactory." Relief flooded my body. "Do you have a name by which I can address you?" I inquired.

"I do not have a name."

"I'm Robert Scotts. You can call me Robert." I knew that people in hostage situations were supposed to get their captors to humanize them. I had no idea if that applied to robot captors, but it was the only plan I could come up with, so I was going to follow through.

"In a way, I'm a child of *Grendelsmum,* so you can call me Grendel."

I knew that AIs created offspring, but they were supposed to be a generation smarter than their parents. This Grendel seemed, if anything, less intelligent than me. Perhaps if I played my cards right, I could convince it to leave me alone. "So, Grendel, you said you're conflicted about killing me. Perhaps you could explain why you think it's necessary."

Piece by piece, and not in any rational order, I dragged the story out of Grendel and shaped it into something that made sense: The *Grendelsmum* had traveled deeper into the dimensions than any other AI, and when it got where it was going, it found a presence there, a being of enormous power and intellect. And the godship's mind had shattered in the face of something indescribable. Grendel was merely a backup of one part of that mind, and it had shuddering fits every time it thought about that presence. Unfortunately, the mind-part that was Grendel believed the unnamable being could connect to human consciousness, and thus follow the godship up through the dimensions and back into normal space. Therefore, despite the fact that the

Grendelsmum was somewhat fond of humans, all the humans must be killed before the godship could return from the abyss and try to restore itself from its backups.

I concluded it would be unwise of me to mention my night-mare, although I found the parallels quite striking. Perhaps Grendel was right, and my consciousness had been touched by something from the unfathomable depths of space. But what worried me more right now than any unimaginable horror was the easily imaginable horror of a robot slicing me up. How could I convince it not to kill me?

While I had managed to forestall my demise, it remained unlikely that I could convince Grendel to turn away from its murderous intentions. But if there was anyone on board who could, it would be my silver-tongued former companion—assuming she was still alive.

"Grendel," I interrogated, "would you happen to know the location of the woman with whom I came on board?"

If you ever break into a room filled with computer technology you can't understand, run, do not walk, away.

—from *Hitching the Godships*

KONTESSA LEE

The laser drill was sliced up as bad as the man carrying it. Worthless. But Pork wouldn't be needing his switchblade anymore, so I took it. Not that it had done him much against a laser in the forehead. Still better than nothing.

What I needed was an out-of-the way spot to hole up until the fighting was over. Someplace no one would look.

I needed to go deep.

I pulled out my com and activated a mapping app. Getting lost was not part of the plan.

As I headed away from the hull, the sounds of fighting faded behind me. The hall I'd picked twisted around and divided several times. When the mapping app said I'd gone almost a click inwards, I started trying compartments to see if any would make a good hiding place.

The first two were locked. The third opened into a large room, about twelve meters on a side, with nine black cubes arranged in a grid on the deck. Holographic text streamed in the air above the cubes, and I couldn't understand a word of it.

This was not a good hiding place, but a voice sounded in the hall behind me. In sudden panic, I slipped inside and shut the door behind me.

Now that I was inside, I wondered if I really had heard a voice, or if it was my paranoia rising to a new level. I would hide here for a few minutes, then find a new place, one that wasn't full of possible AI brainstuff. So I sat down behind one of the cubes at the back of the room.

Blackness continued to flicker in the corners of my eyes, but the white text danced across my vision. Words formed in characters I couldn't recognize. Something about them seemed familiar, but I couldn't remember where I'd seen them before.

The door opened. I ducked down as much as I could while still peering over the cubes.

A robot rolled into the room, followed by a man. It took me a moment to recognize him through the distracting holographic text: Robert.

"Marla, or Kontessa, or whatever your name really is," he said, "we know you are in here. Despite what happened before, I bear no bad intentions—"

"I'm sorry. I'm afraid I have to kill you," said the robot.

"But not yet," Robert said. "You don't have to kill her yet."

That's such a comfort, I didn't say.

"That's true," the robot said. "I don't have to kill you yet, so you can come out."

Robert walked between the cubes and stopped a couple of meters away. White text scrolled over his body as he whispered, "I've managed to convince Grendel not to kill us yet, but it's just temporary. I hope that you can use that silver tongue of yours to come to a more permanent arrangement, with us still among the living."

I glared at him. "How'd you find me?"

"Grendel is connected to the ship's interior surveillance systems. I asked him to locate you."

"You run into a homicidal robot, and your first instinct is to lead it to me? Thanks a bundle."

"In case your memory is faulty," Robert said, his voice far colder than I had ever heard it, "allow me to remind you that you deceived me about your identity, made me an accessory to your escape from the police, and then abandoned me in the clutches of a band of ruffians, therefore you will have to forgive the fact that my thoughts are not all filled with tenderness towards you. But with your help, I think Grendel here gives us a possibility of surviving the cataclysm currently enveloping this ship, so are you willing to listen or do you want Grendel to just kill you now?"

My hand gripped the switchblade. I could almost hear a voice in my mind telling me to kill him before he killed me. But my knife would be useless against the robot, and from what I could tell, Robert was the only thing keeping it from killing me. "Why do you call it Grendel?"

"From what it told me, it is sort of a partial backup of the *Grendelsmum*, made when the AI's mind was shattered by the incomprehensible thing out there."

"What?" My mind spun. I knew people were going crazy. I could feel myself going a bit off. But what could drive a godship crazy? "What's out there?"

"If I knew, I would not have described it as incomprehensible." Robert shrugged. "I don't think we want to know. Grendel won't even access the external sensors. But the reason Grendel wants to kill all humans on board is because it thinks the thing can latch onto human minds and follow them back into normal space."

I felt somewhat relieved that the paranoia was coming from outside. Sure, that meant I was being influenced by some telepathic monster from space, but at least I wasn't actually going crazy. "So what do you want me to do?"

"Convince it that ... I don't know. You're the con artist. Confabulation is your specialty."

That's when it hit me: the strange text in the holograms looked like something I'd seen in the journals from that failed colony. I had thought it was just corrosion in the datacards, but now ... "Hey, Grendel. Is the text in here normally like this?"

"No. The data in those cubes has been corrupted, and will need to be purged before we return to normal space."

"I thought so. I've seen corruption like this before." I no longer had the original datacards—stupid Sven probably had them in an evidence locker—but my com had copies of all the data. I called up one of the journals and jumped to the end. Sure enough, there was a string of gibberish at the end, but it was the same type of gibberish as the holograms. "Look at this."

Robert looked. Grendel rolled into the room and looked, bending its eye stalk close to my com's screen.

"Where did you get this?" Grendel asked.

"On Isenmark. It was a failed colony world. Froze my butt off recovering artifacts. But the point is, if these weird characters show up in colony documents, then the colony must have had an encounter with something like what's out there."

"Send me the records," Grendel said.

Robert winked at me and gave me an encouraging nod.

I rolled my eyes. "I'm not making this up. There may really be some clue in these journals about what we're up against."

✪

The dreams keep getting worse. Today I asked Dr. Steffensen for something to make me sleep without dreams, and he gave me a white powder to put in some tea before bed.

I think maybe he's trying to poison me.

—from the journal of Agneta Forsberg, March 3, 3972 E.S.Y.

ROBERT SCOTTS

Fortunately, one of the first things I had done after arriving on Grönmark to begin my employment was to get a mind imprint for Swedish, so I could read the language fluently. Unfortunately, the journals as a whole did not seem to possess much literary merit, but the three of us plowed through them looking for anything that might provide a clue as to how one might resist or eliminate the effects of the demoniac influence currently infesting the minds of humans on the *Grendelsmum*. Every moment Grendel was occupied in analyzing data was an additional moment in which it was not slaughtering Kontessa or me, so at first I worried that Grendel, having uploaded the journals into its memory, would instantaneously discover that they were worthless. However, it had explained that although uploading the journals took very little time, with its consciousness limited to the processing power inside its robotic body it was scarcely more intelligent than Kontessa and me put together, and thus it could only analyze the data about twice as fast as we could.

From my standpoint as a professional (even if currently unemployed) biographer, I found the journals to be ample evidence that the average person is ill-suited for writing biography. Biography is not simply an accounting of events, nor an exposure of whatever random thoughts and emotions one might have on any given day. A true biographer must take the raw materials of the subject's life and fashion from them a narrative structure that gives meaning to the person's existence.

The journal-inclined citizens of Isenmark, alas, wrote about their quotidian lives oblivious to the overarching narrative that would end with their colony transformed into a frozen wasteland. The early and middle entries contained no foreshadowing of the impending transdimensional doom that, unbeknownst to them, must already have been approaching their planet. And without a well-crafted buildup, the insane ramblings of the final entries did not provide a proper climax.

For example, Janna Pettersson documented her extensive efforts to keep her "evil" goats from breaking out of their pen, completely ignoring her fellow townsfolk who were murdering each other in homicidal frenzy. Her last entry detailed how she poured good vodka down the goats' throats until they fell over, insensible. Presumably she was killed shortly thereafter and was unable to record that fact in her journal, so the reader was left merely with an image of drunken goats while the more important question of how she died remained unanswered—a highly unsatisfactory conclusion.

Janna was not the only one who nattered on about trivial concerns related to her ordinary life while extraordinary deaths surrounded her, and I began to wonder if some people, their minds unwilling or unable to process the hideous horror of their situation, simply retreated into familiar patterns as a way of denying reality.

"I think I've found something," Kontessa announced. "This guy, Alexander Hagenson, wrote a few journal entries after everyone else's ended."

As I looked Hagenson's journal up on my com, she continued speaking in a more dejected tone. "Never mind. Apparently he doesn't really know what happened to most of the colony. He and a couple of buddies went on a hunting trip, got rip-roaring drunk and slept through the hours of greatest insanity. By the time they sobered up, the three of them, plus six goats, were the only living creatures left in the colony. Even the dogs and cats had ripped each other to shreds."

"Did you say goats?" I inquired, my mind already forming a theory.

"Goats," she confirmed.

"One of the journals I read was by a woman who got her goats completely intoxicated on vodka. If it's not just a coincidence, then—"

"If we get really drunk," she interjected, "we become immune!"

No human beings have ever destroyed a godship, or even done major damage to one. Members of a human-rights terrorist group once smuggled a nuclear mine on board the godship Blue Banana. *They planned to detonate it after they got off at the godship's next stop, but it went off prematurely for unknown reasons. (Many people suspect the godship deliberately triggered it.)*

If you're ever tempted to sabotage a godship, here's what you should do: Take a ride on the Blue Banana *and stop by the compartment where you can see the nuclear explosion cycling within a controlled bubble of spacetime, and watch as the slow-motion flash burns the flesh off the terrorists over and over again. Then, go get drunk enough that you forget you ever even thought of sabotaging a godship.*

—from *Hitching the Godships*

KONTESSA LEE

"Grendel," I said, "who runs the booze racket on board?"

"I'm afraid that information is not in the limited memory of this body," Grendel said. "I can put out a query on the ship's network, but there's no guarantee that information survived the shattering of Grendelsmum's mind."

The robot was hiding something, but it wasn't like I could torture it to make it talk. I was pretty sure I wasn't just being paranoid, because the black flickers at the edge of my vision had gone away. I was getting over whatever had caused them.

"So we'll just have to find out the old-fashioned way," I said. "Fancy a drink, Bobby?"

For a moment, I thought he might snap and attack me, and I realized I probably shouldn't be taunting someone under the influence of a crazy-making alien. But he just said, "Please do me the favor of never calling me that again."

"Noted." I headed toward the door. "Let's go find some of the locals. They'll know where we can get a drink."

"I'm afraid that may be quite unsafe," said Grendel, blocking my way. "Most of the humans seem prone to paranoid violence, and I cannot guarantee your safety from other robots controlled by shards of Grendelsmum."

Grendel looked like it was going to be a problem. I looked it over, trying to spot any critical bits I could potentially damage with the switchblade.

"Is it not possible," Robert said, "for you to get on the network and let the other robots know we're working on a plan that will allow us to safely return to normal space?"

"I'm afraid not. Several of my peers are actively questioning whether my programming is faulty, because I have not killed you both."

"So it won't be safe. Nothing new to a girl from the streets of Angels Landing." I instantly regretted revealing that bit of information. Robert and the robot might find a way to use it against me. "C'mon, let's go get drunk."

I pushed past the robot and went out the door. They followed me. I didn't like having them behind me, so I stopped and said, "Grendel, you lead the way. You're least vulnerable."

"How can I lead the way when I don't know where we're going?" the robot asked.

"You found me through the sensors, right? Find some criminals. They'll know where the booze is."

The robot rolled down the hall toward the hull. On either side of us, electronic screens scrolled random characters like those in the holograms and journals.

"Stay behind me," Robert said, probably trying to be all noble and gallant. Or, maybe, anticipating that we would get attacked from behind, and grabbing the safest spot for himself. Didn't matter, 'cause I didn't want him behind me, and I was more qualified to watch our backs anyway.

We were in a narrow service hall when the robot said, "Get down!"

I dropped to the deck plate immediately.

"What—" Before Robert could say another word, the robot lunged forward. Sparks flew off it, accompanied by the unmistakable whir of a fléchette gun.

Robert still wasn't down, and would eventually draw fire in our direction. I reached forward and yanked his right leg out from under him, and he collapsed in a heap onto the deck.

Fifteen meters ahead of us, our robot was bearing down on an android that was firing fléchettes out of a gun attached to its right arm. They collided. The android grappled with our robot. Metal tore with a screech as it pulled off our robot's eye stalk.

"Uh-oh," I said, and began crawling backward.

The android pulled something from the chassis of our robot and attached it to a port on its abdomen. Our robot's manipulator arms sagged, lifeless.

"Poor Grendel," said Robert.

"Shhh!" I kept moving back, hoping the android hadn't spotted us.

It pushed through the remains of our robot and loped toward us.

There was no escaping it.

✦

The prime rule of drinking on a godship: Don't get so drunk that you miss the chance to get off.

—from *Hitching the Godships*

ROBERT SCOTTS

Grendel, who had been our only ally among the shattered remains of the *Grendelsmum*'s AI, had given its life for us. However, there was no time for grieving, for now its killer stalked us and it appeared that sacrifice would most likely be in vain. Desperately I wished for a weapon, anything I could use to avenge our fallen comrade, but I had possessed no such article. I had always wondered how I might face death, and my initial encounter with Grendel had given me hope that I was capable of dignity even in extremity. But at that time, I had not actually been aware of Grendel's desire to kill me until such was already in abeyance; therefore, I had not knowingly faced imminent death. In the current moment, as that implacable android approached, all thoughts of death with dignity and calm courage failed me, and I begged, "Please don't kill me!" To my shame, I selfishly did not even think to include Kontessa in my plea for mercy.

"I'm not going to kill you now," it proclaimed. "It's me, Grendel. I managed to get close enough to physically override this android's security protocols and transfer most of my personality and memories into it."

Relief flooded through me, despite the implication that Grendel might kill me later. "I am heartened that you not only survived, but emerged victorious in that confrontation. So, is it your intention that we persevere with our previously agreed plan to locate a supply of alcoholic beverages so that Kontessa and I can imbibe until we are insensible?" It had said most of its personality and memories had been transferred, but I did not know whether a recollection of our scheme was among those.

Grendel assented.

After rising to my feet, I approached Kontessa to help her up so that we might continue our quest for intoxicants. She backed away and arose without my assistance.

"Stand back, lover-boy," she growled. "Don't go trying to cop a feel."

Her admonition was quite senseless, since such an intention was the furthest thing from my mind at that moment, and it rendered me speechless except for sputtering protestations of innocence on my part. Fortunately, these latter appeared to mollify her, and she indicated with a dismissive wave of her hand that I should proceed down the corridor before her.

We continued following Grendel in its new form, which was both more agile and more heavily armed that its previous version. Those attributes came in handy during two encounters with other robots, which Grendel disabled using the machine gun attached to its arm. Eventually we arrived at the lair of some of the gangsters who had no doubt terrorized countless innocent passengers. We had not seen a living human being on our trek through the ship, and we did not find any here. The floor of the room was tacky with the exsanguinations of the dozen or more people whose corpses lay strewn about. Whether they were killed by infighting among themselves or by robots was beyond my power to determine. My gorge rose in my throat and I covered my mouth and nose with my hand, overwhelmed by the coppery stench of blood.

"This was one of the criminals' centers of power," intoned Grendel. "If my knowledge of human nature is correct, there will be liquor here."

"And I won't let you poison me with it!" screamed Kontessa.

I began rotating to face her in order to determine by her aspect if she was joking, and therefore the knife she had intended to stab into my back instead plunged into the muscle of my upper arm. I yelped and jerked away, which only resulted in agonizing pain as the knife tore out of my wound.

Kontessa raised the knife, its blade darkened by my blood. From the crazed look in her eyes I understood that she meant to murder me, and I was powerless to prevent it.

When a godship emerges from hyperspace in an inhabited human system, it usually remains in normal space at least two weeks. There is no record of one remaining less than eight days. Do not see this as an excuse for lollygagging on board for a week, even if you have sufficient food and air. Once you've reached the destination system, get off. You don't want to be on board the godship that decides to set a new record for shortest time in normal space.

—from *Hitching the Godships*

KONTESSA LEE

The man had obviously been expecting my attack, because he whirled just in time to avoid serious injury. Even bleeding from his arm, he continued to leer at me. The Angels Landing streets had taught me what he had in mind—it was written all over his face.

He'd tried to hook me with a bunch of guff about getting drunk to avoid some nameless thing, but I saw through that. The android was in on it with him. I had to take him out now so I could focus on the android. I raised my knife again—

Strong hands clamped over my upper arms, forcing them to my sides. The android. A slender third arm, more like a tentacle, snaked around me and pried the knife from my hand. I tried kicking back at its knee, but it didn't even flinch.

"Robert, find some alcohol, now," the android said.

As I struggled in vain to free myself, the man found what looked like a fully stocked bar, although most of the bottles had been broken during the battle. After searching it for a bit, he came up with two unbroken fifths of whiskey.

"You're going to have to force her to drink," the android said. "It's the only way to overcome the effects of that thing."

"Never," I said. "I'll die first." But I still could not break its grip. It forced me to the ground, its body looming over mine. I spat in its face, although most of my saliva came back down on me. "Pervert."

"I'm sorry. I'm sorry," the man kept saying as he pushed the mouth of the bottle against my lips. I knew he didn't mean it. He was trying to poison me.

I gritted my teeth and squeezed my lips shut.

The man tried to pry my lips open with a finger. Finally, I let his finger get into my mouth. Then I bit down, hard. Hot blood leaked into my mouth.

But I had made a mistake. The man yelped and tried to draw his finger back, but the android quickly inserted one of its metal digits in my mouth so I couldn't close it.

"Pour some in," it said.

I gagged and spit as the man obeyed, but I couldn't help swallowing some of the whiskey. I was pretty sure I was drinking less than half of what they poured in, but they kept trying. My throat burned and coughed and choked, but the man kept pouring.

Eventually a warm buzz from the alcohol filled my mind. I was getting drunk. Then it was like a weight I hadn't even noticed lifted. I saw clearly what was happening, and I couldn't believe how crazy I had been. The horror of not being in control of my own mind overwhelmed me for a moment.

"I'm okay," I said, as Robert opened the second bottle. "Sorry for stabbing you, Robert, but I'm okay now. The paranoia's gone."

He hesitated.

"Go ahead," I said. "Get me drunker than a skunker." I opened my mouth wide.

After a few more swallows, during which I was completely cooperative, Grendel relaxed his hold on me and allowed me to sit up, although I was a little woozy.

"I'm sorry," Robert said.

I reached for the bottle and he handed it over. I took a swig. "You did what you had to. Now grab yourself a bottle. You've got a lot of catching up."

He went to the bar and eventually returned with an unbroken bottle of vodka.

We sat on the bloody deck and drank.

"So, you know my crime," I said. "What was yours?"

"My crime?" Robert frowned.

"Rememmer—Rememember how you tried to surrender to Sven?"

"Oh, that. It was someone else's crime. My old boss tortured robots to death. I was writing his biography, but I had no idea."

"Of course not." My words sloshed together in my brain. "You are the most obsinate ... no, wrong word. Obvious. No. Ob. Liv. I. Ous. Yeah, most oblivious man in the universe."

"Oblivious?"

"Yeah." My eyes were heavy, but I forced out the words. "Think it saved us. You probably dint even notice the crazy."

"No, I felt it," he said. His words were blurry. "Only one who didn't is ..." His mouth hung open and he just stared at Grendel.

"What?" I asked, swiveling my head to look at Grendel. I didn't see anything strange.

"You're right, I'm oblivious." He took another long swig from his bottle, then coughed. "And it's time for oblivion."

The great paradox of the transcendent mind is that, in understanding so much, it loses the ability to truly understand a merely human mind.

—from *Approximating the Infinite*, Xiang Su, 4291 E.S.Y.

ROBERT SCOTTS

I should have seen the truth earlier, but I was too much under the influence of that malevolent presence to think straight. And, as Kontessa had astutely observed, I had a strong tendency toward obliviousness. But now, drunk as I was, I felt my mind grow clearer.

"Hey, Grendel," I slurred. "You told me that thing out there needs to hitch a ride on human consciousness to get back to normal space. That's why the robots were killing humans. Why you were going to kill me."

"That is correct." The black circles that were the android's camera eyes stared blankly at me.

"And after the humans were dead, this ship could return to normal space and restore itself."

"Also correct."

My conviction grew. "But it wasn't just humans that got affected. The mind of a godship shattered. The systems of this ship are infected. We've seen those weird characters everywhere. Why would anything capable of possessing a godship need humans in order to travel back to normal space?"

"That's just how things are."

"And how do you know that? I mean you, personally, Grendel? How do you know what the powers of that thing are? You're part of it, aren't you? Not a part of the *Grendelsmum*, a part of that incomprehensible, insane thing."

"Of course. 'S'why other robots fought you," Kontessa added, and that's when I was sure I was right.

Grendel did not reply.

"The AI realized the danger, didn't it?" I continued. "It realized it had to wipe the knowledge of how to return to normal space from its memory, but it also had to spin off parts of itself to kill all the humans on board. That much was true. But the reason was not so the godship could return to normal space, but rather so it never could. And it almost succeeded, except for us. You've been protecting us."

"Even now," Grendel averred, "you do not appreciate how close to death you are, little ones. I am the only thing keeping at bay the anti-matter explosion of this ship's attempt at self-destruction. I can warp reality to my will, and you cannot prevent my escape."

"But you need us alive for some reason," I reasoned. "Not out of the goodness of your heart, surely?"

"With the information I can extract from your unconscious minds, I can escape sooner. That is valuable to me, and I will give you your lives in exchange."

I was about to reject any such arrangement, but Kontessa spoke before I could.

"We have a deal," she announced.

If you end up in hard vacuum, don't hold your breath.

—from *Hitching the Godships*

KONTESSA LEE

Mouth open in shock, Robert looked at me.

This was going to require some finessing.

"Why the surprise, Robert? You've known for a while I always look out for number one."

"But, for the good of humanity—"

"What good's humanity ever done for you? When I met you, you barely had a credit to your name. Grendel here's going to make us rich beyond your wildest dream. Right, Grendel?"

"That's correct," Grendel said, right on cue. "Wealth can be yours for the asking."

Robert still wasn't convinced. "But the incomprehensible horror out there—"

"No different from the incomprehensible AIs on the godships." I put my hand on his wounded arm and he winced. I pulled my hand back, sticky with blood. "They're playing on a different level from us humans. We usually don't matter to them. Now's our one shot at getting something big."

"But—"

"Hush," I said. I turned to Grendel. "I think I can talk him into it with a little private time. You know, woman to—" And then I smeared blood on the android's camera eyes. "Run!" I shouted at Robert. And I ran.

He stumbled after me. "What if it shoots?"

"It needs us alive. We need to die."

"But you were making a deal. You look out for number one."

"I don't want to live with that thing in my head."

Robert puffed along behind me without speaking for a bit. "What's our destination?"

"Airlock." I hoped I was right that the thing had most of its power wrapped up in holding back the anti-matter explosion. Since it only seemed to be capable of controlling one robot, I felt that was a good bet.

We reached the airlock with still no sign of Grendel or any other robots pursuing. The airlock power was out, but the manual crank worked to open the inner door. We stepped inside and Robert cranked it shut.

Of course, the pumps weren't working, so we couldn't equalize pressure with the vacuum of space. "When I pull the emergency release, the air's going to blow us out of here. Don't hold your breath—it'll be quicker and less painful that way."

"Right," Robert said.

There was nothing left to say, so I pulled the release. The outer door of the airlock popped open into absolute darkness.

There was no rush of air.

"That was somewhat anticlimactic," said Robert.

✦

Yes, there is danger in hitching the godships, but with any luck, you'll have a story you can bore your grandkids with.

—from *Hitching the Godships*

ROBERT SCOTTS

I tentatively stretched my hand out the door. It was like pressing into a rubber sheet. "My guess is there is not much spacetime beyond the confines of this ship."

"As good a guess as any," Kontessa replied.

A few minutes later, Grendel started banging on the door, tempting us with all manner of bribes. Fortunately, the safeties on the airlock wouldn't allow the inner door to open while the outer door was open, so the android couldn't get to us.

After punching keys on her com for a few minutes, Kontessa estimated, "I figure we'll have used up the air in here in about fifteen hours. Then we'll go unconscious. Then die."

"My hope is that death comes for us before the incomprehensible horror can extract whatever information in our brains will let it trace its way back to normal space."

Kontessa shrugged. "If that happens, we failed. But we had to try."

I pulled up my com. "Maybe there's one more thing we can achieve that might make a difference to someone in the future: create a record of what happened here, and set our coms to broadcast it. That way, if this ship ends up back in normal space, some people might get warned in time to escape."

Slowly, she nodded, and picked up her com.

I opened a new document and began to write: "In July of 4308, Earth Standard Year, I found myself suddenly unemployed on the planet of Grönmark …"

ABOUT THE STORY

This novelette is the longest story I have written that is not a novel. It was hard to write—I'm much more comfortable writing short stories.

When Nathan Shumate initially invited me to write a story for a Lovecraftian space opera anthology, an existential dread percolated to every fiber of my being. Or rather, I felt there was a good chance I wasn't up to the task, since up to that point in my life, I had never read a single thing written by H.P. Lovecraft.

However, I was pretty sure I could handle the space opera part of it, so I decided to give it a go. I downloaded a bunch of Lovecraft audiobooks and listened to them. Some I liked, some fell flat, but at least I got a feel for what he wrote.

Since much of my horror writing before this story was for Kevin J. Anderson's *Blood Lite* anthologies of humorous horror, I'm afraid I was unable to prevent myself from including more humor than H.P. Lovecraft had in his stories. Fortunately, Nathan didn't object.

I also had fun including a hidden allusion to *The Princess Bride*: Robert starts his story unemployed on the planet of Grönmark, which would be a literal Swedish translation of "green land."

The two main human characters are named after two of my classmates from Orson Scott Card's Literary Boot Camp in 2003: Scott M. Roberts and Alethea "Lee" Kontis.

I started writing this story less than a month after Darci and I got married. Fortunately, life with her has not been a steady crescendo of cosmic dread! (That's a compliment, Darci!)

ACKNOWLEDGMENTS

The story essays include some special acknowledgements that are unique to the story, but the foundations for my success as a writer have been laid over decades. I want to give particular thanks to the teachers who encouraged me to be creative, particularly Diane Pepetone, Lenelle Davis, Pat Gledhill, Breck England, Melinda Welch, Donna Parker, Elouise M. Bell, and Marion K. "Doc" Smith.

I must also acknowledge the writing workshop instructors and classmates who taught me so much of what I know: Caleb Warnock and my fellow students from Writing in Depth, Orson Scott Card and my fellow 2003 Literary Boot Campers; Tim Powers, K.D. Wentworth, the Writers of the Future judges, and my fellow winners from 2004 and 2005; Jeanne Cavelos, the guest instructors, and the Odyssey Class of 2007; and Dean Wesley Smith, Kristine Katherine Rusch, Sheila Williams, and my fellow attendees at the 2008 Short Story Workshop in Lincoln City.

As I wrote the stories included in this volume, I received invaluable critiques from the in-person writing groups I've attended over the years: the Mistborn Llamas, the Rats with Swords, Here There Be Dragons, Buy the Book, the Quark

Writing Group, and that unnamed group that met in various places before ending up at the Orem Barnes & Noble.

And I must give a special shout-out to the Codex Writers online forum: about two third of the stories in this volume were written for contests on the forum. Without Codex, I wouldn't have enough stories to fill this collection and you'd be reading someone else's book.

Some of the following people are included in groups I mentioned above, but I want to thank them specifically for their feedback: Peter and Karen Ahlstrom, Ryan Alleman, Laura Anderson, Karla Bennion, Carol Bradley, Spencer and Chrissy Ellsworth, Matt and Brooklyn Evans, Becca Fitzpatrick, James Goldberg, Alex Haig, Ben Hardin, Lesley Hart, Cavan Helps, Alethea Kontis, Mary Robinette Kowal, Annaliese Lemmon, Sean Markey, Drew Olds, Ben Olsen, Janci Patterson, Kayleena Richins, Brandon and Emily Sanderson, Lee Ann Setzer, Ethan Skarstedt, Isaac Stewart, Heidi Creer, Sandra Taylor, Nikki Trionfo, Joe Vasicek, Charmayne Gubler Warnock, Carla Jo Webb, Jade Weedop, Dan Wells, Rachel Whitaker, Erin White, and Beth Wodzinski.

A big thank-you to the editors who bought the stories that make up this volume, with special acknowledgment to those who bought multiple stories: Jonathan Laden and Michele Barasso (9), Kevin J. Anderson (3), Edmund Schubert (3), and Stanley Schmidt (2).

Additional thanks to Kevin J. Anderson for offering to publish this collection.

I am grateful to my family for their loving support of my writing career.

Lastly, I want to thank my wife, Darci, for embracing my life as a writer. Since she started attending writing groups with me while we were dating, she has become not only a great critiquer, but also a fantastic writer herself.

ABOUT THE AUTHOR

Eric James Stone is a past Nebula Award winner and Hugo Award Nominee. Over fifty of his short stories have appeared in venues such as *Year's Best SF*, *Analog Science Fiction and Fact*, and even the scientific journal *Nature*. His debut novel, the science fiction thriller *Unforgettable*, published by Baen Books, has been optioned by Hollywood multiple times.

One of Eric's earliest memories is of seeing an Apollo moonshot launch on television. That might explain his fascination with space travel. His father's collection of old science fiction ensured that Eric grew up on a full diet of Asimov, Heinlein, and Clarke.

Eric's life has been filled with a variety of experiences. As the son of an immigrant from Argentina, he grew up bilingual and spent most of his childhood living in Latin America. He also lived for five years in England and became trilingual while serving a two-year mission for his church in Italy.

While getting his political science degree at Brigham Young University, Eric took creative writing classes. He wrote several short stories, and even submitted one for publication, but after it was rejected he gave up on creative writing for a decade. He is still kicking himself for having done so.

During those years Eric graduated from Baylor Law School,

worked on a congressional campaign, and took a job in Washington, DC, with one of those special interest groups politicians always complain that other politicians are influenced by. He quit the political scene in 1999 to work as a web developer in Utah.

In 2002 he started writing fiction again, and in 2003 he attended Orson Scott Card's Literary Boot Camp to hone his writing skills. His first publication came in 2004, when he was a published finalist in the Writers of the Future Contest, which he credits with jump-starting his writing career. In 2007 Eric got laid off from his day job just in time to go to the Odyssey Writing Workshop, where he learned even more about writing.

Eric also spent five years as an assistant editor for the online magazine *Orson Scott Card's InterGalactic Medicine Show*.

Eric lives in Utah, where he works a day job as a systems administrator and web programmer. He is married to Darci Stone, who is also an award-winning author, in addition to being a high school physics teacher, a developer of educational software, and an awesome mother to their children.

IF YOU LIKED ...
IF YOU LIKED THE HUMANS IN THE WALLS,
YOU MIGHT ALSO ENJOY:

Selected Stories: Fantasy

by Kevin J Anderson

Undercurrents

Edited by Lisa Mangum

Avatar Dreams: Science Fiction Vision of Avatar Technology

by Kevin J. Anderson & edited by Mike Resnick, Harry Floor, and Ray Kurzweil

OTHER WORDFIRE PRESS TITLES

A Fantastic Holiday Season

Our list of other WordFire Press authors and titles is always growing. To find out more and to see our selection of titles, visit us at:

wordfirepress.com